Love
Redesigned

Center Point
Large Print

**This Large Print Book carries the
Seal of Approval of N.A.V.H.**

Love Redesigned

JENNY PROCTOR

CENTER POINT LARGE PRINT
THORNDIKE, MAINE

This Center Point Large Print edition
is published in the year 2023 by arrangement with
the author.

The text of this Large Print edition is unabridged.
In other aspects, this book may vary
from the original edition.
Printed in the United States of America
on permanent paper sourced using
environmentally responsible foresting methods.
Set in 16-point Times New Roman type.

ISBN: 978-1-63808-625-3

The Library of Congress has cataloged this record
under Library of Congress Control Number: 2022947579

For Becca

Your friendship is a gift
I cherish daily.

Love
Redesigned

Chapter One

Dani

Four, seven, eight, thirteen, thirteen, fifteen.
Four, seven, eight, thirteen, thirteen, fifteen.

I rounded the corner and pushed through the coffee shop door, the numbers on repeat in my brain. Four, seven, eight, thirteen, thirteen, fifteen.

"Hey, Dani," Chloe, the barista at the counter, said. "What'll it be today?"

I smiled. "I'll take a number four, a seven, an eight, two thirteens, and a fourteen." There. Done. God bless the owner of Java Jean's for numbering their coffee shop menu. "Wait. Did I say fourteen? I meant fifteen. Four, seven, eight, thirteen, thirteen, *fifteen.*"

Chloe grinned. "Are you sure?"

"Don't question me! If I have to repeat them again, I'll definitely forget."

"The fifteen's for Sasha?" Chloe asked. "The coconut milk macchiato?"

Of course it was for Sasha. My boss lived on air and coffee and little else. "How'd you guess?"

"It's her second one today. She stopped by on her way in this morning."

"And it probably won't be her last." I leaned

9

against the counter and waited for Chloe to make up the drinks. A basket of peaches sat next to the register and I reached for one, lifting the fruit to my nose. I frowned and put it back in the basket. The fruit smelled less like a fresh peach than the scented lotion my roommate slathered onto her legs every night. But then, my standards for fresh peaches were high. I was spoiled by my childhood in South Carolina, roaming my grandma's orchards, eating peaches seconds after I'd pulled them from the tree.

A swell of emotion rose in my chest. It had been years since my grandmother had died, but I couldn't think of home without remembering her.

Granny wouldn't have liked Java Jean's, with its endless options and ridiculous names. "There's only one way to drink coffee, sugar," she'd said to me countless times, the *r* so soft, it all but completely fell off her words. "With lots of cream." The same rule also applied to peaches. I didn't disagree with her on that point. Fresh peaches slathered with cream was a part of my Southern heritage I'd never surrender.

But I *did* love Java Jean's. It made me feel like a New Yorker, like I truly belonged in the city. I mean, I had the entire menu memorized. Surely that balanced out my lingering Southern accent and affinity for pastel floral prints, even in the sea of blacks and grays that filled New York City streets.

"Seriously," Chloe said, handing over the first tray of drinks. "You need to feed that woman a cheeseburger. She'd probably be happier."

I offered a tight-lipped smile. Sasha maybe had a bit of a reputation. She was a woman who knew how to get what she wanted and didn't back down no matter the sacrifice. How else could she have climbed to the top of an elite fashion house design team in less than three years? Naysayers claimed she'd slept her way to the top—she was engaged to marry brand originator and CEO Alicio LeFranc, after all—but I'd seen the way Sasha worked. She was a cutthroat, for sure. But she had gumption.

An administrative position had gotten me through LeFranc's front door, but it was Sasha's recommendation that would get me designing. I couldn't afford to be anything but loyal.

"Just add those to the company tab," I told Chloe.

She nodded. "Sure thing. That's a great dress, by the way. I love the color."

"Yeah?" I looked down at my dress. The pale blue Oscar de la Renta Guipure lace had been a splurge at *Mood*, my favorite fabric store, but the tiny geometric pattern had been perfect for the A-line I'd been sketching. I'd dropped a third of my weekly paycheck without even flinching. I spent the first two hours of sewing cursing my decision—there was definitely a learning curve working with guipure—but in the end, I was thrilled with the results. The lace kept it feminine, but it wasn't too frilly. Cinched at the waist, with a tiny black belt and a boat neck, I loved it.

Still, that was different than someone else loving it. "I just finished it," I said to Chloe. "You really like it?"

"Wait, are you serious? You made it yourself? I've never wished so much that I could afford to wear LeFranc."

My cheeks warmed with her praise. I'd been designing clothes a long time, but it still surprised me when people liked my stuff. "Oh, I didn't design this for LeFranc. Designing is . . ." I hesitated. Designing was my life, my passion, my everything. But that felt a little heavy for small talk with the barista. "It's still just a hobby for me," I said. "But who knows? Maybe someday."

"I take it back then. The fact that they have *you* making coffee runs instead of designing clothes makes me hate LeFranc," Chloe said as she slid a lid onto Sasha's macchiato. "I'll *never* wear it in protest."

"Give me a few more months," I said with a wry grin. "Every day I'm a day closer."

"I like your attitude." Chloe turned back to the cappuccino machine behind her. "Just a few more to go."

I nodded and pulled out my phone, scrolling

through the to-do list Sasha had texted over that morning. I'd already made it through the first half—not bad for a morning's work.

A minute later, a text came in from my brother, asking if we were still on for dinner that night. I inwardly groaned. I'd almost forgotten about dinner.

I should have been excited to see my twin. He still lived in Charleston, so we didn't see each other very often. But Isaac and I—we couldn't be more different. I was Gucci and New York Fashion Week. He was cargo shorts and . . . the couch in his basement. We'd done okay as teenagers. We'd tolerated each other, at least. But then he'd opted out of college to stay home and focus on the YouTube channel he'd developed while we were still in high school. I'd been furious at the time. Colleges had offered him money to come use his brain and Isaac had picked . . . YouTube?

Still, family was family. I keyed out a quick response, confirming the restaurant and time.

When the bell above Java Jean's front door jingled, I didn't even look up. But then I heard a voice that made the blood in my veins run New-York-winter cold.

"I completely understand. I'll take care of it right away. Right. Sounds good," the voice said.

I gripped the edge of the counter, grateful it was there to hold me up. Because hearing Alex

Randall's voice? That was enough to put me flat on the floor.

Chloe leaned toward me. "Dani? You okay?"

I forced a breath in through my nose and out through my mouth. Maybe it wasn't him. Maybe it was some other Southern guy that just *sounded* like him. Some other guy who didn't have wavy chestnut hair or perfect brown eyes or an incredible dusting of freckles across perfectly chiseled cheekbones. I closed my eyes, a sudden swell of anger surging to the surface, making my skin feel hot, prickly. I could envision those eyes like it was yesterday. Like it hadn't been twelve agonizing months since he'd left New York. Since he'd left *me.*

I snuck a brief glance over my shoulder, my heart tripling its speed as soon as I determined that *yes,* the one and only Alex Randall was standing less than ten feet away from me. At once I felt both elated to see him again—I'd loved the man, after all—and furious that he felt like he had any right to place himself within a one-hundred-mile radius of where he knew me to be. Java Jean's was my territory. Maybe he'd introduced me to the place, but he'd ceded it when he'd left. He was the guilty one. The heartbreaking, dream-crushing, soul-stabbing, vanishing act that had nearly been my undoing.

A year-long relationship and he'd left without even sending a text.

If not for my job at LeFranc, and my close friends rallying around me, I might have left New York altogether, but I couldn't have run home even if I'd wanted to. *Home* was where Alex had gone. If I had tucked tail and gone to Charleston, it would have looked like I was running to *him*.

Alexander Ellison Randall III had eased into my life with the grace you might expect from someone named like they belonged in the pages of a Civil War-era romance novel. We'd met at a fancy party on the Upper East Side where anyone who was anyone in fashion was in attendance. From the cultured Southern accent that made me feel homesick and at home all at the same time, to his stories of spending his summers in New York with his stepfather, the legendary Alicio LeFranc who I'd idolized since childhood, it hadn't taken me more than a minute to fall for him.

I couldn't stand there gripping the Java Jean's counter forever.

I had to face him. Unless I wanted to vault over the cash register and belly crawl my way to the backroom. And there was no way my guipure lace was belly crawling anywhere. Taking one last breath, and willing my nerves to calm, I turned around.

We made eye contact. At once, I was grateful I'd heard him come in, that I'd at least had a few seconds to prepare. I'd clearly caught him by surprise; the shock of the moment was written all over his face. He froze, his jaw hanging open, and his cell phone, once secure in his hand, clattered to the tile floor at his feet.

He scrambled to pick up his phone, wiping it on his sleeve before quickly dropping it into the inside pocket of his suit coat. And *oh,* what a suit. The color was good. Blue, not too bright, just bold enough to give him an edge over the more conservative grays and blacks. The fabric was expensive, the tailoring impeccable. His tie was great. Silk. Purple. And his shoes? *Sweet tea and cornflakes.* Medallion toe oxfords in a rich brown leather I immediately wished I could touch. I'd forgotten how good he made clothes look.

"Hi," I managed to say.

For all the scrambling I'd witnessed seconds before, he recovered quickly and was suddenly as poised and polished as ever. "Hey, Dani," he said, the words smooth and soft. "It's great to see you."

I admired and hated him in the same second for having such control over his emotions.

I closed my eyes and swallowed. Not many people made Southern sound as good as he did.

"What are you doing here?" I realized as soon as the words left my mouth how filled with hurt they sounded and I hated myself for being so transparent.

He dropped his eyes and I winced. He'd picked up on it too.

"Work," he said. "I'm just here for a few days."

"Work," I repeated, curious about what that actually meant. Accounting work? Something different?

He'd been an accountant at LeFranc right up until the week we'd broken up, the same week he'd left the city altogether. Office gossip was that he'd been fired after a disagreement with his stepfather. I believed the disagreement part— Alex hadn't been happy at LeFranc for a while— but my guess was that he'd left willingly, on his own terms.

Alexander Randall was not the kind of man who got fired.

A few weeks after he'd left, Isaac had texted me and told me he'd hired Alex to help him with his taxes and some other business stuff. He and Alex had met a few times while we'd been dating, and they'd liked each other enough to exchange numbers; Isaac had texted Alex money questions all the time before we'd broken up. Isaac had worried I'd be upset when he'd told me, but I'd mostly pretended not to care. I'd been firmly in the *rage* stage of my post-breakup grief at the time, when the mere mention of Alex's name was enough to send me flying into a fit. And it wasn't like they were hanging out. Alex was doing his taxes. That only took minutes of inter-action.

Alex took a step forward. "How are you?" he asked, his tone so sincere, a spark of anger flared in my chest. He didn't get to care about me anymore. Not here. Not now.

"Here are your drinks, Dani," Chloe said softly behind me. I gave her a brief nod and mouthed a silent thank you.

I looked back at Alex and shrugged. "I'm fine," I said. "The same, really."

He nodded. "That's good to hear."

We stood there, the air between us so full of awkward and uncomfortable, I half-expected everyone else in the coffee shop to get up and walk out just to save themselves. When Alex didn't say anything else, I picked up the drinks Chloe had left for me and started for the door. I held them up as I walked past, evidence presented before a judge. "I should get these to the office."

"Of course." Alex stepped to the side, but then he called after me. "Dani, wait."

I turned around.

"I feel like we should . . . talk."

Talk. Now he wanted to talk? A full year of silence and he suddenly decided he wanted to work it all out in the doorway of Java Jean's? I almost laughed. "We should have talked a year ago."

He closed his eyes. "I know. You're right about that. I'm sorry—"

"Alex, stop." I cut him off. "Just stop. I can't do this here."

His jaw was tight, his brow creased, but he nodded his understanding. "I'm sorry," he said again.

Countless times I'd imagined what I would say to Alex if I ever saw him again. In my mind, I was always witty and clever, my insults perfectly crafted to hit him where they'd make the biggest impact, like sharpened razors homing in on the tenderest flesh. But now that we actually stood face to face, my words were dried up. All I really wanted to do was cry. Since crying in front of him was *not* going to happen, I did the next best thing.

I fled.

"I gotta go," I said. I turned and blindly pushed toward the coffee shop's front door, with little heed to anything—or anyone—in my way. Until the someone in my way crashed into me, upending four of the six coffees I carried, splashing them all over the front of my dress. I stood there in shock, coffee dripping off the ends of my hair, soaking all the way through to my skin. It was even pooling up in my shoes.

"Watch where you're going, lady," a gruff voice said. I had half a nerve to punch the guy. *I* was the one covered in coffee, not him.

Of course, it only took a second for Alex to reach me. He pulled the two surviving cups out of my hands and set them on the table beside us. "Are you okay?"

I sniffed. "A little damp, but undamaged, I think."

"You're not burned, are you?"

The coffee *was* hot, but not so hot that I felt anything more than a temporary sting.

I shook my head, my shock finally giving way to embarrassment. "I'm fine."

"Are you sure? Can I . . . help at all? Maybe get you a cab to take you home?"

"You know how long cabs take around here. I don't have time to go home, but it's fine. I'll figure something out."

Chloe appeared beside us, a mop and bucket in hand. She handed me a stack of napkins. "I'm so sorry, Dani," she said. "I can remake the drinks you lost."

There wasn't much that sounded worse than standing next to Alex, coffee dripping in between my breasts and into my belly button, long enough for Chloe to make another round of drinks. I looked at the surviving coffee cups, noting that one of the two was Sasha's macchiato. "It's really fine," I said. I used the napkins to wipe off my hands and arms then tossed them into the trash can by the door before grabbing the remaining drinks from the table. "You can owe me next time."

With that, I pushed through the door, the heat

of the late August morning matching the fire that filled my cheeks and burned in my chest. I thought I heard Alex call my name as I crossed the sidewalk and rounded the corner. But this time, it was me who didn't look back.

Chapter Two

Alex

It had been stupid to go to Java Jean's. I should have expected the possibility of running into Dani, knowing full well that she worked right next door. But then, I was an adult. Avoiding her intentionally would have been childish.

I *felt* childish as I walked slowly back to the studio where Isaac was finishing up his photo-shoot. I carried a bag of Java Jean's breakfast sandwiches—our flight had landed early that morning and neither of us had eaten—but any appetite I'd previously had was gone. Seeing her, hearing the sound of her voice, had left me . . . derailed.

Autopilot took me down the street, into the lobby, and onto the elevator which carried me up to the third-floor studio.

When the elevator doors slid open, Isaac was waiting for me. "Dude, where have you been? I'm starving."

I slammed the bag of food into his chest with a little more force than necessary and stalked past him. I needed a place to sit down. Somewhere to think and figure out why seeing a woman I finally thought I'd gotten over had me feeling so torn up inside.

Guilt, maybe. I'd handled the situation with Dani like an idiot and wouldn't deny it. But it felt like more than that.

Isaac followed me to the center of the room where an assortment of couches and chairs they'd used to stage the photos sat clustered together. "What's wrong with you?" he asked. "You look terrible."

I sank onto the nearest chair and dropped my head into my hands. I breathed out a sigh and looked up, finally making eye contact with my friend. "I ran into Dani."

He stared, his eyes wide, then he slowly started to laugh. He shook his head as he pulled out a sandwich, peeling back the paper before taking a large bite. "I don't feel sorry for you, man. You know you had that coming."

"What's that supposed to mean?"

"It means you're the idiot who never called her."

"But she was right there, in person, without any warning," I said. "That's not how it was supposed to be the first time I . . ."

"The first time you what? Saw her again? How was it supposed to be?"

I ran a hand across my face, frustrated that Isaac was being so casual about the entire thing.

"I just thought I would have the chance to explain myself before actually seeing her."

Isaac crumpled the wrapper of his sandwich.

"You're delusional, man. She lives here. Like three blocks away. You had to have considered the possibility of running into her."

"Millions of people live in this city. I just . . ." A thought suddenly occurred to me. "Does she know you're in town?"

"Yeah." Isaac looked away quickly, like he'd been hiding something and was finally going to fess up. "We're um, we're actually having dinner tonight."

"Really?"

That was surprising. Isaac and his twin sister rarely got along. They tried, but the entire time I'd known them, the trying had usually dissolved into fighting somewhere around hour two.

"It was her idea," Isaac said. "Apparently her boss gave her this reservation at some fancy place in East Harlem. I still need to meet with Rizzo to go over plans for the scavenger hunt, so I figured, why not take advantage of the opportunity, meet with Rizzo *and* knock out obligatory family time all at once?"

I still couldn't get used to Isaac speaking seriously about someone named *Rizzo*. When he'd called me and offered me a job three weeks after I'd left New York, I had known saying yes meant entering a sphere completely different than the buttoned-up financial world I was used to. But I'd underestimated just how different. Rizzo didn't even have a last name. Apparently, you didn't need one on YouTube, not according to the millions of subscribers his channel boasted.

Rizzo was the only YouTuber more successful than Isaac who was participating in the upcoming scavenger hunt—Isaac's recent effort to diversify his brand and make more of a positive social impact. The entire thing would benefit a charity organization chosen by the YouTube personalities participating in the event. To have Rizzo onboard was a big deal.

"Two things," I said to Isaac. "First, what else does Rizzo need to know? He was here for the promotional photos and he's already agreed to the terms. Why do you need another meeting? Second, you're having dinner with him *and* with Dani at the same time?"

"Rizzo is in. He gave me his word and he's good for it. And why not have dinner together?"

"You haven't seen your sister in over a year. I'm not sure she'll appreciate having you bring a business associate to what I'm sure she assumes will be a family dinner."

He rolled his eyes. "Why do you suddenly care so much about Dani's feelings? It'll be fine. Rizzo's coming an hour late, so I'll do the family thing with her, then when Rizzo shows up, I'll do the business thing with him. And if I'm lucky, I'll still make it to Carlie's party before midnight."

"Carlie?"

"Carlie the lighting assistant? With the—"

Isaac raised his hands and traced the imagined silhouette of a generously curved woman.

I cut him off. "I get it."

"She said you can come too. I think her exact words were, 'bring your stuffy assistant if you want.'"

My jaw tightened. It had been bad enough watching the photographer's lighting assistant fawn all over Isaac for the better part of the photoshoot. I didn't need to see how bad she'd be in a less professional setting. "I'm not your assistant. Also, how did you make all of these arrangements for dinner and a meeting with Rizzo without my knowledge? I thought you hired me to be your manager."

"I hired you to be my business manager," Isaac said. "This dinner is mostly . . . social."

"Rizzo counts as business. I should be there for your meeting."

"I was planning on you being there. The reservation is for four."

I pinched the bridge of my nose. "You just said this was a social dinner. Why are you expecting me to be there if I'm your *business* manager?"

Isaac rolled his eyes. "For the first part of dinner, you can be there as my friend. When Rizzo shows up, you can play manager for a few minutes. This isn't a big deal."

No, it was a huge deal. "Isaac, I'm not having dinner with Dani."

"Why not? You said you wanted a chance to explain yourself. Now I've given you one."

"But she doesn't even know I'll be there," I said. "Does she even know I work for you? We can't just spring that on her."

"She knows you work for me. I told her right after I hired you that you were helping with my taxes and stuff."

"Hiring an accountant to do your taxes is entirely different than hiring an accountant to be your full-time business manager."

"Right," Isaac said, his voice annoyingly even. "I told her taxes . . . *and stuff.* I didn't tell you not to reach out and clarify your new job description, man. You could have explained things to her yourself whenever you wanted."

Isaac made it sound so simple, but he had no idea how complicated things really were. I wanted Dani to know why I left without any explanation, without even saying goodbye. But there were some things I couldn't explain. Not just because I didn't want to. But because legally, I *couldn't.*

Not as long as she worked for LeFranc.

After settling with the photographer, and agreeing on a deadline to receive the proofs, we took a cab to the hotel. I still had an apartment in the city and wished we could have stayed there. It would have been more comfortable than any hotel room. But it was presently sublet to a pair of Swedish ballerinas who I didn't think would appreciate accommodating a pair of unexpected house guests.

Before pulling away from the curb, our cab driver looked over his shoulder and immediately recognized Isaac. "Dude, are you Random I?" he said, his voice full of enthusiasm. "I love your stuff."

Isaac nodded. "Hey, thanks, man. I appreciate it."

The driver held up his phone. "Do you mind?"

I leaned out of the frame while Isaac leaned forward, smiling into the corner of the guy's selfie.

"I love the weekly kindness challenge," the driver went on. "I had somebody leave me a fifty dollar tip the other day. Hashtag Random I."

"Hey, that's awesome," Isaac said. "It's what I love to hear. Just be sure to pay it forward. That's the whole idea, right?"

"Right on, man," the driver said.

It wasn't the first time random strangers had approached Isaac to tell him about ways his weekly kindness challenges had influenced their lives. The challenges had developed their own cult following; people completed them and then posted and shared videos of their experiences on social media.

"You still haven't told me why you need another meeting with Rizzo," I said to Isaac,

28

once the gushing fan bit from the cab driver had subsided.

He shrugged, not even looking up from his phone. "It's not a big deal. He just wants to review the details one more time."

I raised an eyebrow but didn't question further. At least not verbally. I was a bit territorial when it came to the charity event I'd been planning with Isaac. It was part of why he'd hired me. My primary responsibility was to make sure he managed his money in a way that would help it last, but he also hoped I could help to improve his brand and broaden his reach.

A YouTube channel is a pretty self-serving entity by default, so I admired his desire to turn his success into something more meaningful than the notoriety of his own name. Though, it was admittedly challenging to find a balance between my Harvard educated professionalism and . . . I didn't even have a word to describe what Isaac was.

Still, I couldn't criticize. He was really good at what he did. His tech news was always insightful, his comedy was sharp, and the kindness challenges were obviously making an impact. At the same time, in the last episode I'd seen Isaac film, he'd issued the weekly challenge while sitting in a bathtub full of chocolate pudding.

I respected him, yes. That didn't mean I always understood him.

"You think I ought to let Rizzo have two teams?" Isaac asked.

"Of course not. Why should he get two?"

"He says he's bringing twice as many viewers as the rest of us."

"Is that what this dinner is about?"

"Cool your jets," Isaac said. "We're just talking about it."

I held up my hands. "You cannot cave to his pressure. We've set things up well. Five YouTubers. Five teams. This isn't about him anyway. It's for charity. It shouldn't be about him feeling more important than anyone else."

"Fine, I get it. I'll tell him no on the second team."

"And by you, you actually mean *me*," I said, my tone flat.

He reached over and smacked me on the knee. "That's why I pay you the big bucks."

I scoffed. The salary he paid me was plenty, but it barely compared to what I'd made working at LeFranc.

Though, I'd take Isaac over my stepfather for a boss any day. At least he had a measurable sense of integrity.

Thinking of LeFranc brought Dani back into my mind and I tensed, realizing all over again that I would have to share a table with her at dinner. I had to think of a way to warn her. If she showed up to the restaurant expecting her brother, and I was there too, she might leave.

That wasn't what Isaac needed, and I realized with alarming clarity, it wasn't what I *wanted*.

I pressed my forehead into my hand. She'd looked amazing when I'd run into her. She'd been wearing blue. I'd always loved it when she wore blue, making her eyes explode with color. And then when she'd spilled all that coffee down her dress, her cheeks had flushed with embarrassment and . . .

I ran a hand across my face, an attempt to wipe the image of her from my mind. It didn't work, nor did it remove the guilt I felt that she'd wound up in such a mess in the first place. It hadn't been my fault—not directly anyway. But I *was* the man she'd been running away from.

When the cab pulled up in front of the hotel, I followed Isaac out of the car, but then paused on the sidewalk. A flower shop with a deep blue awning and a bright pink sign sat right next to the hotel.

"I'll be right back," I said to Isaac. And then I went inside.

Chapter Three

Dani

"What, did they make you *brew* the coffee yourself?" Sasha's words were biting when I finally made it back to her office, coffee in hand. I handed over her cup.

"Sorry. There was a . . . long line," I said.

"At eleven-thirty in the morning? I find that hard to believe." She took a long sip of her macchiato. "At least it's still warm."

I swallowed a sarcastic retort. What was with her? Her mood had been declining over the past few weeks to the point that it felt like she always had something to be upset about.

"What happened to your dress?" Sasha asked.

I looked down, embarrassment flooding my cheeks all over again. She was lucky one of the coffees that had survived had been hers. "Someone ran into me on the way out of the coffee shop. It was an accident."

"Ugh." Her lips turned down in disgust. "Well you can't work looking like that."

I glanced again at my dress, pulling it away from my skin. I *really* wasn't loving the stickiness inside my bra.

"I'd say go find something in the sample room,

but . . ." Sasha hesitated, looking me up and down. "With your curves, I'm not sure anything will fit."

Nice. "I'll figure something out," I said, hoping it wasn't a lie. "Sasha, are you okay? You seem . . . agitated."

She gave me a dismissive wave and moved to sit down behind her desk. "I'm fine," she said irritably. "It's just been a long morning."

"Okay. Well, let me know if there's anything I can do for you."

"Actually before you go, Dani, there is one thing."

"Sure. Anything."

"Do you remember the navy dress? The one with the fabric issue? Isabelle called this morning and it's not going to work. For all her experience, she can't seem to make the back-zipper seam lay flat. She says it keeps *puckering.*"

So that was why Sasha was in a bad mood. Changing the fabric had been her idea. I'd designed the dress, but since I wasn't a real designer, she usually took my designs and tweaked them to make them hers. I didn't love the arrangement, but it was all part of the process. Paying my dues. Proving to Sasha I had what it took to design. I was close, too. She'd been dropping hints lately about me being ready for the design team.

Just the same, Sasha didn't love it when it

looked like I knew more about clothes than she did. Which was why the fabric puckering would always be Isabelle's fault and not hers. It didn't help that I'd known the fabric switch wasn't going to work and had told Sasha as much. The fabric I'd used in the prototype was a thicker knit, with just enough stretch for ease of movement, but with much more structure.

The charmeuse she'd swapped it for was meant to drape loosely, softly. It was *not* meant for box pleats. But Sasha had refused to take my advice, demanding we create an additional sew-by in the charmeuse. The sew-by sample was the most important one, acting as a gauge for what the piece would require in production and how much it would cost. If Isabelle—the best seamstress at LeFranc—couldn't get a sample made correctly? There was no way the piece could go to manufacturing.

"Do we still have the original sample?" Sasha asked. "The one in the navy with the tiny, pink pinstripe?"

I tried to hide my irritation. She was talking as if I might not know exactly which dress she meant. Like it wasn't the dress I had made at home, on my own time, after she'd foisted the sample fabric on me and begged me to turn it into something "stunning."

"We do," I said, my face emotionless.

"Good. We'll have to send that one as the

sew-by. There simply isn't time to make another one."

Six months ago, I might have been thrilled by the victory. My design, unchanged, on the racks at LeFranc. But this time, the victory felt hollow. As far as anyone else knew, Sasha was the designer. "I'll take care of it," I said halfheartedly.

Sasha's voice softened. "This is a win for you, Dani. That's your dress going to production. Your design."

No, a win would be presenting the design to Alicio myself. Letting him know it was mine and getting the credit I deserved. A win would be making the same salary the designers made instead of doing Sasha's job for a third of that amount. I hated that money even had to be a part of it. My friend Chase was already a LeFranc designer and had told me he'd take me on as an intern without a second thought. But I couldn't take a nonpaying internship, even if it meant face time with the design team. Living in New York City wasn't free.

"I know," I said, hoping I'd sufficiently masked my disdain. "And I appreciate it. I'll pull the original sew-by sample and send it over."

"Good girl," Sasha said. "Did you decide about the reservations tonight? At Rao's?"

I nodded. "My brother's in town so I invited him to go with me."

She frowned. "Your brother? How *nice*."

35

She moved to the edge of her desk and perched herself on the end, one Prada-clad foot crossing over the other. "Did you know that's where Alicio and I first had dinner together? Five years ago today, actually. That's why we're going away this weekend. To celebrate the anniversary of when we first—" She paused. "Well. I suppose you don't want to know the details of all that."

"I'm sure it was wonderful," I said, happy she'd spared me the details. It was Sasha's favorite subject—just how *in love* she and Alicio were—but I wasn't in the mood to relive her first *anything* with Alicio, dinner or otherwise.

As Sasha rambled on about the trip she and Alicio were taking to the Caribbean, my thoughts drifted back to Alex. What had happened with his stepfather that day? And more importantly, why couldn't he have talked to me about it? A familiar tightening filled my belly and I forced myself to breathe, to stay in control of my emotions. I'd carried the sting of his rejection for months— long enough that it had dulled to something I could almost forget about from day to day. But when I'd run into him at Java Jean's, it was like the bandage I'd placed over my wounds was ripped away, taking half my skin clean off.

"Did you hear me, Dani?" Sasha asked, a slight edge to her voice.

"What?"

"My three o'clock appointment?" She waved

her hand in front of her like I ought to know exactly what she was talking about.

I *had* to get Alex out of my head.

"Oh, right. You want me to . . . confirm?"

She breathed out an annoyed sigh. "I want you to push it to tomorrow morning. What's gotten into you today?"

"I'm sorry. I'm just distracted. I'll take care of the appointment."

"Thank you. But go clean yourself up first. You're starting to smell."

Chase sifted through a rack of sales samples from last season. "How do you feel about black?" He pulled out a black sheath dress and held it up.

"Black is great, but no way these hips are fitting in that dress."

Chase looked me over. "True. What about this one?" He pulled out another. "With the flared skirt, you'd have a little more room."

"Here. Let me try." I stepped behind another rack of dresses and peeled off my wet clothes before shimmying into the new dress. It was strapless—a little more Friday night than regular workday—but it fit great and it was dry. I spotted a white button-down on a different rack and reached for it. "Can I have this too?" I asked Chase.

"Fine by me," he said over his shoulder, his back respectfully turned while I changed. "This is all heading down to the basement for the sample sale next month. No one will miss it."

I put on the shirt, cinching it up and tying it just under my bust line, then rolled the sleeves up to the elbow. "There. Does it work?"

He turned around. "Throw on a chunky necklace and you just improvised yourself a killer outfit." He picked up my discarded dress and hung it up. "And this . . . this is definitely a Dani original." He fingered the lace. "I like."

I shrugged my shoulders playfully. "I know a thing or two about fashion."

"More than Sasha, that's for sure."

I looked over his shoulder at the closed sample room door. It wasn't likely anyone would walk in and hear us, but the door wasn't locked, which made me nervous. Chase was the only person at LeFranc who knew just how much involvement I had with Sasha's designs.

"Do you remember the navy dress she pulled out of the collection last week?"

"Yours, right? Except, she wanted to do it in teal charmeuse?" He rolled his eyes.

"Isabelle couldn't do it," I said with a grin. "She called Sasha this morning and said she can't make the fabric work."

"Of course she couldn't. Alicio himself couldn't make box pleats work with charmeuse. Does that mean we're doing it in the navy?"

"Yep."

He held up his hand for a high five. "Look at you, getting a dress into a premiere LeFranc collection."

I raised my hands in mock victory. "And look at me not getting credit for it."

His face fell. "I hate that woman."

"Don't hate her. She's good to me."

"She's good to you so she can keep using you."

"It's not like that," I said. Even as I said it, I knew my words weren't true.

"It's exactly like that," Chase said. "And it's about time you wake up and see it."

My shoulders slumped. "Please don't, Chase."

"Don't what? Tell you you're better than this? That she doesn't deserve your loyalty?"

"Don't stomp all over my hope," I said.

"No." He waved a finger in front of my face. "I'm not letting you pin your hopes on her. How many times has she told you she's going to talk to Alicio about your designs? How many times has she promised she'll introduce you, let him know"—he held up his fingers in air quotes and pitched his voice high in a remarkably accurate impression of Sasha—"just what you're capable of? You don't need that woman," he continued. "You've got more talent in the end of your nose than she has in her entire surgically enhanced body. And that's why I don't think she's ever going to tell Alicio about you. You're a threat. Right now, she's got you where she can control you. You do the work, she gets the credit. As long as you're willing to do her bidding, I don't see her screwing that up. At least not on purpose."

My jaw tensed. "It's easy for you to be critical because you already have your dream job. What else am I supposed to do?"

There was more he wanted to say. I could tell by the way the corner of his mouth kept twitching. But he was too good a friend to push me further. "Just don't rely on her alone, okay? Watch the job board. If anything in the design room opens up, tell me and I'll submit a recommendation for you."

He'd made the offer before. But odds were against anything opening up. Internships, sure. But not the real deal. Working at LeFranc was a dream job for *any* designer, not just me. Turnover was rare.

"You know I'll stand by your work, Dani." He reached over and squeezed my arm. "You deserve it."

I pulled my still-coffee-sticky hair into a messy bun on top of my head, pulling a few strands loose around my face. "What do you think?" I asked Chase. "Passable?"

He looked up from the tray of jewelry he'd been sorting through. "Perfect. You just need this." He held up a strand of chunky turquoise pearls, motioning for me to turn around so he could secure the clasp around my neck.

"Seriously? Can I keep?"

"Like I said, no one will miss anything from in here." He turned me around, hands on either shoulder. "There. Now you really are perfect."

I leaned forward and kissed his cheek. "Thank you."

Chase grabbed the coffee-stained dress before turning toward the door. "I'm getting this cleaned for you."

"You don't have to do that." I reached for it. "I'll drop it off on my way home."

He waved my hand away. "Whatever. I want to. Plus, I know a guy. It'll look as good as the day you made it."

"You're too good to me."

"Speaking of how wonderful I am," Chase said, tossing me a grin, "I almost forgot. Darius asked me to give this to you." He pulled a thumb drive out of his pocket and handed it over. "He said you'd know what it was and would probably scream the second it was in your hands."

My eyes went wide. "Seriously? It's done?"

Chase threw up his hands, the dress draped over his wrist bumping into my side. "I have no idea. Darius told me nothing."

"Oh my word. It's done, it's done, it's done!" It was all I could do not to actually jump up and down with excitement.

"Why are we so excited?!" Chase whisper yelled.

I took a deep, calming breath. "It's Elliott Hart's new album. Darius did the sound mixing and he told me he would sneak me a copy as soon as it was finished. I thought I still had weeks to wait."

"Elliott Hart. Is that the piano guy you love so much?"

"Yes!" I followed Chase to the sample room door. "And it's been forever since he released any new stuff. I guess he got married and had a kid or whatever. But this!" I held up the thumb drive. "This feels like gold in my hands."

"That Darius," Chase said. "He's quite the charmer, isn't he?" He opened the door and led the way to the elevator where he pushed the button to take us back up to the fifth floor.

"Oh, he's my favorite," I said, my face serious. "No question. I mean, I know I technically met you first and that maybe you deserve some sort of loyalty for that, but really. Darius is special."

Chase thrust the dress back at me. "I take it back. You can take care of your own dry cleaning."

I sniffed primly. "Maybe I'll ask Darius to do it."

Chase chuckled. "He'd probably do it. I'm the nicest person in New York City and he still makes me look like the kitten-kicking uncle no one wants at Christmas dinner."

The man Chase had married five years ago

really *was* embodied perfection. He was gorgeous, for one, tall and suave, with beautiful brown skin and this velvet voice that sounded like music even when he was saying the most basic things. But he also had the best heart—better than anyone I'd ever known. He was gentle and forgiving and always gave everyone the benefit of the doubt.

His relationship with Chase kept me hoping I'd eventually be in love again myself. They effortlessly supported each other with this quiet, steady devotion; it was the kind of relationship I might not have believed was actually real if I hadn't known them both so well, if I hadn't witnessed it firsthand on an almost daily basis.

It was also the kind of relationship that might have made me burn with jealousy if I hadn't loved them both as much as I did.

The elevator doors dinged open and Chase and I stepped inside. "You're going to get him fired if you don't stop begging for advance copies," Chase said. "You know he'll never tell you no."

"Darius is the best sound engineer Blaze Records has. They won't fire him. Plus, I don't beg. This is the only album I've ever asked him for."

"If we don't count the Jenna Fields album he gave you last Christmas."

My mouth dropped open. "That was a gift!"

Chase laughed. "Right. And you didn't drop *any* hints that you wanted it."

I smiled sheepishly and shrugged my shoulders, the thumb drive held tightly in my hands. "Please tell Darius thank you and I love him dearly."

Two hours later, I was back at my desk, earbuds in my ears and sketchbook open in front of me. I still had fifteen minutes of a lunch break I'd finally managed to squeeze into the afternoon hours, so I used the time to brainstorm new dress ideas. I cranked up the volume on the new Elliott Hart album, which was every bit as fantastic as I had expected. Ten seconds into the next song, Chase pulled one of my earbuds out and stuck it into his own ear. "How is it? Everything you hoped for and more?"

"Yes. Amazing. Brilliant. Astounding. I love him and wish I could marry him and his amazing piano hands."

Chase dropped into the chair across from my desk, then tossed a furtive look over his shoulder.

I followed his gaze but didn't see anything that looked alarming. "What's up with you?"

He gave his head a tiny shake. "Quick. Act natural. Like I've got a reason to be here."

"What? Why?"

He tossed another glance over his shoulder. Who was he expecting to see? "Because Mylie told me not to tell you anything. She didn't want me to ruin the surprise."

"What are you talking about? What surprise?"

He scratched his chin thoughtfully. "How's your dating life?"

"My dating life?"

"Sure. You met anyone new?"

"Chase, what is going on?"

"Why don't *you* tell *me* what's going on?"

I shot him a look. "I have no idea what you're talking about."

He looked for Mylie one more time, then leaned forward, leaning his elbows onto my desk. "Spill it, Dani. Who's the man?"

I echoed his movements, leaning forward so our faces were barely a foot apart. "What man?"

He threw his hands in the air and sighed. "Gah. You're impossible."

Seconds later, Mylie, LeFranc's receptionist, rounded the corner, a long, thin box in her hands. When she saw Chase, her smile dropped. "Seriously? You had to run ahead and tell her?"

Chase smiled innocently. "Tell her what? We were just chatting." He crossed one leg over the other and leaned back, revealing his socks— bright pink and yellow paisley. It made me smile.

As a gay man in his twenties, living in New York *and* working in fashion, Chase almost had a moral obligation to be respectably fashionable himself. His look wasn't flashy at all—very tailored, very clean—but his socks were reliably colorful, a pop of something to echo the color of his tie, or the pinstripe of his vest.

As a designer, Chase's eye for color was his greatest strength. He was a master at pulling out accent colors, adding just the right something to make pieces work. For the other designers, it was maddening. How he could look at a piece and say with astounding conviction, "It needs turquoise," or, "Cut the yellow and add peach instead." The smart ones listened to him. As long as I'd known him, he'd never steered me wrong.

Mylie huffed and dropped the box onto my desk. "These were delivered for you, Dani." She eyed the card.

I didn't move from my chair. Just sat there, my arms folded across my chest. "Thanks."

She tapped her toe impatiently. "Aren't you going to read the card?"

I was completely baffled as to who might have sent me flowers, but there was no way I was going to satisfy Mylie's insatiable need to know everyone else's business. I lifted my shoulder in a casual shrug. "I don't need to open it. My dad sends me flowers on my birthday every year. I know they're from him."

"Oh," Mylie said, making no effort to conceal her disappointment. "That's not very exciting." She turned and walked back toward her desk.

"Your birthday's not for another three weeks," Chase said.

I reached for the card. "But Mylie doesn't know that."

He grinned. "Then there *is* something you need to tell me."

"I swear there's nothing to tell! Your guess is as good as mine as to who these are from." I slid the square card out of its envelope. The paper was thick cardstock, with a tiny satin trim.

"Fancy," Chase said over my shoulder.

"Seriously? I can't even read it first?"

"Fine, fine," he huffed. He took a step back but arched his neck like he was still trying to see.

Dani—I feel responsible for what happened at the coffee shop. I know flowers can't replace your dress. Hopefully they can brighten your day. I want you to know I'll be at dinner tonight with you and Isaac. I didn't want you to be blindsided. —Alex PS. I hope this is enough to cover the dry cleaning.

Two twenty-dollar bills fluttered to my lap, but I hardly noticed them.

I handed Chase the card and sank back into my chair. *Alex* would be at dinner?

How? Why?

"Wait, is this *Alex* Alex? Your Alex?" He lowered his voice to a whisper. "LeFranc's Alex?"

I nodded. "But why is he going to be at dinner with my brother?"

"Uh, more importantly, why didn't you tell me you ran into him at Java Jean's?"

Chase had been Alex's friend as much as he was mine. Which was maybe the reason I *hadn't* told him. He knew too much. And he knew *me* too well. He'd hear in my words exactly how unmoored I felt, like a skiff in a flood tide. I sat, unmoving, so Chase reached for the flowers, carefully lifting the lid off the box. He whistled and handed the box to me. A dozen roses lay inside, their petals a vibrant orange.

"I think you need to tell me what happened," Chase said.

I shrugged and shook my head. "There isn't much to tell. I ordered coffee, he came in behind me. We spoke for twenty seconds, he tried to apologize, I told him to stop, then I ran away."

"Right into the Cappuccino machine," Chase said, his voice light.

"Shut up."

"So how was it to see him again?" Chase asked. "How did he look?"

I sighed. "He was wearing Armani."

Chase echoed my sigh with his own. "Armani," he repeated softly.

"I guess this is for you," I said, holding up the cash. "For the dry cleaning."

Chase pushed it away. "I don't want it. I'll never catch Darius at this rate."

I grinned. "Catch Darius in the imagined nice-ness competition that doesn't actually matter because I love you both the same?" I held up one of the bills. "Split it with me?"

He rolled his eyes. "Fine." He tucked the money into his pocket. "It wasn't him you ran into, right? It was nice of him to think of the dry cleaning."

"It was a random guy at the door. But if I hadn't been running away . . ."

"Hmm. Good point. Alex always *was* thoughtful, wasn't he?"

I held up a finger. "Don't get distracted. We are not reminiscing here." I pushed the flowers aside and pulled my cell phone out of my top drawer. "I can at least figure out the answer to one question." Determination filled my voice.

I tapped out a text to Isaac. *Why is Alex Randall coming to dinner tonight?*

B/C I invited him, Isaac immediately replied.

I rolled my eyes. *Thanks for the information, genius. WHY did you invite him?*

I drummed my fingers on the desk waiting for Isaac to respond. *He works for me,* he finally texted. *I told you that right after I hired him.*

He had to be kidding. *TO BE YOUR TAX ACCOUNTANT. Are you the reason he's in New York?*

He's not my tax accountant. He's my business manager.

I froze. Why did Isaac need a business manager? *WTH??? Why? Doing what?*

Making the Nutella sandwiches, Isaac said. *Why are you being weird about this?*

"So?" Chase asked. "What's the verdict?"

I put my phone down, my brows drawn close together in confusion. "He's my brother's business manager."

Sasha's door opened and she appeared. "Dani, have you—" She paused. "Oh. Hello, Chase. Nice to see you working so hard." As a senior designer, Sasha technically outranked Chase, but she wasn't his boss. Other than her influence with Alicio, she couldn't do much to hurt him.

He stood, shooting her a look I'd never have the nerve to give and sauntered past her. "I'll go toe to toe with you any day," he said. "Later, Dani."

"A little less socializing, a little more working, Dani," Sasha said. "Don't make me ask you again."

I hastily replaced the lid on the flower box and shifted it to the back of my desk. "Of course. Sorry about that."

"Did you take care of the navy dress?"

I nodded. "Everything's all set."

"And you checked on my appointment for tomorrow morning? If I'm not out of here by noon, it will ruin the entire weekend."

"Everything is confirmed," I said. "The writer from *Elite* will be here at nine. And I've arranged for the samples from the spring line to be brought to your office by five today so they're ready for her preview in the morning."

"Perfect. That's what I wanted to hear." She pulled her handbag onto her shoulder and slipped a pair of sunglasses onto her face. "If that's all taken care of, I'm going to head out early."

"One quick reminder," I said before she'd gotten past me. "I have the day off tomorrow."

She paused and lifted her sunglasses, her lips pursed into a frown. "Did I know about this?"

"You did. For my best friend's bridal shower."

Her face fell. "Oh. Right. I suppose I do remember. Well, enjoy your weekend."

She paused as she passed by, her finger tracing the edge of the sketchbook I'd inadvertently left on the desk when Chase had bombarded me with flower news. "What's this?"

I quickly pulled the sketchbook away and closed it. "It's nothing. Just some doodling."

She gave me a curious look. "It looked like a wedding gown."

I shrugged and held the sketchbook tightly against my chest. "Oh, you know how it is. Single girls always dreaming of their weddings."

"Sure," she said, her brow furrowed. "Well, all right then. I guess I'll see you Monday."

I watched her walk down the hallway until she turned the corner toward the elevator and disappeared out of sight. I took a deep breath and opened the sketchbook to the page Sasha had seen.

I would design dresses for Sasha all day. Dresses, pants, jackets, whatever she wanted for LeFranc, I'd do it. But this? This was mine.

It wasn't the first wedding dress I'd designed, but it was by far the prettiest. It was the prettiest thing I'd ever designed, period. And that was what my roommate, Paige, deserved. She'd been my best friend since elementary school and had more than earned her right to a custom dress. Paige had spent hours as a human dress form while I pinned and tucked and draped fabric over her body, then graciously performed runway shows for my parents, she the only model, and I, the glowing designer taking the stage at the end of the show. A wedding dress was the *least* I could do. My fingers started to itch just looking at the sketch. It was already half-sewn back at my apartment, and I couldn't wait to finish it.

Thoughts of working on Paige's dress only half-distracted me from the flower box perched on the edge of my desk. The flowers, and all that they stood for.

Alex worked with Isaac. Alex would be at dinner.

Alex.

Alex.

Chapter Four

Alex

I stood in front of the restaurant, nervously looking up and down the street. It was still fifteen minutes before Dani was supposed to arrive, but fifteen minutes didn't feel like enough cushion. The last thing I wanted was for her to show up while I was standing out front talking to Alicio.

Well, probably not Alicio. I doubted he'd show up himself. He'd said he had something to give me, but Alicio rarely did anything he could have someone else do for him.

A sleek, black car pulled up in front of the restaurant, slowing to a stop. I took a step forward, anxiety gripping my gut with an unyielding fist. I hadn't seen anyone from my stepfamily in almost a year.

Gabriel climbed out of the car and the tension in my shoulders eased.

"Alex," he said, a surprising measure of warmth in his voice. He held out his hand. "It's good to see you."

We shook hands and I nodded. "Good to see you too. How are . . . how's everything, I guess?"

Gabriel raised his eyebrows as if surprised I had even asked. "Good. Great. And you?"

I'd never been close with either of the LeFranc brothers. A few years older than me, they'd considered me little more than a nuisance growing up. But Gabriel hadn't been as cruel as his brother. Whenever Mom had wanted me to feel welcome during my summer and holiday visits, she'd always used Gabriel as her emissary. That she had sensed some measure of good in him and trusted him not to be a jerk went a long way; I suddenly wondered if he'd volunteered to come and meet me, if he'd understood he was the only one that might manage the task civilly.

I shrugged. "I can't complain. It's nice to be back in the city."

The silence stretched between us until Gabriel cleared his throat and pulled an envelope out of his suit pocket. "Right. So I'm supposed to give you this." He held out the envelope.

I took it and opened it long enough to check the contents. A magnetic key to a storage facility in Chelsea sat inside. I nodded, slipping the envelope into my own pocket. "Thanks."

"There isn't much in it," Gabriel said. "Some furniture. A few photo albums and jewelry. Some artwork. I guess when Sasha started moving stuff around at home, she wanted to just get rid of it."

I narrowed my gaze. "She would have thrown away Mom's old photo albums?"

Gabriel shrugged. "They're from before she

married into the family. She probably assumed you had your own copies."

I scoffed. "Right."

"Anyway. You have Justine to thank for saving it all. She's been paying the storage fee out of her own pocket so it might be nice for you to compensate her for all that. She was the one that asked Alicio to reach out to you."

Suddenly the entire situation made a lot more sense. The text from Alicio a few weeks back had been unexpected, but Justine—his housekeeper—had always been kind to me. That she was behind the gesture was less surprising.

"Right," I said again. "I'll take care of it."

Gabriel stepped back toward the car. "I guess that's it then."

"Thanks, Gabe," I said. "I appreciate you meeting me."

He opened the car door, pausing before climbing inside. "They're going to invite you to the wedding."

I nodded. "Okay."

"It'll be in Florida. On Islamorada. Victor's probably going to call you and tell you not to come. But you should ignore him and come anyway." He shrugged. "If you want."

It was a very small olive branch, and only from one member of the family, but even that was more than I'd expected.

"Just think about it," he said before I could

55

respond. Then he climbed into the car and was gone.

I moved into the restaurant and sat next to Isaac, trying to sort out my thoughts. I would sometimes go months without giving the LeFrancs more than a passing thought. I did not need them in my life; I didn't really even *want* them in my life. Yet, Gabriel's invitation had felt sincere enough to trigger a dormant hope for something I'd never gotten among the LeFrancs. *Acceptance.*

I didn't like what that said about me. I wasn't supposed to still care. I *didn't* care.

At least, I thought I didn't.

I drummed my fingers on the table and glanced at my watch. 7:34. I'd been nervous all afternoon about seeing Dani again, but I suddenly welcomed the distraction she'd be. Four minutes wasn't really all that late, and yet, I couldn't keep myself from glancing toward the door every fifteen seconds.

"Alex," Isaac said, his voice dry. "You're going to pull a muscle if you don't relax and sit still."

I huffed and settled back into my chair. "Shut up."

"Why are you so stressed out about seeing her? I thought it was all over between you two."

"It is. It . . . was. You just could have given me some warning. I don't appreciate seeing her again under these circumstances."

Isaac gave his head a derisive shake and reached for his phone. "Under what circumstances? Don't pretend like this is my doing. It's not like I kept you chained to the radiator in Charleston. You could have come up to see her anytime. Whatever you feel right now is completely on you."

My jaw tensed with frustration, but Isaac was right. As much as I hated to admit it, I was the only one responsible for the awkwardness between Dani and me. And that was the problem. Shame was a *very* uncomfortable feeling.

While Isaac was good at spouting off generalities regarding my relationship history with his sister, in truth, he didn't know much about what had happened between us. Isaac was a friend, but he liked to keep things surface level. I had my own theories about why that was, revolving largely around personal insecurities and fear of rejection—one didn't spend years (or at least summers) in family therapy without picking up a few scraps of useful information—but I hardly had room to throw mental health diagnoses at Isaac. I was clearly just as much a mess as he was. I was, after all, the one who had walked out on Dani. The one who had walked out on everything.

I took a deep breath and rolled my neck, cracking it on one side, then the other—a vain attempt to clear my head. When I looked up, Dani approached the table.

I stood, my breath lodged in my throat. She looked amazing. Her blonde hair was . . . and her blue eyes . . . and her dress. I'd seen it before. It was the dress she'd had on when we first met.

I'd first spoken to Dani on the balcony of an apartment on the Upper East Side, at a party I'd had no desire to attend. I'd only been there because my stepbrothers had dragged me along, insisting it was part of my responsibility to "represent the brand," to think of "the family image." It wasn't that I didn't *like* fashion. I'd always appreciated a well-tailored suit, but I didn't like the networking. The fierce competition. The hobnobbing with socialites. Working for LeFranc, I was required to be on display at all times. It was exhausting.

But then I'd seen Dani, the wind lifting the curls from her neck, and my heart had nearly stopped. She'd been having a conversation with my stepbrother, Victor, and looked so uncomfortable, I'd immediately decided she needed rescuing. It wasn't a stretch to assume Victor was being rude to her, so I took a gamble and lied, telling Victor his secretary had called me looking for him. As soon as he excused himself to call her back, I took his place on the balcony next to Dani.

"Seriously, thank you," Dani had said as soon as Victor was out of earshot. "Even a LeFranc isn't worth the way he stared at me."

"Like he's a lion, and you're lunch?" I'd said.

"He's my stepbrother. Unfortunately, he doesn't improve with time."

"Stepbrother," she'd repeated. "So you're a LeFranc too?"

I'd never actually cared about being a LeFranc until that moment. Until I realized how much Dani wanted me to say yes. I should have recognized her desire as the warning it was. "I'm not as much of a LeFranc as Victor," I'd said instead, "but Alicio still claims me and lets me work for him. That must count for something."

She smiled wide, the sight making my breath catch in my throat. "It definitely counts." She held her hand out. "I'm Dani. Danielle, actually. But friends call me Dani."

Her hand had felt warm and soft in mine. We'd spent the rest of the evening together after that, and then I'd walked her home.

We'd had lunch the following day, and dinner the next Friday, texting multiple times a day in between. After that, things had happened quickly. For almost a year we were nearly inseparable.

Until I'd left.

A new wave of shame washed over me. For a moment I wondered if she'd worn the same dress on purpose. Was she trying to tell me something? Remind me of something?

If so, she'd hit the mark. She left me speechless. I swallowed and willed myself to breathe slowly. "Hi," I managed, my voice strangled and cracked.

I cleared my throat and tried again. "Hello."

She met my eyes only briefly, a small smile of acknowledgment flitting across her face before she settled her gaze on her brother, who still sat at the table, *his* gaze glued to his phone.

"It's nice to see you too, little brother," Dani said.

Isaac held up his hand, one finger raised in the air, while his other hand continued to tap something out on the screen. A few seconds more passed before he nodded, turning his phone over with a thud of finality. "There. Done." He stood and pulled his sister into a hug, though from my view, neither of them seemed particularly happy about the physical contact.

"How are you doing, Dandelion?" Isaac asked as we all sat at the table.

I watched Dani cringe at the nickname, her hand reflexively reaching for her hair. She'd told me once how much she hated it—I remembered the conversation—but I couldn't remember where it had come from. Isaac would tell me, and probably jump at the chance to embarrass his sister, but the look on Dani's face warned me away from the subject.

"You're never going to stop with that, are you?" Dani asked as she opened her menu.

Isaac grinned. "Not as long as I know how much it bugs you."

She pursed her lips but didn't look up, her eyes

flitting from one thing to another far too fast to actually be reading them.

"It was nice of you to share your reservation with us," I said, glancing from Dani to Isaac and back to Dani again. "Rao's isn't an easy table to get."

Dani looked up, her expression sharp. "It's easy enough for a LeFranc," she said, an air of . . . *something* in her voice. "Sasha is a *very* generous boss."

My fist clenched under the table. So that was how the evening was going to go? I leaned back, not breaking Dani's gaze and raised my eyebrows. "Yes, Sasha is very good at getting what she wants."

Dani smiled, her lips tight. "Isn't that part of being successful? Getting what you want isn't such a bad thing."

I wanted to keep pushing. Getting what you want at the expense of everyone else hardly made you successful. But Sasha's problems ran much deeper than being a little bit of a cutthroat. She was a criminal, guilty of fraud and extortion.

At least, I thought she was.

I'd only been working on the financial side of LeFranc a couple of months when I'd started seeing things that didn't line up. But I wasn't important enough to have access to all of LeFranc's accounts and couldn't really dig for answers without it. Then my stepfather had threatened to disinherit me if I continued to ask questions. *That* had made it easy to walk away.

But that wasn't an argument I could have with Dani. I'd tried. The last conversation we'd had before I left New York had ended in an argument about my suspicions.

Dani loved working for Sasha and had insisted I was wrong. She had even gone so far as to suggest I disliked Sasha simply because she was marrying Alicio, somehow replacing the memory of my mother. Funny—Alicio had made the same argument.

"I take it things at work are still going well," I said. That Dani had so quickly reminded me of her loyalty to Sasha, and to LeFranc, left a bitter taste in my mouth and reminded me of why I'd felt like I'd had to leave in the first place.

A shadow of doubt flitted across her face, but she shook it off so quickly, I wondered if I'd imagined it. "Things are great," she said. "Better than ever."

I narrowed my gaze. Dani had a glass face. Her words were telling me one story, but it wasn't one that matched her emotions.

A surge of anger pulsed through me. Anger at Sasha, at Alicio, even at Dani for falling victim to Sasha's duplicity. Someone was eventually going to get hurt, and it killed that I was powerless to stop it.

Chapter Five

Dani

Even with all afternoon to prepare for Alex's presence at dinner, it was still ridiculous to see him sitting there next to Isaac. Taking myself completely out of the equation, I couldn't begin to wrap my head around the idea of him working with my brother.

Alex was Armani suits and perfect hair. He loved art museums and classical music. I mean, he'd had season tickets to the New York Philharmonic. The only classical music Isaac had ever intentionally heard was my eighth-grade orchestra recital in which I'd very badly played the cello. To imagine my video-game-playing, tech-nerd brother hiring a Harvard-educated accountant? It didn't add up.

"So, how did this happen?" I said, motioning to the two of them.

They glanced at each other.

Alex cleared his throat as if to answer, but Isaac beat him to it. "*Random I* has been doing really well. Well enough it seemed like having a business manager was a smart move."

That didn't come close to answering my question. I mean, Isaac having a business manager was still a lot to swallow. But he'd hired my ex-boyfriend. I needed more explanation. I looked at Alex.

He appeared sheepish, as if he knew Isaac's answer hadn't really addressed my concerns. Well, *good*. Served him right.

"All the accountants in the world, Isaac, and you hire my ex-boyfriend?" I raised my eyebrows.

At least Alex had the good sense not to say anything. He kept his eyes down, his hand resting on the table beside his plate.

"I didn't want just anybody," Isaac said. "I knew I could trust Alex. You seemed to like him okay. I figured that was a good endorsement. Plus, have you seen the man's resume?"

"But he didn't *work* for me; he was my *boyfriend*. How is that an endorsement?"

"If he were dishonest, or a criminal, or a terrible person, he wouldn't have been your boyfriend. Seems pretty straightforward to me. Plus, he was already in Charleston. Hiring local meant I didn't have to offer a relocation package."

Weirdly enough, Alex had grown up not ten minutes from my childhood home back in South Carolina, though we'd definitely run in different circles. My parents had done pretty well for themselves, and we'd lived in a nice part of town, but we were *new* Charleston money. The kind that lived in the suburbs. We played on

Charleston's historic peninsula. Shopped there. Ate there. Walked through the waterfront parks. But we didn't *live* on the peninsula. That took an entirely different kind of money. The kind that went back generations to when streets were made of cobblestone and everyone had names like Alexander Ellison Randall III. It wasn't weird that Alex had gone back to Charleston when he'd left New York.

It *was* weird that he'd started working for Isaac.

"What if we broke up because he's dishonest and a terrible person?"

Isaac rolled his eyes. "That isn't why you broke up. I talked to Mom."

"You talked to . . . ?" Heat rose in my cheeks. Having a conversation with your brother about why you and your boyfriend split up *in the presence* of said boyfriend was *not* a good idea. Imagining him talking the whole thing over with my mother felt even worse.

My shoulders slumped. "You should have told me."

Isaac didn't even break eye contact. "I did tell you."

"You didn't—" My argument froze in my throat. Technically, Isaac was right. It was nothing but my own judgments against Isaac's professionalism that had led me to assume he'd only needed Alex for tax purposes.

"We haven't kept it a secret, Dani," Isaac said.

"He's been on the show a few times. In pictures on Instagram. I think we both figured you knew."

My eyes darted to Alex who lifted his shoulder in a shrug.

So this was on me?

If I was a better sister, followed Isaac's career more closely, I'd have known my ex-boyfriend and twin brother were new best friends?

Moisture gathered in my eyes and I squeezed them shut, not sure if it was the injustice of their accusation or the truth behind it that triggered the tears. I willed my emotions to settle; neither reason was good enough to cry in public.

"It wasn't enough," Alex said softly. "I shouldn't have agreed to work with Isaac without talking to you first. That's on me."

Warmth surged through my chest at his admission but acknowledging as much felt like a betrayal. I wasn't supposed to feel any warmth toward Alex. It had taken me a solid six months to get to the point where I could even think of him without wanting to scream. Warmth of any kind could *not* creep back in. It was too risky.

The conversation shifted to more neutral topics, which would have been a relief had Isaac not called me Dandelion no fewer than five times. It was a nickname assigned to me in childhood when he and his friends decided my light blonde hair, when frizzed by heat and Southern humidity, looked like dandelion fuzz. The nickname had stuck around way too long. He knew I hated it. And because he was still a toddler, that hatred only fueled his desire to use it.

"Have you talked to Mom lately?" Isaac asked, midway through the main course.

I put down my fork and slid my plate forward, happy to latch onto a subject as benign as our parents. "Not since last week," I answered. "Have you?"

"Yeah, yesterday. But just about house stuff."

"What's wrong with the house?" My parents had been out of the country on an extended tour of Europe—which sounded way too fancy for our middle-class upbringing—for close to six months. They'd converted their house into a temporary vacation rental before leaving and hired a management company to do the heavy lifting, but Isaac still ended up making decisions, overseeing repairs, and doing other tedious stuff that made me grateful I lived out of state.

"One of the renters reported a ceiling leak through the vacation rental website. It's minor, and the house is still functional, but we'll have to fix it eventually. Before hurricane season, for sure."

I studied my brother. The way he spoke of the repairs so matter-of-factly, without any disdain or annoyance, felt . . . *different*. I would have expected him to grumble about the extra work or make some snide remark about cleaning up after our parents while they basked in the European sunshine. But there wasn't a trace of malice in his voice. Before I could reflect further on the *why* behind Isaac's behavior, the check arrived, and Alex picked up the tab.

"I can cover mine," I said, reaching out for the check. "Please. I want to."

Alex shook his head. "It's a business expense. *Isaac's* business expense and I promise he can afford it."

Before I could argue further, Alex cleared his throat and motioned over my shoulder to Isaac. I turned around and saw a man in a bright blue bomber jacket and yellow-tinted aviators walking toward the table. Isaac stood and greeted him with a weird handshake turned half-hug shoulder pat thing. "Rizzo. Good to see you," he said. He motioned for Rizzo to join us at the table.

I looked at Alex, eyebrows raised in question. He gave me an apologetic look and shrugged his shoulders as if to say it wasn't his idea for Rizzo to join us.

"The pleasure's all mine," Rizzo said. He nodded a hello to Alex—they'd apparently met before—then turned his attention to me. He lifted his sunglasses, revealing a pair of dark brown eyes and thick, curly lashes. His mouth lifted in a sly, half-grin. "There is a beautiful woman at the table that I have not met," he said. He looked at Isaac. "How can we amend this situation?"

Amend the situation? Who was this guy?

"Rizzo, this is my twin sister, Dani," Isaac said. "Dani, my friend, Rizzo."

It still wasn't clear why Rizzo was at our dinner table, but it didn't take long for me to figure it out. Apparently, he was a YouTuber like Isaac, only with more subscribers, and more overall success. Rizzo *really* liked to talk about himself. He'd been invited, by Isaac, to join us to finalize details of a charity event Isaac and Alex were planning to which Rizzo had been asked to contribute.

That enough was a lot for me to wrap my brain around.

Isaac was planning a charity event?

"So I'm not a hundred percent sure I'm following," I said, as soon as there was a break in the conversation. "How does the scavenger hunt play into the actual party? And it's all happening here in New York?"

"The five YouTubers that are acting as sponsors," Alex said, "two of whom are Isaac and Rizzo, are from all over the country. New York felt like a great place to meet up. Plus, we needed somewhere populous for the scavenger hunt to work—somewhere with no shortage of people that could use help."

"The scavenger hunt?"

"So here's the basic gist of it," Isaac said. He leaned forward, both elbows on the table and excitement in his eyes. "We're calling it the Compassion Experiment. Each YouTuber will sponsor a team of five people. They can choose their team however they want. Auditions, random selection, whatever. It's up to them. All five teams will report to the main event, happening Christmas Eve here in New York. The time will start, and each team will head out into the city. Instead of *looking* for certain things, the teams will have to accomplish certain tasks. Charitable stuff. Acts of kindness. They'll document it as it's happening, and we'll live stream the video feed from each of the teams online, and at the main event. The winning team, whoever completes the tasks and makes it back first, wins twenty grand."

"But more importantly," Alex added, "all the proceeds from the entire event will be donated to charity. All the ticket revenue, which should be substantial, plus everything from the auction. It will all be donated."

"The auction will conclude that night, at the main event, but it will also be happening online," Isaac said. "Which is kind of the beauty of the entire thing. People at home will be able to attend virtually and participate from wherever they are."

"Right." Alex picked up where Isaac left off. "And there will be entertainment throughout the night as well. We're still working to line up a few acts connected to the YouTube community, but we're hoping to get at least one big name that might draw in a new audience."

I perked up. My piano playing Elliott Hart had gotten his start on YouTube. He was legit famous—had risen far above YouTube notoriety—but I couldn't keep myself from asking. "Entertainers like Elliott Hart?"

Isaac didn't know to make fun of my question or he probably would have. But Alex immediately smiled. He knew firsthand how much I loved Elliott Hart and, from my influence, had quickly become a fan himself. I felt a sudden urge to share the advanced copy of Elliott's new album that Darius had given me with Alex. The second track was a classical interpretation of a Coldplay song he would love.

"I actually asked the same question," Alex said. "But we think he might be a little more than we can afford."

"Even for a charity event?" I said. "It can't hurt to ask, right?"

"Elliott would be great, but his fans are mostly millennials and younger, the same age bracket where *my* audience already hangs out," Isaac said. "But Red Renegade is releasing a revival album next year. I'm kind of thinking a Christmas Eve performance would be a great way for them to reach a new, younger audience."

"Wait," I said. "Red Renegade, the band you

idolized for all of seventh and eighth grade? Weren't they kind of old, even back then?"

"They were not old. They were amazing. *Are* amazing," Isaac said.

Alex leaned toward me. "Red Renegade is even more of a stretch than Elliott Hart. I've tried to reach out to their agent but haven't gotten a response. From what I understand, the band hasn't performed together in years."

I almost asked him if he'd tried texting Darius but thought better of bringing it up in front of Isaac. It would for sure get his hopes up, and even with Darius's connections, odds were probably still low.

"Either way," Isaac said, "we'll figure it out."

"What charity will it benefit?" I asked.

"It's an organization called Thrive," Isaac said. "It focuses on increasing educational and social opportunities for underprivileged neighborhoods through mentoring and outreach programs."

I nodded. "They have programs in Charleston, don't they? I recognize the name."

"The Charleston chapter has been very supportive," Alex said. "They put us in touch with the Thrive national leadership team, who recommended a corporate event planner who has coordinated charity events for them in the past."

"We have a meeting with him tomorrow," Isaac said.

I studied my brother carefully. He was excited,

that much was clear. But something didn't add up. Not with the Isaac that I'd always known. My confusion over his mature handling of our parents' roof repair suddenly tripled.

"So, what's in it for *you?*" I asked.

Isaac stared without blinking. "You would ask that, wouldn't you?"

"I'm not judging, I'm just asking. Surely there's a benefit to you if you're going to all this effort." Maybe I *was* judging. But this was Isaac we were talking about. Isaac who, in my mind, wasn't all that different than he had been eight years ago at age seventeen. His show and channel had evolved over the years, but it was still basically the same thing, none of which struck me as very adult-like. Climbing into an ice bath full of lemon-lime soda. Setting his own hair on fire. Fitting fifty-seven cinnamon bears into his mouth at one time. A massive charity event just for the sake of charity didn't feel very . . . congruent.

It was Rizzo that finally volunteered an answer. "Money," he said smoothly. "An event generates attention. Attention brings subscribers. Subscribers bring hits, hits bring cash. Simple as that."

Isaac didn't look up. "That's not—" He sighed. "Forget it. You wouldn't understand."

"Obviously exposure is never a bad thing," Alex said cautiously, "and there will be multiple internet personalities involved so Isaac's fan base does have the potential to grow, but we're trying to approach this as more of a giving back scenario."

I was momentarily distracted by the soothing lilt of Alex's voice, the way his g's were almost silent, the way his words rolled into each other like tiny ripples of sound. Isaac and I sounded Southern—but not next to Alex. Our mother was from Maine; we grew up sounding more like her than our Lowcountry father. But Alex was all South Carolina. A longing, deep and intense, swelled inside my chest. I missed *home.*

I forced my brain back to the conversation in front of me. To the way Alex had called Isaac an internet personality instead of just a YouTube star. Somehow, he'd managed to give the entire thing an air of professionalism I'd never associated with Isaac before.

"So, will . . ." I wasn't sure how to formulate my question. "I mean, I think it sounds amazing, but do you think there's that kind of money in your viewership? The kind of money that attends charity events? Or buys stuff at an auction?"

Isaac looked at Alex. "See? I told you she wouldn't get it."

I backpedaled. "I didn't say I didn't get it. I think it sounds amazing, like a really good idea, I just—"

"No, it won't be the kind of event where people wear LeFranc dresses," Isaac said with a measure of contempt that made me uncomfortable. "I know it's hard for you to imagine life outside your fancy, high-end fashion world, but the point of this entire event is for it to be accessible. It's going to be for regular people. For regular fans. Anyone who can get to New York."

"And anyone else who wants to watch the live stream," Alex added. "We had a photoshoot today with Isaac, Rizzo, and the three other hosts to create some promotional material. We're confident the event will be well-attended, and well-watched from home."

I had so many doubts. So many questions. So many reasons to think this was a terrible idea, headed for miserable and certain failure. But I knew better than to doubt my brother again. At least not out loud. He had a lot riding on this; I could tell. "I think it sounds really amazing," I said.

Isaac looked up and met my gaze, a question in his eyes.

"Truly. It's a good idea."

He shrugged, noncommittally, but the lift of his eyebrows told me he was pleased to have my approval.

The rest of the evening was easier. Lighter. Oddly enough, Rizzo influenced the mood for good. For a brief moment, I almost forgot I was at a table with a brother I didn't really get along with *and* my ex-boyfriend. I didn't even mind the stories Isaac told about growing up as a twin.

"So many stupid questions," Isaac said. "Do you have the same thoughts? Do you have a secret language?"

"Are you identical?" I chimed in.

"Oh, that one always killed me," Isaac said. "And then when we'd say no, people would come back with something like, 'oh, yeah, I guess your eyes aren't the same color.' Right, right. Eye color is absolutely more definitive than gender." He pressed his hands against his forehead. "I mean, seriously, people."

"I'm intrigued by the idea of always having someone around like that," Alex said. "I was mostly an only child, at least when I was in Charleston with my dad."

"But you had your stepbrothers in New York," I said.

"Who were genuinely awful at every turn."

"That about sums up having siblings," Isaac said.

Rizzo and I laughed, but Alex didn't. He just sat there, his lips pressed into a tight line. From what he'd told me about his childhood in the past, and it wasn't much, I didn't think the awful he'd referenced was the same kind of awful Isaac and I had been to each other. We'd fought like only siblings could, but ultimately, we came from a loving family. Our parents taught us to respect each other, to love each other. We didn't have to like the same things or have the same friends, but we had to have each other's backs, no matter what. That was what being a family was all about.

I only half-listened as Isaac started another story, my thoughts stuck on Alex and his relationship with Victor and Gabriel. Alicio's sons both worked at LeFranc so I saw them around the office occasionally. Gabriel, I didn't mind too much. He was the quieter brother, always polite and quick to say hello when he passed by, but Victor made me want to jump out of my skin. The way he looked at me. The way he spoke with entitled arrogance and contempt. Even worse, the way he looked at Sasha, who would soon be his *stepmother.*

"I seriously thought I was going to have to throw a rock through the window to get their attention," Isaac said, pulling me back to the present. He scraped up the few remaining crumbs on his dessert plate with the back of his fork. We'd already paid the bill, but Rizzo had ended up ordering a bottle of wine for the table and desserts all around. "There I was, trying to do the kind and decent thing by giving them a heads up," Isaac continued, "and they don't even look up. They keep going at it, hands and tongues going everywhere. So I keep banging, louder and louder, and they finally look up literally seconds before Dad walks in."

"Wait, what are we talking about?" I asked.

Isaac laughed. "Prom night, junior year. When I saved your make-out session from a Dad-flavored interruption."

I raised my hands to my cheeks. "Oh my word! I was seriously so grateful for you that night. But in my defense, we did have a movie on, and the volume was up pretty loud which is a really good reason why we didn't hear you knocking the first time. Also, there was no *going at* anything. We were just kissing. And badly. Jeremy had braces and I was scared I was going to hurt myself."

Isaac pulled out his phone and clicked a few times before handing the phone to Alex. "Did Dani ever tell you she made her own prom dress?"

Alex took the phone. "Really?"

"You do not have that picture on your phone." I leaned over, trying to see whatever Alex was seeing.

"Of course I do," Isaac said. "It was amazing."

I looked at my brother. I would have expected him to be joking, but he looked genuinely sincere, like he actually *did* think my badly made high school prom dress was amazing.

"You should have seen the things she made," he continued. "Out of nothing, too. She could take the ugliest clothes and turn them into the most incredible stuff." He met my eye across the table and grinned sheepishly before taking his phone back from Alex and passing it to Rizzo.

"Ah, high school," Rizzo said, looking at the photo. "So you're a designer?" He turned his attention to me. "You make clothes?"

My eyes reflexively darted to Alex before I forced them to the table. "Oh. Well, not yet. I work for a designer, but I'm still just a PA."

"She could be though," Isaac said. "She could go out on her own and be incredible." He looked at me one more time. "You still could, you know. It'd be better than getting coffee for the stuffed pricks you work with now." His gaze darted to Alex. "No offense, man."

Alex nodded. "None taken."

The whole conversation had stunned me into absolute silence. Isaac had a picture of my high school prom dress on his phone. And he thought the clothes I'd made in high school were amazing. *And* he thought I should be designing on my own? I mean, he'd always joked about it in high school, but only at the same time that he'd called me a wannabe and a sell-out for wanting to work in New York fashion. I'd always assumed his opinions were a result of his general anti-establishment view of the world.

But now he actually sounded like he thought I was good at what I did. Or, rather, what I *wanted* to be doing. It was disconcerting, to say the least.

Moments later, Isaac brought the evening to a sudden halt. "Well, it's been real, Dandi," he said, "but I've got somewhere I need to be."

"You do?" I picked up my phone and glanced at the time. It was getting late, but not *that* late.

"I promised a friend I'd stop by her party." He looked at Rizzo. "You want to come? There might be some company that interests you, if you know what I mean."

I rolled my eyes at the subsequent exclamations of machismo, but it could have been worse. He could have included Alex in his invitation. And while the thought of my brother party-hopping in search of women was bad, thinking of Alex alongside him was enough to make me feel like I'd eaten curdled cream and rotten tomatoes.

I followed Isaac and Rizzo out of the restaurant, Alex behind me, feeling suddenly deflated. It had been months, years even, since I'd spent any time with Isaac that hadn't felt strained and uncomfortable. The dinner had definitely held moments of tension, but the last few minutes when we'd talked about growing up, laughing at old stories, had felt good. *Really* good. Like maybe it was possible for us to figure out a way to actually get along. But then he'd ended the evening so quickly, and in a juvenile way that reminded me of all the reasons why I found him so irritating.

Isaac stopped when he reached the sidewalk in front of the restaurant and turned to face me. "Will you get home okay?" he asked.

I stared. "I live here, Isaac. I know how to get myself home."

"Right. Okay. I was just checking." He looked to Rizzo. "Ready?"

Rizzo nodded.

"I'll see you back at the hotel?" Isaac said to Alex, who nodded in response. Almost like an afterthought, Isaac turned to me one more time, wrapping his arms around me in a vice-like squeeze. "Bye, Dandi. You know I love you, right?"

I shrugged out of his grip. "Fine, fine. Good-bye."

I watched Isaac turn the corner and disappear out of sight, then looked at Alex, still standing beside me. "He's something else, isn't he?"

"He is . . . the most entertaining person I've ever worked for. I'll say that much." Alex pushed his hands into the pockets of his suit. "Do you want to walk for a bit?"

I hesitated. Did I?

Curse his deep brown eyes. If he hadn't looked so handsome standing in the glow of the dim streetlight overhead, I might have had the courage to say no.

Instead, I shrugged my shoulders. "Sure," I said. "Walking sounds good."

Chapter Six

Alex

We walked side by side for half a block or so, my hands shoved into my pockets, her arms folded tightly across her middle. We probably looked like a walking argument to anyone observing from the outside. I wasn't all that sure myself why I'd asked her to go for a walk. But I wasn't ready for us to part ways. I'd been bitter over the comment she'd made about Sasha, but as dinner had progressed, I remembered more and more of the things I'd loved about her. Maybe we had different opinions about LeFranc, but I'd hurt her. Abandoned her. And my integrity wouldn't let me forget that. If there was a way to make it right, I had to at least try.

"Thank you for the flowers," she said without looking up. "They were beautiful."

Relief flooded through me. It wasn't like I'd been dwelling on the flowers all night, but knowing she'd appreciated the gesture and not felt weird about it was no small thing. "It felt like the least I could do. Is your dress going to be okay? It was one you made, right?"

She looked at me, surprise evident on her face. "You could tell?"

I shrugged but couldn't keep myself from grinning. She'd made a lot of her clothes while we'd been dating; the dress she'd had on that morning had looked particularly *Dani*. "Is that such a surprise?"

Heat crept up her cheeks, barely visible in the dim light cast from the streetlamps above us. "Chase is getting it cleaned for me. He says he knows a guy."

"Like a guy that isn't just a dry cleaner?"

She smiled at the question. "This is Chase we're talking about. An ordinary dry cleaner would never do."

I chuckled. "How's he doing?"

"He's perfect, as always," Dani said.

"I'm glad to hear it." Silence stretched for several paces before I tried another topic. "I don't think I realized just how different you are from your brother until I started working with him."

"You don't know the half of it. Tonight was actually better than it usually is."

"I don't remember you guys fighting all that much."

"We're really good at avoiding each other," she said. "But it's more that we just can't relate. It's like there's this fundamental difference of understanding that we've never been able to overcome."

"Understanding about what?"

"You name it. Life, work, everything." She ran her hands up and down her arms. The temperature had dropped during dinner and while it was still mild, she was obviously feeling chilled.

I shrugged out of my suit coat and offered it to her. She shook her head no and increased the speed of her step, lengthening the distance between us.

"Dani, just take it," I said. "You're cold. I can tell."

She hesitated, but finally turned back and reached for the jacket. She draped it over her shoulders without slipping her arms through the sleeves. "Thank you," she said, a definite edge to her voice.

We walked in silence a few more moments before she asked, "Was it really his idea?"

"Was what his idea?"

"The Compassion Experiment. I mean, I don't mean to discount what he's trying to accomplish, but Alex, your fingerprints are all over it."

Before graduating and taking a job working for Alicio in New York, I'd spent a semester abroad in London interning for a nonprofit. I hadn't been an actual part of the event planning, but we'd been a small team. We had all been involved in every aspect of the organization. Dani knew my history there. She'd see right through me if I tried to deny any influence on Isaac's event. "Isaac did say he hired me because he knew what his weaknesses were and hoped I could compensate for them."

"So, what? His weakness is that he's shallow and self-centered?"

"His weakness is that he has zero business experience and has no idea how to build a positive brand image."

"So he called you? An accountant? To help him with his *image?*"

I stopped. "My undergrad degree was in business. I took marketing classes. You know all of this about me. Why does this matter so much?"

She turned to face me. "It just feels so unlike him."

"Just because a charity event was my idea doesn't mean Isaac didn't have a desire to make a bigger difference. He's the one who has figured out all the details. I might have planted a seed, but he's doing all the work."

She scoffed. "That feels even more unlike him."

"Dani, can I say something as a friend?" The minute the words came out of my mouth, I regretted them. I was asking for more than I deserved.

"No Alex, I don't think you can," she said, her voice cool.

"As Isaac's friend, then."

She raised an eyebrow, which I took as encouragement to press forward. "I want to preface this by saying that obviously, I am also very different from your brother. We have different opinions on everything, from what we find entertaining to what we feel constitutes appropriate work attire. But even acknowledging those differences, I don't think you give him enough credit."

She took a deep breath. It felt intentional, like she was measuring her next words very carefully. "What makes you think I don't give him enough credit?"

"He does," I answered without hesitation. "He wears your disapproval on his sleeve. I think that's why he hesitated to even tell you the details of this event. He's really excited about it, and he didn't want you to—"

Her shoulders slumped. "Do exactly what I did? Doubt him? Squelch him? Rain on his shiny YouTube parade?"

"See?" I said. "You really don't like what he does for a living. And he feels that. Keenly."

She closed her eyes, one hand clutched around the edges of my jacket, the other pressed to her head, thumb and forefinger rubbing her temples. "Did Isaac ever tell you he was accepted into MIT?" she asked.

My eyebrows shot up. "No, he didn't."

"He was also offered a full ride to Clemson, *and* Georgia Tech," she said. "I used to hate it. How hard I had to work when it was always so easy for him. He was so smart. Test scores higher than everyone else we knew. And for what? For a little bit of YouTube notoriety? How long is that going to last? When all of his subscribers grow up and turn into adults who no longer want to watch *Random I*, what then? He could have done so much with those smarts."

"Okay. I see your point."

"It's not so much that I disapprove. I've watched a few of his early episodes and I almost get it. I don't always understand the randomness, but he's funny. I'm willing to give him that much. And I like that he's always challenging people to be kind. But I can't stop thinking about what he could have accomplished had he gone to college."

"There's more than one way to find success," I said. "His isn't the most conventional path, but it's still his. And he's accomplished a lot, even without a fancy education."

"I suppose that's true," she said with a sigh.

I wondered if she actually believed it. I'd heard Dani talk about her own career. She had a very clear definition of success and it had a lot to do with progress based on merit and hard work, and not things like YouTube views or notoriety. Even convincing her to go to the interview I'd set up for her at LeFranc had been tough. Because she hadn't "earned" it and didn't want her path to senior designer tainted by a favor from her boyfriend or even just a stroke of good luck. She would have the job because she deserved it, or not at all.

"Can I ask you a question?" she asked.

"Sure."

"I don't . . ." She hesitated, her eyes focused somewhere at my feet. "I'm not sure I'm up for talking about why you left New York. But . . . why *Isaac?* It's not like you're lacking qualifications. Anyone would have hired you."

"Anyone would have hired me to keep doing what I was already doing at LeFranc. But I didn't *like* my job at LeFranc. Isaac offered something different. Plus, I needed a place to stay and the job came with one."

Her eyes jumped to mine. "You couldn't go home?"

I ran a hand through my hair. "I did, at first. Malorie said I was welcome to stay. But her girls are teenagers now. All they did was giggle whenever I was around."

My father's second wife was well-intentioned. She technically lived in *my* house—the one I'd inherited from my father when he'd passed away a few years back—but Dad's will stipulated that she and the girls could live in the house until the youngest graduated from the private school he'd also paid for in his will. They'd been happy together; I couldn't begrudge Dad wanting to take care of Malorie and her girls. Still, the two weeks I'd spent living with them before moving in with Isaac had been long enough.

Dani chuckled. "They still don't feel like family, huh?"

"Not hardly. And Malorie was . . . flirty. It was weird."

"Oh, wow. That's awkward. She isn't that much older than you, is she? I can't remember."

"Ten years, I think?"

Dani started walking again and I fell in step beside her.

"Is it weird for you? To own a house you can't live in? I mean, she and your dad were only married for what, three, four years?"

I shrugged. "Seven years. And three of those, Dad was sick. She took care of him better than anybody else could. She probably deserves to live in that house forever."

Dani pulled my suit coat closer around her. "I remember the night you told me about losing both your parents." She shook her head. "It still doesn't seem fair."

A memory flooded my mind of Dani in my arms, our legs propped up on the coffee table in front of the sofa in my New York apartment. "I remember that night, too. You cried."

She huffed out a small laugh. "It was a really sad story."

Losing both parents to cancer within a couple of years *was* a sad story. I was generally used to the sympathy expressed whenever people found out. But Dani had given me more than sympathy. She'd taken a little bit of my sadness and felt it like it was her own. I'd never forgotten how different that felt, how she'd made the burden feel a little lighter for her willingness to help me carry it. "That's the night I really started to fall in love with you."

She stopped on the sidewalk, gripping the lamppost beside her. She closed her eyes, her lips pressed together in a thin line. "Don't, Alex," she said, leaning toward the lamppost, her voice so soft I almost couldn't hear. "You can't say things like that."

"I'm sorry."

She pushed away from the post and walked down the sidewalk at a good enough clip, it was clear she wanted to put some distance between us. I followed behind, respecting the distance, waiting for her to make the next move.

Finally, she turned around, the fire in her eyes evident even in the dark, across six feet of sidewalk. "So Isaac knew you were back in Charleston because my mom told him about our breakup?"

I nodded. "I think so, yeah."

"And he just called you up and offered you a job?"

"Basically, yes. He sent me a resume request through LinkedIn."

She pressed the heel of her hand to her forehead. "There are so many weird things about that sentence."

I grinned. "It felt a little weird to me, too. But I appreciated him trying to keep it professional."

"Is it just you and Isaac living together?"

Ha. If only. "No; the whole team lives there. It's a pretty big house."

Her eyes went wide. "Tyler? Vinnie?"

I nodded. "And Mushroom. I've never actually figured out what his real name is. Oh, and Steven. He's the co-host Isaac hired last year."

"Mushroom's name is . . . Marvin? No. Marshall. Which almost sounds like Mushroom? I haven't met Steven."

"They're all friends from high school, right? Except Steven?"

She nodded. "From elementary school, even. At least Tyler and Vinnie have been around that long."

"It's a very interesting group," I said. "But honestly, it hasn't been as difficult as I expected it to be. We all get along, and I appreciate how much they look out for each other. They treat each other like family. And they are genuinely the most nonjudgmental group of men I have ever been around."

"Hey-hey, you do you, bro," Dani said, in a voice lowered to sound like her brother.

"That was an unnervingly accurate impression,"

I said. "But mocking aside, that *is* why I like it there."

"I bet *you* were overdressed your first day of work."

I laughed. "I feel overdressed when I'm wearing the most casual thing I own."

It couldn't last, not with the history between us, but it was nice talking back and forth like we used to. It felt good to laugh with her.

After a few moments of silence, she stopped one more time to face me. "I hear what you're saying, but I'm still not sure it adds up in my brain. You and Isaac living together, working together every day. I don't want to make it all about me, but he's *my* brother. Is that part not weird for you?"

I sighed. "It was, at first. It felt a little like I was torturing myself just by being around him. But I was desperate. Things with Alicio got really bad. I had to separate myself from him, from the whole company, and it didn't feel like I could do that without leaving the city. I looked for work in Charleston, but nothing felt right. When Isaac reached out to me, he tossed me a life preserver. I actually didn't plan to move in long term, not initially. I thought I'd find my own place somewhere, but then your brother made it really easy to stay, and odd as it may seem, I feel *accepted* living with him and his friends. I never felt that living here in New York."

She breathed out a painful half-laugh, half-cry. "You didn't feel accepted by me?"

I closed my eyes. "Of course I did. At times, anyway. But Dani, our life was so wrapped up in LeFranc. And the LeFranc version of myself— the parties, the entertaining, the high society networking—that *isn't* me."

She turned and started walking again and I hurried to catch up.

"Is that supposed to make it easier for me?" Her steps grew faster as she spoke. "That after you abandoned me without any explanation, you had a Kum-ba-yah experience at my brother's house and found your true self? Why didn't you call me, Alex? You can't even claim out-of-sight, out-of-mind on this one. You work with Isaac! A living, breathing reminder that I, his twin sister, exist."

"I know that. I know I treated you badly and if given the choice to do things differently, I would take it a thousand times over. But I felt betrayed, too. There was so much pressure from Alicio. Keeping up appearances, playing the role of a LeFranc in New York society. I was such a disappointment in that regard and yet, it was a world that seemed so important to you. That version of me was the one you wanted to be with. I tried to talk to you about Sasha, but you *always* took her side. Your star was rising, and my concerns were nothing but a flaming arrow that might shoot it down. I didn't know what to say to you. I didn't think you would understand."

"I didn't love you because you're a LeFranc."

"I'm not a LeFranc," I shot back.

She huffed. "You know what I mean."

Her words sparked something deep inside me and a dormant insecurity flickered to life. It was *only* a flicker now, a year after we'd broken up, but it was easy to remember the raging inferno it had been when I'd walked out. She'd *said* she didn't love me because of my ties to LeFranc. And maybe she was telling the truth. But she'd never managed to convince me.

"Maybe you didn't," I said, my voice doubtful despite my effort to remain neutral. "But my connections didn't hurt."

She shook her head and rolled her eyes in a way that felt familiar; it wasn't like we hadn't had this argument before.

She paused a long moment, her eyes trained on the sidewalk. "You said things got bad at LeFranc. Was it because of Sasha? Was any of what you believed true?"

I shook my head. "I wasn't given the opportunity to prove anything before I left."

My jacket dropped off her shoulders; she caught it, pulling it back up and finally slipping her arms through the sleeves. "But you still believe it."

I ran a frustrated hand across my face. "Dani, I can't talk about this with you."

She frowned. "You can't, or you won't?"

"Legally, I can't."

"Legally? What does that even mean?"

"It means Alicio sent me a cease and desist order." Frustration filled my voice. "It means I can't talk about anything related to LeFranc with *anyone,* particularly those still employed by the company."

She dropped her gaze, her head shaking sadly from side to side. She shrugged out of my coat and held it out to me. "So I guess that's supposed to make it okay that you left without talking to me." Her voice was distant, cold. "I was just another company employee." The light of the streetlamp above her cast shadows over her face, but I could still see tears brimming in her eyes. "Here," she said, shaking the jacket she still clutched in her hand. "I'm going home."

Chapter Seven

Dani

My Uber driver was chatty. He was nice enough, but it was taking every ounce of my willpower not to burst into tears. I really didn't want to hear about his accounting classes in business school, or his roommate from Nepal, or his four-year-old niece no matter how cute she was. The relief I felt when he finally pulled up outside my apartment was palpable.

Outside the car, I paused on the sidewalk long enough to rate my ride and leave a tip for the driver. When I closed out the Uber app, there was a text notification on my screen.

Dani, I'm sorry about the way our conversation ended. I never meant to hurt you, and I hate that I seem to have only made it worse. It wasn't my intention. I only wanted to say I was sorry.

Fresh tears filled my eyes and I closed out my screen, hiding the message from view. I didn't want to read his apologies. Before I could drop the phone back in my bag, another notification lit up the screen.

One more thing. Please be careful at work. Trust Chase, and your own instincts. But no one else. I'm sorry I can't say more than that.

What was that supposed to mean? Be careful? Careful doing what? If he couldn't tell me everything, I'd almost rather he tell me nothing at all. Plus, he gave up his right to care whether I was being careful or not.

I hurried up the stairs to the loft I shared with Paige. Well, sort of shared with Paige. She was a full-time nanny and had a room at her employer's home. She didn't always sleep over, but it was a little bit of a haul to get from the Upper East Side all the way down to Chelsea so she often chose to stay at work. She was home on the weekends most of the time, but with all the traveling she did with the family, I never knew when to expect her. Still, she paid half the rent. I'd have never been able to afford the space without her help.

The loft was tiny. Anything even remotely affordable in the city always was. But it had high ceilings and huge windows and a funky, modern kitchen with Art Deco subway tile and light fixtures that looked like they belonged in an art museum. We were fairly certain the lights were courtesy of the previous tenant, an artist who had also left a mural that took up the whole of Paige's back bedroom wall.

I hadn't seen Paige before dinner, much to my disappointment—it would have been nice to talk through my Alex anxieties with her—so when I saw her purse and coat hanging on the chair by the door, I really did start to cry.

"Paige?" My voice cracked. "Where are you?"

She appeared in the doorway that led to the short hall separating our two bedrooms, her face wrinkled with worry. "What's wrong? Are you okay? Did someone die?"

I shook my head and dropped my bag on the table by the door. "I'm so glad you're home."

We met on the couch where I walked her through the entire day, from running into Alex in the coffee shop, all the way through dinner and the disastrous walk afterward.

"Wow," she finally said, after I'd finished. "You've had some day."

I huffed. "Tell me about it."

"I saw the flowers when I came home and wondered where they came from. That was at least nice of him, to tip you off about dinner. Can you imagine if you'd shown up and found him sitting there with Isaac?"

I sniffed and wiped my eyes on the back of my hand. "I'd have died. Alex was always like that. I'm not surprised he sent flowers."

Paige gave me a knowing look. "Ohhh, no."

I narrowed my eyes. "What?"

"You are so not over this guy."

"Yes I am," I said, but the new tears welling up from her words indicated otherwise.

She opened her arms and pulled me into a hug. "Oh, honey," she said, patting me on the back. "No, you're not."

"I'm still so mad at him, Paige. And I can't even begin to make sense of things he said tonight. Stuff that he can't legally tell me? What does that even mean?"

Paige shifted and I sat up, pulling a blanket off the couch and wrapping it around my legs. "What do you remember about the last time he *did* talk to you about LeFranc? Before he left."

"I don't remember specifics. He had suspicions about Sasha, which made me defensive because I'd just started working for her and I loved my job. She was letting me design, you know? And he seemed so determined to bring her down. I guess I didn't feel like he had a lot of convincing evidence."

"But if he had, you would have believed him, right?" Paige said. "If he'd had actual proof that she was doing something shady, you would have taken his side."

I thought back through the conversations Alex and I had had those last few days before he left. We hadn't spent a ton of time talking about work. I loved LeFranc, and Alex had only seemed to tolerate it. He'd loved that I wanted to be a designer, but he'd always had complaints about the way Alicio did business, and he was particularly hard on Sasha. He'd never liked her—even less so when she and Alicio had become engaged.

And I'd always defended her.

"What if I didn't listen to him?" I asked Paige, fear creeping into my voice.

Paige grimaced. "You did have Sasha-shaped stars in your eyes those first few months. But, Dani, this is Alex we're talking about. You cared about him. You would have listened."

I shook my head, forcing out the sympathy that had slowly been creeping into my brain. "You know what? It doesn't even matter if I would or wouldn't have listened. He could have done a thousand different things to let me know he was leaving. Even *if* he thought my loyalties were to LeFranc, I didn't deserve to be cut off."

I thought of all the texts and emails I'd sent him in those first weeks after he'd left. Ranging from curious, to a little more desperate, to downright distraught and worried. A surge of embarrassment coursed through my veins.

"He doesn't get a pass on this," I said, with an air of finality. "I'm glad he apologized. Maybe it'll help him get some closure, but it doesn't change anything."

"Fine," Paige said, with a defiant fist pound onto the back of the sofa.

"Fine," I echoed.

She grinned. "Do you feel better?"

I wasn't quite ready to smile back, but I did breathe out an audible sigh. "Maybe a little."

"Good. Can we sort of change the subject?" Paige asked. "Also, are you hungry? I'm hungry."

"I'm starving. I was too nervous to really eat my dinner."

Paige stood and started rummaging through the kitchen—rather, the tiny counter behind our tiny living room where we kept our food. She returned to the couch with a loaf of French bread, a block of Wensleydale cranberry cheese, a bowl of strawberries, and a knife wedged between her teeth.

"Bless you, woman," I said, reaching for a strawberry. She unloaded the impromptu meal onto the coffee table, but before sitting down, returned to the kitchen, this time retrieving a pint of Talenti gelato from the freezer, and a couple of spoons from the drawer. The girl had a killer metabolism, which I probably should have found annoying, what with my own petite and curvy frame. I loved it though. She wasn't quite tall enough to actually *be* a runway model, but she was still lean and lanky and was perfect for when I wanted to make something for a normal-sized human, as opposed to the miniaturized clothes I made for my own not-quite-five-foot-three self.

"What are we changing the subject to?" I asked, reaching for an offered spoon.

"Right, yes," Paige said, settling back down on the couch. "Why on earth did Isaac need to hire a business manager?"

"I know!" I said. "Weird, right?"

"And someone like Alex. He's so business-y. And Isaac is so . . . Isaac."

"Seriously. They're so different. It seems like such a weird combination. Alex made it seem like Isaac was ready to diversify and do something more profound with his money. So that's why he brought him on."

"How much money are we talking, here?" Paige asked. "Is he really that successful?"

"I have no idea. I mean, he bought a house, so that's something, I guess."

"What kind of house?"

"I don't know, but . . ." I reached for my phone. "He sent Mom the address the other day in a group text. I guess I can google the address."

Paige looked over my shoulder. "Uh, he bought a house on Church Street?" she asked, as soon as I pulled up the text. "I bet it's historical."

I copied the address into Google. A listing on one of those "value your home" websites pulled up. I quickly scanned the information.

Isaac hadn't just bought a house. He'd bought an early nineteenth century single house in the heart of the Charleston peninsula.

"Built in 1804," Paige read, leaning closer to the screen.

I swallowed. "And worth more than two million dollars."

I swiped through the photos of the home, likely

the ones that had accompanied the last real estate listing.

I gasped at the next photo that filled my screen. "Paige! Look at this garden!" Brick walkways, Carolina jasmine curling around a wrought iron fence. Flowers everywhere.

Charleston city ordinances required historical homes to stay historical, keeping the outside looking just like it would have when it was originally built. It gave the city an old-world feel that my entire family had always loved. Cobblestone streets, gas lamps, and beautiful gardens like the one in the photo.

But loving downtown and *living* downtown were different things. That Isaac was living there indicated a measure of financial success I could hardly fathom.

"Um, Dani?" Paige held her own phone now, the gelato temporarily forgotten. "Have you checked out Isaac's YouTube channel lately?"

"What? Why?"

"He has over ten million subscribers."

My jaw dropped. "Are you serious?"

"I'm pretty sure that makes him like, legit YouTube famous. Ten million subscribers is a lot of people."

I'd never felt so out of touch with my brother's life. I remembered a few years before when he'd hit the one million subscriber mark. And I'd known then that it was a pretty big deal. But, ten million? "So I guess we know why he needed to hire a money guy," I said.

"I should say so," Paige agreed, through a mouth full of gelato.

"They're planning this big charity thing on Christmas Eve," I said. "An online scavenger hunt called the Compassion Experiment to benefit some charity organization. I'm totally baffled by the whole thing."

"More baffled than you are by a two-million-dollar house?" Paige asked. "*I* just can't believe they didn't tell you they were working together. Such a dude thing to do. Did they seriously think you wouldn't find out? Or wouldn't care when you did?"

"Isaac *did* tell me. I guess it was my mistake for assuming it was just to do his taxes."

"Yeah, but Alex should have said something too." Paige sighed. "So lame. I'm sorry, Dani."

I shrugged. "At least it's over now. He'll go back to Charleston, I'll go back to work, and we'll both go back to not ever seeing each other."

"It sucks," she said. "Nothing like grinding a little bit of sand into your sunburn."

I reached for the gelato and scooped up a generous spoonful.

"Does Sasha ever ask about Alex?"

"Not really," I said. "I mean, she knows everything. She was pretty sympathetic when he left New York. She gave me the day off, even. But no one at work really talks about him much. He's not actually a LeFranc, you know? And he was there such a short time. I don't know that he ever really felt like a part of the company. Sasha definitely doesn't talk about him like she talks about Gabriel and Victor."

"Isn't Sasha only slightly older than Gabriel and Victor?"

"Oh, she's younger than Victor," I said. I fluttered my eyelashes with dramatic flair. "But she's going to be such a good stepmom."

Paige frowned. "I know you say she's good to you, Dani, but there's a lot about that woman that bugs me."

I stared into my gelato, not sure if I was ready to admit how I was really feeling. For almost two years, Sasha had been my everything. She was my ticket—the one who held all the power to give me my dream job. I had given everything to LeFranc. Worked ridiculous hours. Answered the phone no matter the time of day. I'd designed at home, giving Sasha my designs without question, without demanding anything in return because I *knew* she saw my value and would, as soon as she could, promote me to the design team.

But when?

More and more lately, I'd been feeling a lot more *used* and a lot less appreciated. "Honestly, she's been bugging me lately, too."

"In what way?"

"I don't know. She's talking so much about how privileged I should feel that she's taking my stuff to the design team. But she's not giving me any credit for it. Literally, no one but Chase knows I know anything about clothes."

"So you're basically doing her job for her, but she's getting all the credit?"

"I'm not doing her job. Not completely. But she's using more and more of my ideas. Which is great, but—"

"But it sucks not to get any validation yourself."

"Exactly. It's not really that I care so much about getting credit. I just wish I could be in on the collaborating. I'm never in on the talks about fabric or theme or overall style. So I'm really just sort of stabbing in the dark hoping I come up with something Sasha can use. It would be so much more rewarding if I got to be a part of the actual team."

"I'm sure your time will come." Paige reached over and squeezed my knee. "In the meantime, you could always go out on your own doing wedding gowns." She smiled wide and lifted her shoulders in a playful shrug.

I narrowed my gaze. "Did you peek?"

She placed her hand on her heart. "Cross my heart. I promise I . . . did."

"Paige!" I jumped off the couch and flew to my workspace. "I told you not to look!"

Our loft wasn't spacious enough for me to

have an actual work*room*. For that reason, Paige deserved a ton of credit for tolerating just how much of our shared space was dedicated to fashion. Racks lined two of the four walls in the living room, full of things I'd made through the years. And the back half of the room—the half I'd commandeered as wedding dress central— was the happiest of my happy places. My sewing machine sat on a table against the back wall, underneath tall windows that let in tons of natural light. On either side of the table, huge bins held fabric, buttons, zippers, and other notions I might need while working. Years of collecting had yielded a pretty impressive assortment— impressive enough that I probably shouldn't have been spending a third of every paycheck at Mood. But it was hard to resist the siren call of a great fabric store. Paige's obsession was shoes. My mom couldn't resist buying pretty paper and fancy pens. But me? Fabric was my weakness.

I crossed to the back corner where a dress form was hidden by an old sheet. Paige was great. Not Bridezilla at all. But working with someone watching over your shoulder, observing the minute-by-minute progress of a dress they hoped to eventually wear was intensely stressful. Creation was a process. And rarely did the finished product look anything like the first few versions. By the end of week two of dressmaking, I had stopped working on the dress whenever

Paige was around, covering it with a sheet when I wasn't home, and threatening to turn it into a mermaid dress with puffy sleeves if she came within three feet of my sewing area.

Little cheater.

I pulled the sheet off the dress form and studied the half-made dress, intentionally angling my body to block Paige's view.

"Oh, come on!" Paige called.

I turned around to face her, my hands on my hips. "Did you seriously look?"

She stood and walked toward me. "Of course I didn't. But I really wanted to."

"The skirt isn't even finished yet," I argued. The dress *had* a skirt, but it was just simple white satin. I still needed to embellish and make it pretty.

"But you said the bodice was done, right? Please oh please? Just one tiny peek?"

I bit my lip. I wanted her to see it. Because I was pretty sure she was going to love it. But I was still terrified. That she trusted me to make something this big, this important to her was huge. It felt a little like I was standing in front of Heidi Klum on an episode of *Project Runway*. "Okay," I finally relented. "But you can't try it on yet. I still have to stitch the lace in place and secure the buttons up the back."

Paige raised her eyebrows. "Oh. I thought—"

"We did." I interrupted her. "We decided an

open back was best. But I couldn't stop thinking about how much you loved the idea of buttons, so . . ." I turned the dress form around and pulled off the sheet. "I'm hoping maybe this will work."

Paige's hand flew to her mouth and she gasped. "Ohhh, Dani. It's beautiful!"

"Do you really like it?"

"It's perfect." She reached out and touched the back of the dress. "So this whole middle part is completely sheer?"

"Right. You'll barely see it when it's against your skin, except for the buttons, obviously, and the little bit of lace that comes over your shoulder here and trims the opening. And then, look." I turned the dress back around. "The same lace wraps around to the front and will continue down the skirt."

"All over?"

I crossed my fingers. It was a sheath dress, per Paige's request, so no giant full skirt walking down the aisle for her. With such a simple outline, lace all over was exactly what I was hoping for. "I really think it will be beautiful."

She nodded. "Oh, me too!" She reached out to hug me. "Seriously. This is the nicest thing anyone has ever done for me."

"I can't wait to see it *on* you. There might still be a few pins on the skirt, but a few more hours of work and I should have it ready for you to try on before your mom leaves town."

Paige smiled. Her mom was slightly less confident in my ability to make a wedding dress than Paige was. To have a finished product to show her would probably do a lot to relieve some of the wedding tension Paige was feeling. She got along with her mom. Most of the time, anyway. But they'd definitely had it out over more than a few wedding details. "I'm so glad. I didn't want to push you, but man, Mom's been driving me crazy over this dress."

"She's here through next Thursday, right?"

"Yeah, but her flight is super early Thursday morning, so it'll have to be on Wednesday."

Six days. I looked back at the dress. "I can finish in six days."

Paige gave me a hug, squeezing extra hard before letting me go. "Alex is stupid, Dani," she said, her voice close to my ear. "Don't even give him another thought."

Chapter Eight

Alex

"How long has it been?" Isaac leaned forward, stretching his arms far over his head.

I closed out the book I was reading on my phone and looked at the clock. "Three hours," I said. "We've now officially been on the airplane on the ground, twice as long as we will be in the air. If," I added, "we ever leave the ground." The flight crew had cited ambiguous "delays" and a backlog of planes trying to leave JFK, but three hours? I'd done a lot of flying over the years and had never waited so long before takeoff.

Isaac groaned. "I think Charleston is going to sink into the ocean before we make it home."

"Probably not," I answered dryly. "But you aren't going to be home in time to film. Did you leave anything for Tyler to post?"

He scrubbed his hands across his face. "No. I thought I'd be home in time."

"Can he do it without you?"

He pursed his lips. "Most of it, yeah. But also . . ." His voice trailed off as he looked around the plane. "I think I'll do a little something from here, too."

"From the plane? Can you do that?"

"Why not? I'll talk to a few people, do some trivia, then we can send the footage back to the studio and Vinnie can splice it in with Steven's tech news stuff. I mean, look around. Everybody's bored. This will be fun."

For the next thirty minutes, I watched in awe as Isaac morphed into a full-scale entertainer. All he did was talk to people, ask them questions, play a few random trivia games. But he had a way of engaging people that was unparalleled. My part was easy. I simply followed behind him with a digital consent agreement I'd worked up on the fly and made sure everyone who appeared on video signed it and gave us rights to publish.

It was fascinating seeing Isaac in his element. I'd watched his show, and the process of filming and production countless times, but this was different. Isaac was interacting with people— many of whom knew who he was and seemed very excited for the interaction—face-to-face. It brought him to life in a way that his studio stuff didn't quite capture.

"You're good at that," I told him, as he prepped the video to send to Vinnie.

"What? Talking to people?"

"Yes," I said. "A lot of people should have been annoyed by you shoving a camera in their faces, but somehow you charmed them all into complicity. It was pretty impressive."

He smiled. "It's not something they teach in the Ivy Leagues, huh?"

"Even when I'm paying you a compliment, you can't stop making fun of my education, can you?"

He chuckled. "I appreciate your education. Someone has to keep the doors open at Harvard, otherwise, who would I make fun of?"

"Is it just the Ivy League you dog on or would you, I don't know, make fun of an MIT grad too?"

He shot me a knowing look. "You've been talking to Dani."

"You forced me to talk to Dani."

"Whatever. I saw the way you looked at her at dinner. Don't tell me you weren't enjoying yourself."

I leaned back into my seat. I had enjoyed her company. But there were so many complications. My phone buzzed with an incoming call; I was happy for the distraction until I glanced at the screen and saw my stepbrother's name across the top.

Speaking of *complications.*

I thought of Gabriel's warning earlier that week that Victor might try to tell me not to come to the wedding. I silenced the call. If there was anything truly urgent, Gabriel would have mentioned it when he saw me in person.

The voicemail notification popped up at the

same time the pilot's voice sounded throughout the plane, announcing we were finally next on the runway. I opened the voicemail, my jaw clenched as I listened to Victor's message.

Alex, it's been a while. Listen, I know you'd rather not associate yourself with the LeFrancs considering our criminal business habits, but what can I say. Alicio is more forgiving than the rest of us. You're getting an invite to the wedding—Alicio says it's the polite thing to do—but just a heads up, we don't actually want you there. This is Dad's day. Please don't ruin it by showing up.

I closed my eyes. Typical Victor.

I had only been four years old when my mother had met Alicio LeFranc while he'd been vacationing in Charleston. Her divorce from my father had only been final a couple of months when she'd married Alicio and moved to New York. I'd been too young to understand the implications of how quickly everything had happened. But as an adult, I knew better than to assume anyone's innocence. Even my mother's.

In retrospect, I was just glad I'd been able to stay in Charleston with my dad and only live with my mother during the summer. Once she'd married Alicio, her life quickly became one of glitz and glamour and social importance. Alicio's sons had been older than me when they'd gained a new stepmom, but they'd still been young enough to look the part of "darling children." The press had loved to picture the four of them at fashion shows and other social events. Happy. Stylish. A perfect family.

It's not so much that I wanted to fit into their world. I was probably better for not having been a part of it. My father had been a philosophy professor at The College of Charleston and had given me a good life full of books and music and culture. But my mother was still my mother. I couldn't turn my back on the family she'd loved, whether they'd ever loved me or not.

It didn't help the situation that Alicio, at my mother's insistence, had bankrolled my entire education. The private schools I'd attended while growing up, then four years of Harvard undergrad, plus a master's in accounting. That was the reason I'd agreed to go and work for him in the first place. My mother wanted it—of course that was the biggest reason—but I also felt obligated. So much money invested. How could I say no?

I remembered going to see Mom in the hospital as soon as I'd arrived in the city to let her know I'd decided to take the job. She was dying, her cancer terminal, the doctors mostly just trying to keep her comfortable, but I'd never forgotten her face when we'd talked that day. The hope she'd had in her eyes that I would build relationships with Gabriel and Victor, find a place in the family she'd grown to love over the years.

"You do belong here, Alex," she'd told me. She'd reached up and cupped my cheek with her hand. "You're so smart, and you have such good business sense. They need you. They may not realize it now, but once they see what you're capable of, you'll blow them away."

I frowned, discouraged by the memory. I suspected accusing them all of fraud and threatening to go public wasn't quite the "blowing them away" she'd had in mind.

Before leaving New York, I'd visited the storage unit Justine had filled for me. It was a little like entering a time capsule, except the woman reflected back in the clutter of belongings wasn't someone I actually recognized. A few pieces of art I recognized as things I'd seen hanging in her bedroom in New York, but there was an old chair, worn and weathered, and a vintage-looking lamp that I'd never seen in any of the homes Alicio owned. The photo albums Gabe had mentioned were in a milk crate in the corner, their pages yellowed with age. Most of the photos I'd never seen before. My birth, my parents pre-divorce, still smiling and happy in each other's arms, our house in Charleston. In one of the photos of the house, I'd noticed the lamp in the background. So she'd taken it with her.

It had brought a measure of comfort to realize

Mom hadn't completely abandoned her old life, but at the same time, it was as painful as it was comforting. Because where *was* this part of Mom for all those years? Hidden in a closet somewhere? Why hadn't she ever shown these photos to me?

Finally on the ground in Charleston, I stayed mostly silent until we were crossing the parking lot toward Isaac's jeep.

"You okay, man?" Isaac asked. "You seem bugged by something."

"I'm good," I lied. "Just tired, I guess."

He unlocked his jeep and opened the back, sliding his suitcase in before turning around and reaching for mine. "Here, I got it," he said.

"Thanks."

A few minutes into the drive home, Isaac broke the silence. "Hey, listen, I'm sorry about making fun of you on the plane. And about Dani, and all that."

"What?" His apology caught me off guard. Isaac made fun of everyone, all the time. And he never apologized.

"I know it was real between you two. I'm sorry if I made things worse by . . ." He waved his hand dismissively. "I don't know. By making you see her, or whatever."

"Oh," I said. "Well, thanks, I guess."

"So we're cool?" he asked.

"Sure. Of course."

"Cool."

I hadn't expected an apology. Hadn't really even felt like I needed one. But after listening to Victor's message, then replaying it in my head over and over throughout the flight home—*just a heads up, we don't actually want you here*—it was nice to feel any measure of sincerity, whether from family or in Isaac's case, a friend.

The simplicity of his apology reminded me of my father and a familiar ache welled up in my belly—a subtle tightening that lasted a moment then disappeared. I missed my mother, was sad that we hadn't had more time together, that we hadn't had a closer relationship. But missing my father was visceral—a physical reaction that squeezed and tugged and needled like no loss I'd ever experienced before. It had dulled over the past two years since his death, but I still felt it. Still wished for the chance to have one more conversation with him. Still wished to just . . . belong somewhere.

Chapter Nine

Dani

I clenched my fists together, willing the nerves in my gut to stop with the somersaults. Paige stood in the middle of our living room, wearing the dress—the perfectly crafted, made-for-her-body, gorgeous-in-every-way dress—while her mother circled around her. It had been a good week. Paige's little sister was maid of honor and she'd pulled off the long-distance planning of a New York City bridal shower from her home in Boston with freakish skill. The shower had been perfect. We'd also managed to squeeze in bridesmaid's dress shopping and had found a great deal on invitations. And I'd spent *hours,* most of them in the middle of the night, finishing the dress.

I didn't technically need Ms. Perry's approval to be proud. I knew I'd designed a winner, and Paige's approval was all that truly mattered. But I still wanted her mom to like it. I wanted the validation of someone not already bound by friendship loving my work.

Well, and validation from Ms. Perry was particularly significant. Her maiden name was Pinckney—which meant something if you lived in Charleston. It was one of the oldest and most prestigious names in the city. Charleston society held firm to culture and tradition and Paige's family was one of the great pillars of that society. I mean, Paige had had an actual debutante ball when she'd turned eighteen. Big white dress, formal presentation to society, the whole deal. Paige never really bought into it, but for her mom, it was everything. The fact that they could, if they so desired, afford to pay top dollar for a designer dress made the pressure even greater.

Ms. Perry tapped her perfectly manicured finger on her chin. "Danielle, I admit, I've always assumed your love for fashion was nothing more than a hobby, but I think you've got something here."

Paige smiled. "Really, Mom? You like it?"

"It's perfect," she said, reaching for Paige's hands. "You look just as I always imagined."

"And you're still going to let me wear your veil?" Paige said.

"Of course! I actually think it will coordinate with the rest of the dress perfectly." She turned to face me. "Well done, Danielle. If you like, I'd be happy to spread the word among friends. You keep designing dresses like these, and we'll make you famous in no time at all."

"That's kind of you to say," I said. "Thank you."

Paige, visible over her mother's shoulder, smiled wide and raised her fists in silent celebration. "Hey, Mom," she said, throwing me a pointed look, "did I tell you Dani is up for a design position at LeFranc?"

I glared at her. What was she thinking? I wasn't up for a position. Well, not officially. Earlier in the week, Sasha *had* mentioned they were toying with the idea of a paid internship she thought I would be perfect for. I would for sure apply, but there was no guarantee.

Ms. Perry's eyebrows lifted. "LeFranc? Really?"

"It's not a sure thing yet. I should know something in a couple of weeks," I said.

"A LeFranc wedding gown. Now that'd be something to tell my friends."

"Oh, but that's not . . . I mean, LeFranc doesn't do gowns. Even if I get the job, it still wouldn't be—"

"Dani, can you help me with this zipper?" Paige interrupted, giving me a pointed look. She hauled me toward the bedroom. "We'll be right back, Mom."

As soon as we were out of her mother's earshot, she spun around, hands on hips. "You've gotten her blessing," she said. "How about we don't say anything to ruin that?"

"Fine. But she can't tell people it's a LeFranc dress. *Especially* if I get the job. It's not like they'd be cool with their designers doing a little bit of freelance work on the side."

"Ohh, good point." She turned around. "Here. For real unzip me. I'm hungry and there's no way I'm eating in this thing."

I helped her out of the dress and carefully hung it up.

"So let's say you do get the design job," Paige said. "Hey, can I wear the black dress? The one you stole from work?"

"Sure." I crossed the hallway and retrieved the dress. Paige and her fiancé, Reese, were taking her mom out to dinner. They'd invited me to tag along, but I was on too much of a budget to eat the kind of food they'd be enjoying. Back in her room, I tossed her the dress. "If I get the design job . . ."

"Right. If you get the job, would you consider showing them the dress?" Paige asked. "I mean, really, Dani. It's the most incredible thing you've ever designed. It might help you make a name for yourself."

I sat on her bed. "There wouldn't really be a reason to. LeFranc doesn't do wedding gowns."

"Really? Not at all?"

I shook my head. "I asked Sasha about it once. She says it's always been an idea they've kicked around, but the timing has never been right to really go for it."

"But maybe they would go for it if they saw what you're capable of."

I laughed. "You are loyal, and I love you, Paige,

but I'm a nobody. LeFranc doesn't care that I made one gorgeous wedding dress. Besides, I made that dress for you. You loving it is good enough for me."

She pulled a pair of heels out of her closet.

"Want to borrow my wool coat?" I asked. "You'll freeze otherwise."

"No, the sleeves are too short. It makes me feel like a giant whenever I wear it. I was thinking my red one would do. You think?" She pulled it on. "Not too casual for the dress?"

"Not if you put on the gray scarf. With the little bit of shimmer?"

She pulled it off the back of the chair in the corner. "This one?"

"Yes. Perfect," I said. "You look great. Not that it matters. You could show up in yoga pants and Reese would still think you look fab."

"Reese? Yes," she said with a cheesy grin. "My mother? That's another story."

I looked toward the bedroom door. "Your mother has been alone in our living room for a very long time," I said. "Should we check on her?"

"I'm ready anyway," Paige said. "You sure you don't want to come to dinner with us?"

"Positive," I said. "You guys have fun."

A week later, Paige was home on a rare weeknight, her employers out of town, for once, without her. I'd made her try on the dress again, so I could adjust the way the lace hung along the bottom hem. It was also possible I was having a hard time relinquishing my sewing needle.

"Dani, seriously. One more quarter-inch adjustment isn't going to make a difference. It's perfect. You have to stop." Paige stood in front of the full-length mirror I'd hauled from my bedroom out to the living room, turning this way and that, admiring the dress from every angle.

"Just stand still for two seconds and let me fix this one spot," I said.

She huffed. "Fine. Two seconds. That's all you get."

"Where did the Hoffmans head off to this week?" I asked her.

"They're on a cruise, I think. Somewhere in the Caribbean."

"Seriously? And they didn't want you to come along?"

"I've heard the childcare on cruises is available something like twenty-four hours a day. I guess they figured if the boat is providing it for free, why pay to bring me along?" Paige said.

"Yeah, because the Hoffmans are definitely hurting for cash."

She scoffed. "Ha. True. Whatever their reason, I'm not complaining. I haven't spent two nights in a row with Reese in months. The next few days are going to be bliss."

"You're not with him now, though. Is that my fault?"

"No, he's working. But he finishes his shift in an hour, so, you know, don't dawdle back there." She looked over her shoulder, angling her head to try and see what I was doing.

"Stop moving!" I tugged on the dress. "Unless you plan on walking down the aisle leaning sideways. I just need this hem to hang evenly."

She sighed a dramatic sigh. "What if the Hoffmans took a different nanny on the cruise?"

I stood up straight. "What? Why would they do that?"

"Because I'm getting married. And they need to replace me, and maybe this is like a trial run."

"So you're for sure quitting after the wedding then?"

"Yeah, I have to," she said. "It's hard to give up the pay, but the commute from Reese's place would kill me."

"So what then, you'll teach?" I dropped my pin cushion onto my sewing table. "You're done," I told her. "It's perfect."

"Probably. I mean, it's about time I use the degree I paid for, right?"

I sank onto the arm of the couch. "The Hoffmans have been good to you. But I'm excited that you're moving on. It's fun to imagine you in your own classroom somewhere."

My phone rang, interrupting our conversation.

I looked around. "Do you see my phone anywhere?"

Paige picked it up from the sewing table. "It's Sasha. You want it?"

"Really? What on earth does *she* need?" As demanding as my boss was during business hours, she wasn't one to typically take her work home. For her to reach out to me this late was weird.

I stood and quickly crossed the room, answering the phone before it went to voicemail. "Hello?"

"Oh, Dani, darling, I'm so glad I caught you."

Dani darling? "What can I do for you?"

"Actually, I'm in the neighborhood. Well, I think I'm in your neighborhood. You live above the pet shop, right? The one with the red awning?"

My eyes went wide. Sasha was outside my apartment. *Why* was Sasha outside my apartment? "It's a clothing store for pets," I said. Not particularly relevant, but it was the best my brain could come up with.

"Oh. How charming. You're the red door? Can I come up?"

"Um, is everything all right?"

"Of course. I just have a quick question, and since I was walking by, I figured I might as well drop in and ask you in person. Besides, it's past time I see the place where my favorite assistant spends her time away from the office."

My brain kicked into hyperdrive. Sasha in my apartment. Sasha seeing my workspace, my designs. It wasn't terrible, necessarily. And yet, it still felt like an incredible invasion of my privacy. "Actually, my roommate isn't feeling great right now. I can come down to you if that's okay. Are you here right now, as in, right outside?"

I crossed to the window and peeked down at the street, not wanting her to see me. "Oh, actually your neighbor just let me in—thank you, yes," I heard her say to whoever had opened the door for her. "I'm on the phone with her right now, so I'll just go on up. Okay," she said back to me. "I'm coming up. See you in a minute."

I dropped my phone onto the couch. And then proceeded to full-on panic.

"What is it? What's wrong?" Paige asked.

"Sasha's here."

"As in coming up the stairs *here* here?"

I froze and looked at Paige. "You've got to get out of that dress."

"What, right now? Who cares if she sees the dress?"

I cared, but for a reason I couldn't quite define. Sasha had been nosier than normal the past few days. When I'd returned from lunch earlier in the week, my sketchbook had been out and open on my desk, flipped to the drawings of Paige's dress, even though I distinctly remembered putting

127

it away before leaving. And Sasha's questions had been pointed and unusually wedding dress themed. I'd rebuffed her inquiries as best I could. Ultimately, she had no reason to care if I was designing a wedding dress in my apartment. But obviously, she *did* care. Why else would she have shown up unannounced?

"Paige, please. I don't want Sasha to see the dress."

"You're being paranoid. I do want her to see it. Because once she does, she's going to give you that internship."

"I just have a weird feeling about it." Alex's warning snaked through my brain. "I'm not sure I can trust her."

A knock sounded at the door. "It's just nerves, Dani. Trust me." Before I could stop her, Paige swung the apartment door wide open, head held high. Sasha stepped into the apartment, her eyes glued to the dress. She didn't even look up, not at me, not at Paige. "Turn around," she said softly, motioning with her fingers for Paige to spin.

Paige smiled, and shot me a knowing look, then turned, showing Sasha the back of the dress. It was my favorite part, the sheer back, save a tiny line of lace-covered buttons.

Sasha gasped, her hand covering her mouth. "Oh, it's perfect." Finally, she looked up, her eyes scanning the room. When they landed on me, she smiled. "I knew you were hiding something from me." She walked toward me. "But I've seen the sketches in that little book of yours. The one you keep tucked away in your purse?" She held up her fingers like she was ticking off all the evidence she'd collected against me. "Then the bag of lace you left on your desk. Do you remember? You went to Mood on your lunch break and came back with all this gorgeous lace. I *knew* you were working on a dress. I knew it!" She presented evidence, but I still couldn't figure out my crime.

"I'm not sure I understand what you're trying to say," I said, my words careful, deliberate.

"Why didn't you tell me about this dress?"

I raised my eyebrows. "It didn't have anything to do with work. My best friend is getting married, so I made her a dress."

Paige waved. "Hi. That's me," she said with a goofy grin. "I'm the best friend."

Sasha turned back around and looked at Paige. "You don't understand. This is more than a dress, Dani. It's exquisite. It's magazine-worthy."

My heart started pounding in my chest. "Thank you."

"Now, I came over here hoping to discover that my suspicions were, in fact, founded in truth. Since they are, I have a proposition for you." She steepled her hands in front of her, her fingers tapping together.

I folded my arms. Something about the entire situation felt off. Why couldn't she have just asked me? Why all the secrecy and spying and late-night visits? "I'm listening," I finally said.

"Well, it's still technically a secret. The press release won't drop until next week, but LeFranc is debuting its first-ever line of wedding gowns in January. The Sasha Wellington Collection."

"January? That's so soon." As Sasha's assistant, I felt like I knew every single aspect of her business life. How had she planned the launch of an entire line of wedding gowns without me knowing?

"It took forever to convince Alicio it was a good idea, but he's finally on board and I'm determined to make this work."

My brain still struggled to keep up. "LeFranc has never done wedding gowns before."

Sasha tossed her hair over her shoulder in a gesture that might have made me gag had I not been so distracted by her news. "LeFranc has never had me before either." She held out her hands. "Welcome to the new face of the company."

I swallowed. The whole entire company? "What does this have to do with me?"

"And my dress?" Paige added.

"Dani, I'm going to have a lot of influence when it comes to these gowns," Sasha said. "I'll need people I can trust—designers I can trust— on my team."

"Are you . . . ?"

"Asking you to design for me?" She motioned to the dress with a slight tilt of her head. "Are you willing to give me that dress?"

I hesitated. "It's Paige's dress."

"Well, I'm sure she can still wear it," Sasha said. "I'll just need to borrow it for a bit first." Sasha's offer was enticing. Almost too good to be true. But, for the hours I'd put into that dress, it took all my logical reasoning not to sleep with it tied to my wrist.

"Dani, I think you should do it," Paige said.

"I think you should too," Sasha said.

I willed the knot in my stomach to loosen. This was a good thing. But something was making me hesitate. And I was pretty sure it had a lot to do with Alex and the text he'd sent warning me to be careful.

But this could mean designing.

It could mean finally landing my dream job.

"If the line goes live in January, the dresses are done. That's not even five months away. You can't add an extra dress to an already finished collection."

"I'm in charge," Sasha said. "I can do whatever I want. We have half a dozen dresses to debut, and they're very good. It's why you've had to help so much with the spring line, Dani. I've just been so consumed by these dresses. And they're fantastic. Truly. But this," she motioned to Paige, "is too perfect not to be featured."

"I still don't know. Does it even fit with the rest of the collection?"

Sasha rolled her eyes. "They're all wedding gowns. They're white. There's lace. Isn't that enough of a unifying theme?"

Her lack of understanding grated on my nerves. How had she managed to get so far with so little understanding of how design actually worked? I shook my head. "I'd need to see the other dresses. Maybe if you let me see them, I could find some ways to tie them together, to—"

"Fine, fine," Sasha said. "Whatever you want. But you can't do a thing to *this* dress."

I looked at Paige and she gave me an encouraging smile. "Will my name be on the dress?"

"Darling, you can bow from the runway at Fashion Week beside me. This is your big break, Dani. It's time for your talents to truly shine."

Paige squealed as she ran across the room and threw her arms around me.

"So I guess I'll bring the dress to work on Monday morning?"

Sasha moved to the apartment door. "And not a day later."

"Wait," I called, stopping Sasha with her hand on the doorknob. "When will I actually start designing?"

"Start whenever you want. You're a designer now. The faster you start, the better. Though"—

she hesitated—"things are still *hush, hush* around the office. And I might get some push back bringing on my *assistant* as a lead designer on the new team. It's probably best that you don't say anything for now. Even to Chase. Not until we're ready to go live with the big announcement."

My heart sank. So I wasn't *really* a designer. I would still be her assistant. At least for the time being. "But you said I should start designing?"

"Well, start sketching, at least. And you have a perfectly *functional* workspace here," she said, though the look on her face said she found my loft anything but functional.

I nodded. "Okay. Sounds good."

Sasha offered one last smile. "Good things are going to happen for you, Dani. Your loyalty won't be forgotten."

Chapter Ten

Alex

The wedding invitation came a few days later. I tossed it onto my desk unopened, disgusted by everything it stood for. Even though I'd accused *everyone* at LeFranc of corruption—my anger might have had some influence—my suspicions had originated with Sasha. I didn't have concrete proof, but what I did know always seemed to trace back to her. It killed me that I hadn't been able to stop what she was doing. Find the proof that she wasn't what Alicio believed her to be.

I scrolled through the screenshots I'd saved before I'd quit—images of the corporate expense accounts and how they'd changed over the years. Every senior designer had access to a company credit card. So much of designing was finding the right fabric or accessory; Alicio had always said he wanted his designers' inspiration to have free rein. Of course, the accounts were monitored, and purchases indexed. If anything looked amiss, it was easy to track the overspending to the individual making the purchases.

I had had access to just enough of the numbers to see patterns develop from month to month—the rise and fall of the expense accounts over time. And I'd *definitely* noticed patterns. Specifically, a steady rise in expenses that coincided, quite conveniently, with the month Sasha was promoted to senior designer. Following a hunch, I'd tried to gain access to the individual accounts so I could see for certain that she was responsible for the increase. I'd been stopped before I'd been able to learn anything. The gatekeeper to the expense accounts? Senior accountant and older stepbrother, Victor.

"You're digging for something that isn't there," he'd told me. "Relax. Take a vacation. Use your own expense account for once."

It had only gotten uglier from there. It was possible, even probable, that I'd let my personal motivations color my professional ones. I didn't like Sasha. She'd started working for Alicio just before Mom had died and had given me a bad feeling right from the start; she had pandered to Alicio when his focus should have been his dying wife. Instead, he'd catered to Sasha's every whim. Regardless of my personal animosity toward the woman, facts didn't lie and the numbers justified digging deeper. So I'd kept pushing and pushing.

And pushing.

When I stormed into an executive board meeting, demanding an internal audit, all but accusing Sasha outright, Alicio had calmly asked me to leave the meeting and wait for him in his office.

I left, all right.

Out the door, down the elevator and away from LeFranc forever.

When I ran into Dani at Java Jean's, it was the closest I'd been to the building since walking out.

I never did talk to Alicio face-to-face. Victor sent over a nondisclosure agreement for me to sign upon my "resignation," cutting me off from everyone presently employed at LeFranc and issuing a gag order—I would not speak to the press about my suspicions under any circumstances. A phone call from my stepfather was more than enough to let me know that should I choose not to sign it, I would swiftly reap the consequences; he wouldn't hesitate to send over the documentation for the retroactive student loan account he'd be happy to set up in my name to cover my very expensive Ivy League education.

It was a dirty move, and in my mind, more than cemented the fact that Alicio, or *someone* on the inside, had something to hide. Just the same, it was enough to make me sign.

So I had.

And I regretted it every single day.

My phone buzzed and I looked away from my laptop screen, closing it with a huff. I'd spent too many hours staring at numbers, wishing I could see what they meant. A distraction was welcome.

I retrieved the phone off of my bed and

stretched out across the mattress to see who'd texted.

Dani.

My heart rate climbed just from the sight of her name.

What do you mean, be careful? she'd texted.

I closed my eyes. How could I answer? It had been a risk saying that much. I'd only wanted her to know I still thought Sasha was up to something and I didn't think she should let her guard down. But there was no way I could actually answer her question.

Instead, I answered with another question. *Is something going on?*

Don't answer my question with a question, she responded.

I smiled, despite the seriousness of our conversation. I missed Dani's fire.

I can only speak in generalities, Dani. I'm sorry I can't be more specific.

It took a long time for her to respond. For how long the little dots bounced at the bottom of my phone screen, I expected a much longer text. Instead, it was just one sentence.

But you don't think I should trust Sasha.

At least that was a question I could answer. I'd made no secret of my distrust for Sasha, even before I left LeFranc.

No. My feelings about that haven't changed.

Several minutes went by with no response. I

waited, occupying myself with a scroll through Dani's photo feed on Instagram. It was mostly her clothes—she worked hard to maintain a professional online presence—but there was an occasional photo of her face. I lingered on those the longest.

After ten minutes with no response, I texted her again.

Dani, are you in trouble?

Again, no response.

I dropped the phone on my desk with a heavy thud, a knot of dread forming in my stomach. Something was up. And there wasn't a thing I could do about it. I tried to tell myself it wasn't my problem. It wasn't, even if Dani was in trouble. She'd made her choice and I'd made mine. There wasn't a reason for me to keep thinking about her, and yet, I couldn't escape.

I looked around the sparsely furnished bedroom I occupied in Isaac's home. A bed, a small desk. A chair in the corner. Without even realizing it, I'd furnished the room to look like a slightly grown-up version of my childhood bedroom. The furniture held the same clean, simple lines and the muted blues and grays of the bedding, and the chair in the corner was an echo of what my father would have chosen. Dani's question hovered in my mind. Why *did* I live with Isaac? It wasn't as though I couldn't afford to live on my own. I'd meant what I told her about believing the job was only temporary, but even after I'd decided to continue the work, why did I stay? Why hadn't I found my own place?

Laughter sounded down the hallway, Tyler's booming laugh, followed by Steven's lower-pitched chuckle. Isaac knocked on my open door before sticking his head in. "Hey. Mushroom brought home fried chicken. Want to eat?"

I nodded. "Sure. I'll be right there."

"Cool." He banged his hand on the door jamb before disappearing back down the hall and into the kitchen. "He's coming, ya'll," I heard him say. "Save him something."

I'd opted to furnish my space with new furniture—it didn't feel right taking things Malorie was presently using—but I'd gathered up several boxes of personal belongings that I'd missed while living in New York. There was a conch shell I'd found one morning on an early jog on Sullivan's Island, as well as several sand dollars I'd collected through years of summer bonfires on the beach. There was my stack of Pat Conroy novels and the Mason jar of traditional Charleston moonshine my dad had purchased for me the summer I'd turned sixteen. He'd promised we'd open it the night I turned twenty-one. He'd already been sick by then, distracted by cancer treatments and his efforts to still care for his new family. It had felt wrong to bring it up, to make it a priority when he had so much else going on.

The randomness and clutter that filled the room would have looked wrong in my New York apartment, all sleek and modern. It would have looked wrong *anywhere* in that version of my life. And maybe *that's* why I'd stayed at Isaac's so long. Because the world I'd built for myself living in New York didn't feel like a real life. It felt like a magazine cover—like a representation of who the world expected me to be, even though it had very little to do with who I actually *wanted* to be. But this place felt so much more like someone I recognized.

My eyes fell on the sweetgrass basket I'd purchased on a whim a few weeks back after striking up a conversation with a woman selling them in front of the courthouse downtown. Dani had told me once she'd always wanted one and had often talked about saving up for one of the handmade treasures. In retrospect, it was clear I'd bought it for her, though I wasn't sure I'd ever actually give it to her. I wasn't sure she'd take it if I tried.

I picked up my phone and scrolled through my photos, going back to when Dani and I had been together. I'd told her that my New York life hadn't been an accurate reflection of the person I wanted to be, and that had been the truth. But that didn't mean there wasn't truth to our relationship. A lot of what we'd had had been real—as real as the room I'd carefully built for myself in Charleston. But what about how she felt? What could I possibly be to Dani if all I had to offer her was a single room in her brother's house?

More importantly, why did I suddenly care?

I scrolled through a few more photos, Dani's face filling my screen. Dani on my couch, the tall windows overlooking the city behind her. Dani in Java Jean's. Dani behind the sewing machine in her tiny loft in Chelsea, her nose wrinkled in concentration. Dani leaning against the pillows in my bedroom, blonde hair tumbling down her shoulder. Dani and me together in front of the marquee sign for *Hamilton* right after I'd surprised her with tickets. It was the night of our first kiss.

I tossed the phone back onto the bed and pressed my face into my hands in frustration. I couldn't think about Dani this way. It was too dangerous, too painful. I'd been gutted over our breakup, though she'd likely find that hard to believe. Life had only just begun to feel normal again.

I fled to the kitchen, hoping company would help. I dropped into a chair next to Mushroom and reached for a plate.

"Dude, what's wrong with you?" Mushroom asked. "You look angry."

I sighed as I piled potato salad onto my plate. "Not angry. Just . . . distracted, I guess."

"Woman trouble?" Tyler asked. "I'm guessing woman trouble."

I met Isaac's eyes across the table and shrugged. "Something like that."

Tyler waited, his fork poised above his plate, a look of expectancy on his face. "And?" he said when I didn't offer any additional information. "Elaborate and maybe we can help you."

"There isn't anything else to say. It's not *recent* trouble. I ran into an ex in New York and seeing her messed with my head a little bit."

"You need a distraction," Vinnie offered through a bite of fried chicken. "Someone new."

I hadn't given much thought to dating over the past year. I'd talked to a few women here and there but getting over Dani had felt like full-time work. Anything beyond talking had felt almost impossible. But maybe it *was* what I needed.

"Text Jasmine back," Isaac offered from his end of the table. "Hasn't she asked you out a dozen times or something?"

Jasmine was an old friend of Isaac's. She'd gone to high school with him and Dani and recently moved into an apartment a few blocks away. A few weeks back, Isaac had invited her and a few friends over for an afternoon barbecue. I'd barely talked to her, but before she left, she'd asked for my number and we'd been texting off and on ever since. I didn't know much about her. She had a dog that she often walked up and down Church Street. She was tall and had dark hair and a nice smile, and Isaac had known her long enough he wouldn't have suggested it if she was crazy.

"Jasmine's the tall chick with the dog?" Vinnie asked.

"Chicks are baby birds," Mushroom said, not even lifting his eyes from his food. "Not women."

The whole table froze, all eyes trained on Mushroom.

He looked up to meet the silence, his face flushing red when he realized everyone was staring at him. "What?" he finally said. "I'm just saying. It's the twenty-first century. We should know better."

Laughter spread around the table; I agreed with Mushroom. That wasn't the funny part. I'd just never expected the comment out of *him*. Maybe I'd underestimated the guy.

"Jasmine *is* the tall . . . *woman* who owns a dog," Tyler said, glancing sideways at Mushroom. "And she's attractive . . . not that that's the most important thing," he quickly amended. "I'm sure she's smart and . . ." He shook his head, clearly tiring of being so careful. "Whatever. Isaac's right. You should ask her out."

I pulled out my phone. "It feels wrong to be asking someone out because I need a distraction."

"But maybe you'll like her," Isaac said. "Have an open mind. You never know."

A part of me still felt guilty as I typed out a text asking if she wanted to get together, but

I was desperate. Seeing Dani again had ignited something in me I'd worked a long time to suppress. I had to find a way to stamp the flame back out again, for my sake, and for hers.

Chapter Eleven

Dani

I looked up to see Chase walking toward my desk. A welcome distraction. I glanced one more time at my phone, the texts from Alex still visible on my screen. Even though I'd received them weeks ago, they kept pulling me back, taunting me. Reminding me of his warnings.

Was I in trouble? His question had irritated me, mostly because I didn't know the answer. Something was definitely up with Sasha. And the longer I was left in the dark, the more I worried it had everything to do with me. I had a huge stack of sketches I wanted to show her, and three different dresses I'd started to work on at home. I'd assumed she'd want to see them, discuss them. Be a part of the design process. But I'd only gotten seconds of her time over the past few weeks. She'd encouraged me to keep working and responded with a *Yes, of course* when I'd asked if I could be reimbursed for the fabric and other notions I'd purchased to start the new dresses. But that was it. Which didn't make sense.

It was the end of September—barely three months from debut month. When, exactly, was Alicio going to tell the design team about Sasha's new venture? What was more, I had no idea if anything had been done in preparation for the launch. Had there been a photoshoot? Would there be a magazine spread? Promotional material of any kind? I didn't know everything about debuting a fashion line, but I'd been working at LeFranc long enough to know that we normally worked almost a full year in advance. When everyone was just starting to wear our fall line, we were finalizing what would hit stores in the spring. It didn't seem realistic that this close to January, there wasn't a word about Sasha's dresses anywhere.

Chase dropped the latest edition of Elite Fashion onto my desk with a dramatic thump. "Page seventy-two. Quick."

I shot him a look—I hated being bossed around—but flipped open the magazine anyway. There didn't seem to be much on page seventy-two, just a few random blurbs of industry-related news. But then I saw, in the bottom right corner, a photo of Sasha and Alicio on the red carpet of some awards show they'd attended together. I quickly read the caption.

Wedding bells approach for designer Alicio LeFranc and his fiancée, Sasha Wellington. In a recent press release, it was revealed that Wellington—a senior designer at LeFranc— will debut the first in a line of signature gowns bearing Wellington's name and backed by the LeFranc brand at their December wedding, a preview of the rest of the collection, debuting in January. "I've been working on the dress for months," Wellington told Elite in an exclusive interview. "It's the truest representation of my style and what I want this line of dresses to be. I can't wait to share it with the world." For those of us in the fashion industry, that's one wedding dress we can't wait to see.

"So she's finally gone public," I said. It had been nearly three weeks since I'd handed over Paige's wedding gown to Sasha's greedy hands.

"Wait, you knew about this?" Chase said, pulling my attention back to the article. "How has she kept an entire line of wedding dresses a secret from the rest of the design team?"

"I don't know much," I said. "But she did mention it." I bit my lip, hesitating before admitting what Sasha had specifically asked me not to tell Chase. "She actually asked me to be on her design team for the new line. I've been working on dresses at home."

Chase's eyes went wide. "Dani! That's excellent news!"

I shook my head, cutting short his congratulations. "I thought it was too, but I don't know, Chase. Something isn't right."

He narrowed his gaze. "What do you mean?"

I looked over his shoulder, making sure we were well and truly alone at my desk. "Sasha has been completely avoiding me since we first talked about it. She's hardly been at work. She's avoiding my phone calls. She told me the line is supposed to launch in January, I guess right after the wedding," I said, motioning to the article, "but she hasn't said anything about the actual dresses. She made it seem like they already exist, but they might still need a little tweaking so that they coordinate with Paige's dress and I thought she was going to have me do that. But she doesn't seem to be concerned about any of it. If she wants me to be lead designer, why is she avoiding me? Why aren't we collaborating? Brainstorming? *Working?*"

Chase gave me a worried look. "Dani, why do the dresses all need to coordinate with Paige's dress?"

Doubt welled up in my stomach. "Because I gave it to her. To include in the line."

"But you haven't seen *any* of the other dresses?"

"Well, no, but they have to be somewhere." I pointed at the magazine still open on my desk. "I mean, she's *wearing* one of them. I can't imagine Sasha's wedding dress being anything but top priority for everyone involved."

"That's just it, Dani. Who is everyone? No one else on the design team knows anything about this. The article says she designed the dress herself. Do you *really* have confidence in Sasha's ability to create a designer wedding gown on her own? She can't design *anything* on her own. Something doesn't add up."

"She told me she has a new design team that's handling the dresses. Maybe they're off location somewhere?"

"I guess that part makes sense," Chase said. "Of course she would need a separate location. That way no one here has to know she isn't actually designing the dresses herself."

"Truly? You don't think she could design a gown?"

Chase put a hand on my shoulder. "Dani, Sasha's only contributions that actually get taken seriously are the pieces you design for her. The woman is a cheat and a master manipulator. That she's convinced Alicio to give her a line of wedding dresses is evidence of that. Because she doesn't have the talent to justify it."

"But designers get help all the time," I argued, feeling the futility of my words even as I said them. Chase had never spoken so blatantly about Sasha before. "Alicio has a full team of people who work for him. He still gets to put his name on the clothes."

"But it took him years to build his brand. He did the work, in the trenches. He earned that right. But what has Sasha done? She hasn't earned her place with her design skill, I can tell you that much."

"So you think she's using other designers to create her dresses, and she's doing it away from LeFranc so no one knows she's actually a fraud?"

"Exactly," Chase said, his tone gentle. "But my hunch is that whatever underlings she hired don't have what it takes to create a wedding dress good enough for her to wear herself. She had to find someone else with that kind of talent."

I closed my eyes, a hand pressed to my stomach. "Someone like me?"

Chase nodded. "She already has Paige's dress? Like, *in* her possession?"

I leaned back into my chair. "I think I'm going to be sick."

Chase picked up the magazine and started fanning me with it. "Talk me through it, Dani. Tell me what happened."

"She showed up at my apartment. I guess she'd looked through my sketchbook, and then Paige was actually *wearing* the dress when she came in because I'd been fixing the hem, and then she just told me so many amazing things. Talked about bowing from the runway at Fashion Week. She didn't give me any reason not to believe her, Chase."

"I'm sure. She's very convincing."

And yet, I *had* had a reason not to believe her. Alex's warning had told me not to trust her.

"How long would I have kept picking up lattes and answering her emails before I realized it was all a lie? I'm her pawn. Her puppet. That's all I've ever been to her." I forced a breath out through my nose. "No decent designer in all of New York would stand for Sasha Wellington claiming one of their designs as her own. But she knew I would, right? Because I've been doing it for months." Tears welled in my eyes and I pushed a hand against my forehead. "Why am I so gullible?"

Chase reached for my hand, then scooted around and sat on the edge of my desk, our clasped hands resting on his knee.

"I'm an idiot," I said.

He rubbed slow circles on my back. "Hey. We're going off our hunches here, right? We don't know anything for sure. Maybe she's telling the truth."

"She promised me she'd turn me into someone. Said I would be a part of something special." I hiccupped a laugh. "And I fell for it."

"Shhh. Maybe you still will be. You could absolutely be freaking out for no reason."

"I appreciate the encouragement, but I'm done being optimistic. She stole my dress. Simple as that."

Chase was silent long enough, he had to agree with me. "So what do we do about it?" he finally said.

Good question. "Make another one?"

"You could, though you run the risk of her accusing you of stealing *her* idea."

My shoulders fell. If it actually *did* come to that, no one would ever believe me over Sasha. I pulled my sketchbook out of my purse and opened the page to the finished rendering of Paige's dress. I flipped the book around and handed it to Chase.

He whistled, running his hands across the image. "It's stunning, Dani. It's no wonder she wanted it."

"I feel like such an idiot."

Chase leaned forward and kissed my temple, giving my shoulders a final squeeze. "Let's find out the truth first. Don't lose heart until you absolutely have to."

Later that night, a text came in from Paige. *Staying at work tonight so don't wait up. How's my dress?*

I paused the *Friends* reruns I was bingeing and stared at Paige's text. I couldn't tell her. Not until I knew something definite.

Gorgeous as ever, I responded. It was a lie, but I had to buy a little time somehow. How was I ever going to tell Paige the truth?

Chapter Twelve
Alex

"Alex!" Isaac called to me from somewhere—the kitchen, maybe?—with a volume and intensity that might have alarmed me three months ago. I'd since grown used to Isaac reacting to everything from running out of paper towels to burning his toast with the same vigor he would an approaching hurricane.

I closed my laptop with a weary sigh and stood from the concrete bench in the corner of the side garden. The garden was frequently the quietest place in Isaac's house. Fortunately, our other roommates didn't spend very much time outside.

"Should I get you a bell you can ring whenever you want to find me?" I dropped my laptop onto the table and gave Isaac a wry look. "A cowbell, maybe? Or one of those gongs used to call people—"

Isaac shushed me and motioned to his phone laying face up on the kitchen table.

So he was on a call.

"Rizzo, I get it, man, but it's too late to restructure. Invites have already gone out. Your name is on all of our promotional materials."

My jaw tensed. Rizzo backing out would not

be good for the event. I shot Isaac a questioning look.

He shrugged his shoulders, then waved his hands in front of him, a clear mark of his annoyance.

"I don't want to drop out," Rizzo said, his voice calm and smooth. "I want you to give me what I want."

"Explain, please," I whispered to Isaac.

"Hey Rizzo, hold on a minute, will you?" Isaac pressed mute without waiting for Rizzo to respond. "He doesn't want to contribute to the cash prize."

I scoffed. "Seriously? It's only four grand. He makes that much in twenty minutes."

"And," Isaac continued, "he doesn't want to stop charging for his live stream."

"Wait, I don't understand. What do you mean charging for his live stream?"

Isaac raked a hand through his hair. "A lot of YouTubers do it. When they live stream, you make a donation in exchange for access to the feed. For the event, we've asked that the donations go to charity instead of to the content creator."

"Right. Of course. That's the entire point of the event."

"Except, he thinks that's asking too much. He says he's willing to match whatever *my* live stream brings in, but anything above that is his to keep."

"Great guy," I said. "So generous."

"Tell me about it," Isaac said.

"What he's not thinking about is what backing out would do to his public image." I reached over and unmuted the call. "Hey, Rizzo, Alex here."

"Hey, Alex, my man. You talk some sense into Isaac for me?"

Ha. Not exactly. "I want you to answer a question for me."

"Okay. Shoot."

"How long does it take you to make four thousand dollars?"

He was silent a moment, then he chuckled. "Not very long."

"We aren't changing the terms of our original agreement. You made a commitment and we're holding you to it. You're free to back out if that's what you decide to do, but if that happens, I want you to know I'll be obligated to work up a press release explaining exactly why you backed out of the event—the *charity* event that has the potential to bring in thousands and thousands of dollars to benefit America's underprivileged neighborhoods. I might mention how long it takes you to make four thousand dollars and will be sure to make the point that, in your mind, the small amount of time it takes you to make more money than what most of your viewers earn in weeks, even months, was more important to you than your participation."

"It's not just about the four grand—"

"Are you confident your public image could stand the hit of being the guy who backed out of a charity event because of his own greed?"

"Now you're just playing dirty," Rizzo said.

"No, playing dirty would be including a picture of your multi-million-dollar mansion in the press release."

He was silent for a beat before finally relenting. "Fine."

I smiled. "Always a pleasure to talk with you, Rizzo. We'll see you in December." I hung up the phone and Isaac let out a whoop of victory.

He straightened an imaginary tie and slipped on a pair of imaginary sunglasses. "Always a pleasure to talk with you, Rizzo," he said in an exaggerated Southern accent. "We'll see you in December."

I socked him in the arm. "You're welcome."

"Seriously, you are one convenient man to have around," Isaac said.

"I have a list of things I need you to go over when you have time," I said, moving to the fridge. I pulled out the leftovers from last night's Chinese takeout. I opened the container and sniffed. Maybe it wasn't last night. "When was the last time we had Chinese?"

"The fact that you can't remember probably isn't a good sign."

I tossed the leftovers into the trash, instead

grabbing an apple from the basket on the counter. "I talked to the event planner this morning. She had questions about the food and sent over a few different designs for the decorations. She wants you to pick the one you like the most."

"It's happening on Christmas Eve. I assumed it'd be decorated for Christmas."

"The designs are all holiday-themed, just different styles. You'll see what I mean when I send them over."

"Cool. I'll take a look. But you know you could probably just decide and never tell me we'd actually had options and I wouldn't know the difference."

"You and Dani really aren't anything alike, are you?"

He chuckled and shook his head. "Not hardly. You should send *her* the designs. She'd know exactly which one to pick."

A pang of regret pulsed through me. Dani *would* know. She'd be the perfect person to consult. Instinctively I reached for my phone.

She hadn't texted, not since she'd asked me about Sasha. But that didn't stop me from compulsively checking for new messages. I dropped the phone back on the table, annoyed that I could so easily forget the reasons why I'd left. I'd only ever wanted to escape the LeFrancs and the world they lived in. I couldn't do that with Dani. She was too connected. Too loyal.

An image of my mom flashed through my mind, one arm looped through Alicio's, the other resting casually on a ten-year-old Victor's shoulder. Gabriel stood beside him, his hand holding onto the hem of my mother's jacket. It was a popular photo—one of the first ones that popped up when you googled Alicio's name.

Just the four of them.

Their perfect little happy family.

Dani hadn't been the only person to choose LeFranc over me.

My phone dinged with an incoming text and I lunged for it, grateful for the distraction, hating that I couldn't tamp out the hope that the message might be from Dani.

My shoulders fell, but I typed out a response anyway.

"Who's texting?" Isaac asked. "Somebody terrible?"

I shook my head. "Jasmine. Confirming our date for this weekend."

"Wow," Isaac said, his expression even. "I can already tell it's going to be a party and a half."

"Shut up," I said, tossing my apple core into the trash. I left the kitchen, grabbing my laptop off the table on the way, and headed to my room.

I would go on a date with Jasmine.

I gritted my teeth.

I would go and I *would* have fun.

Chapter Thirteen

Dani

Two days of sneaking around, following Sasha and tracking her every move at LeFranc and I finally had my proof. It came in the form of a tiny Swedish tailor named Julian who spoke terrible English, but not so terrible that I couldn't milk out the information I needed.

After an uncomfortable back and forth in the elevator, he confirmed that yes, he was working with Sasha on her wedding gown. Not designing. Just altering, tweaking a dress that was already made. The thought of my gown being tweaked to fit her body made me feel sick, but I pushed aside the discomfort. If I had any hope of getting it back, I had to stay focused.

Back at my desk, I sent Chase a text. *Basement. 3:30 p.m. Outside the elevators.*

Message received, he texted back.

Chase was already in the hallway when the elevator finally deposited me on LeFranc's bottom floor at 3:37 p.m. He leaned against the wall, his foot nervously tapping against the floor. "What took you so long?" he asked, grabbing my arm and pulling me out of the elevator.

"I couldn't get rid of Mylie," I said. "She kept asking me questions about Hank up in accounting."

"Hank? Really?" He motioned to his head. "With the . . . hair thing?"

I shrugged. "Maybe she likes bald guys?"

"No, no. Being bald is different than being bald and wearing a toupee. You're not allowed to put both kinds of men in the same category."

I looked up and down the hallway. "Have you seen anyone else?" I asked him.

"Are you kidding? No one ever comes down here. I don't think these rooms have been used since we made all our clothes in-house."

I started down the hallway, motioning for Chase to follow. "Which is exactly why Sasha would meet Julian down here."

"Who's Julian?"

"He's the tailor who's altering Paige's dress to fit Sasha. At least, I *think* he is."

"Ohhh, the plot thickens."

I tried a door to my left. Locked. "We've got to find a place to hide."

"What? Right now?"

I glanced at my watch. "She has a fitting scheduled at four. If I can just see the dress and know for sure, then . . ."

"Then what?"

I sighed and looked at Chase. "I don't know. I guess I'll figure it out when it happens."

Chase crossed his arms. "Dani, this could cost you your job."

I put my hands on my hips. "I know that. But I can't let her steal the dress. How would I ever tell Paige?"

He nodded. "I get that. It's just . . ." He pulled his bottom lip between his teeth. "I'm here for you, all right? You know I've got your back. But I can't lose *my* job. On principle, I wish I could, but Darius's mom isn't doing great and we've been sending money to her every month, and there's—"

"Chase." I stopped him. "I would never ask you to jeopardize your job."

He shook his head, his eyes full of sadness. "It's not right what she's doing to you."

"It's not right that I've let her get away with it for so long." I took a deep breath. "Just be my moral support, all right? Stay hidden with me; don't let me lose my nerve." I tried the next door in the hallway, expecting it to be locked, and almost hit the ground when it swung open, depositing me into one of LeFranc's old workrooms.

Chase followed me in and reached for my elbow, steadying me. "You okay?"

I nodded, giving the room a quick scan. I looked over Chase's shoulder. "Do you see a light switch?"

Chase glanced at his phone. "I wouldn't risk the

light. She could be down here any second." He turned on his flashlight app and swept it around the room. "What if the fitting is happening in here?"

"The dress would be here if it was," I said. "She wouldn't risk carrying it around the office."

"But she wouldn't just leave it down here in an unlocked workroom either," Chase said.

The debate became pointless when we heard the elevator ding from down the hallway. Chase's eyes went wide. "What now?" he whispered.

I motioned Chase out of the doorway and pulled the door to the mostly closed position, leaving a tiny crack of light seeping into the dark room. "We wait," I whispered back.

Seconds later, what had to be Sasha's high heels clicked down the hallway, the shuffle of someone else's footsteps following behind her. "I do hope you managed to fix the hemline," Sasha said. "It must be perfect in time for the photoshoot next week."

I gripped Chase's hand. Photoshoot?

Sasha neared the door that hid Chase and me from view, keys jangling in her hand. My heart pounded in my chest, and I squeezed Chase's hand even tighter. There'd be no explaining if she found us hiding together in the basement.

"If she opens that door," Chase whispered into my ear, "we're going to start making out."

I held back a snort, my near panicked state

making his comment seem even funnier than it was. "Don't make me laugh!" I whispered back.

When Sasha passed by, we both breathed a sigh of relief. We listened as she opened a door further down the hallway. "Julian, why is this door unlocked?" she said, her voice shrill. "Didn't I tell you to always lock the door behind you? I can't risk anyone seeing this dress before the reveal."

Julian muttered something I couldn't understand. My heart dropped into my gut as I realized what her comment implied. Had I searched a minute or two longer, I might have found the dress, unlocked, unprotected.

"You wouldn't have made it out of LeFranc before she caught you," Chase said, clearly reading my mind. "It wouldn't have mattered."

I swallowed, my throat dry and tight. "I know."

"Now what?" Chase asked for the second time.

I took another long breath, willing my nerves to calm down, squeezing my trembling hands into fists. "Now I go and confront her."

Chase took me by the shoulders. "Don't let her walk all over you, Dani. You've got this."

I nodded. "Wish me luck."

It wasn't like I didn't know what to expect. I *knew* she'd stolen my dress. I *knew* she was planning on wearing it. But it still felt like a full-on punch to actually see her in it. The door to the workroom where Julian had been working swung open with a squeak. Sasha spun around, her eyes wide with surprise.

"You have some nerve," I said, my voice icy cold.

She smirked. "Dani. How lovely to see you."

"I want my dress back. *Now.*"

"Your dress?" She ran her hands down the front, a possessive glint in her eye. "I don't think so."

I stood there, frozen by her gall, her utter disrespect for anything but her own shallow desires. "You told me Paige would still get to wear the dress."

She slid her hands over the lace that cascaded down the front of the dress. "But I'm wearing it so much better, don't you think?"

"You can't do this. I'll . . ." Fury ate my words. I'd what?

"Tell the boss?" She grinned and walked toward me, her hands on her hips. "Go ahead and try. You want to place bets on whose side Alicio will take?" She stopped in front of me, her eyes holding mine with a ferocity that immediately made me feel sick. Because I could see, with perfect clarity, just how far Sasha would go to get ahead. And how little she actually cared about me.

"You never intended to let me design with you, did you?"

She rolled her eyes. "Oh, please. You're a good designer, Dani. But you'd never make it in this industry. Fashion is cutthroat. And you, with your little doe-eyed innocence and trust, would *never* make it. You'd be eaten alive. Really, I'm doing you a favor by telling you the truth now."

Tears welled in my eyes. "I'll expose you. I have . . . proof. My sketches, my designs." I swallowed. "I'll take it to the press."

She grimaced, leaning forward with a menacing stare. "Go ahead and try," she seethed. "It'll be my word against yours and I guarantee I have a lot more friends in the press than you do." She reached out and gripped my arm, her fingers digging into my flesh. "You don't want to fight with me, Dani. I play dirty. You breathe one word against me to anyone, anywhere, and I'll make sure you never work in fashion again. You'll be ruined in New York. No internships. No working as an assistant. When I'm through with you, you'll be lucky to get a job designing big-box store knock-offs." She finally released her grip on my arm. "Or you can go back upstairs like a good girl and pretend like this never happened. Your choice."

I breathed through my nose, anger and frustration roiling inside me. "I'll make another dress," I said, indignant. "I still have the designs. You'll be the one wearing a knock-off. A copy."

"Oh, sweetie, it's so cute you think anyone

would believe that I'm the one who stole from you."

She smiled and crossed back to Julian, who stood patiently, tape measure around his neck, pins in his hand. She stepped onto a stool in front of him, and he bent over, adjusting the hem of the dress to accommodate Sasha's smaller-than-Paige frame.

"You won't get away with this," I said, but the fire had already fizzled from my voice.

"That's just it, Dani," Sasha said through a sneer. "I already have."

I took a step backward, still furious, but too defeated to keep pushing. I retreated to the door but then turned back. "You know what?" I said. "I feel sorry for you. It must be hard keeping up the façade—convincing everyone that you actually have talent. I wonder how long you'll be able to keep it up? Especially since you won't have *me* to steal from anymore." I reached for the door handle. "I quit."

Chapter Fourteen

Alex

"She really was like my best friend," Jasmine said, for what felt like the fifteenth time. After lunch at The Brown Dog Deli, we wandered around downtown until we hit the battery, aimlessly wandering past centuries-old mansions and sprawling live oaks. It was a warm afternoon for fall—almost too warm—which only added to my discomfort.

Jasmine had been talking about Dani nonstop.

I had to wonder if she knew Dani and I had a history. Constantly talking about an ex-girlfriend seemed like a weird way to spend a date. But then I figured out Jasmine didn't actually care about Dani. Or me. It was all about Isaac.

"We shared a cabin at summer camp one year, did I tell you that?" Jasmine said.

I nodded. "You did. So have you been up to see her then? In New York?"

Jasmine paused. "Oh. No, well, I'm not super big on traveling."

Right. I bet that was it.

"Isaac goes to New York a lot, right? Does he take you with him? As his assistant?"

"Business manager," I said, my tone short. I

167

was trying, but the woman was making propriety really hard.

"What?"

"I'm his business manager. Not his assistant."

"Oh. Well, whatever. I'm sure his life must be so glamorous."

For another hour we walked around the city. Had we not stopped at Kaminsky's to get dessert, the day might have been a complete failure. But eating her ice cream kept Jasmine quiet long enough that I was able to enjoy my milkshake in peace. And a Kaminsky's milkshake was an experience all its own.

I was back home by four-thirty, my shoulders sore from the tension they'd been carrying all afternoon. I'd gone on a date to get Dani *off* my mind and instead experienced the exact opposite. I dropped onto the couch in the living room.

Isaac pulled off his headphones. He was, miraculously, alone in the spacious room. "How'd it go?"

I groaned my displeasure. "I think she only dated me hoping to get closer to you."

"Really? Jasmine?" he said, in a tone that said he already knew. "You think she's into me? Interesting."

"She's already tried to ask you out, hasn't she?"

He grinned. "Did she talk to you about summer camp?"

I tossed a pillow at his face. "Why didn't you warn me?"

He dodged the pillow with a chuckle. "I thought you might like her."

"I hate you." I threw another pillow, this one hitting him square in the face. "Where's everyone else?"

"Went to see a movie," Isaac said.

"And you didn't go?"

"Naw. Didn't feel like dealing with people. Sorry the date sucked. I kinda hoped she'd like you enough to stop talking about me. I mean, she's not bad to look at."

"No, but she's not . . ." My words trailed off. Because finishing the sentence meant admitting to something I didn't want to say out loud.

"She's not Dani?" Isaac finished for me.

I sighed. So much for ignoring *that* truth. "Nobody is."

I leaned back into the cushions. The first time I'd kissed Dani, it had been all her. I'd taken her to see *Hamilton* on Broadway and right there in the theater, minutes before opening curtain, she'd turned to me, taken my face in her hands, and kissed me. "Thank you for bringing me here," she'd whispered.

It had surprised me in the moment, but the longer I got to know her, the more I'd realized that was simply the way she was. She lived passionately. Intentionally. She valued experience, learned from and embraced the world around her, and never hesitated to fight for what she wanted.

"Hey, you busy in the morning?" Isaac asked.

"You tell me, boss."

"Nah, this isn't work-related. I have to go to my parents' house and let in the guy who's fixing the roof. I thought you might want to tag along and see the place."

A surge of desire swelled in my chest. I likely would have agreed to go anywhere with Isaac just to keep him company. He was a good friend and he'd earned my loyalty. But seeing the house where Dani had grown up intrigued me in a way that surprised me. We'd dated close to a year; it was weird that we'd never traveled to Charleston together. But Dani had been so determined to make it in New York and to do it on her own. She didn't make enough to afford the travel or the time off work, and she would have never let me fund the trip. It was hard enough to buy her dinner.

To get an inside glimpse into Dani's life, even after our breakup, felt like an opportunity I couldn't pass up. I tried not to sound too eager. "Sure," I said to Isaac, with a dismissive shrug. "I'll come. I don't have anything else to do."

Isaac gave me a knowing look and I grimaced. My feigned indifference must not have been too convincing.

"You could call her, you know," Isaac said, his eyes focused back on the video game screen. "Tell her you're thinking about her."

I stood. "It's not that easy. She still works for my stepfather. And that's not a world I want to be in, even if she's in it."

Chapter Fifteen

Dani

Chase fell in step beside me as I hurried to the elevator. "That was the bravest thing I've ever heard you say," he whispered.

I bit my lip, determined to keep the tears at bay. Not for Chase's benefit. He knew me well enough to handle tears, no matter their reason for falling. But I had too much pride for anyone else at LeFranc to see me skulk away with my tail between my legs. I leaned against the wall of the elevator while Chase pushed the button for the third floor. I almost stopped him. It felt so much easier to stop in the lobby and walk away without a backward glance. But my phone and my purse were both at my desk.

"You okay?" Chase asked.

I shrugged. "No. But I think I will be. Eventually."

"We can still find a way to make this right, Dani. You can't stop fighting."

I shook my head. I *could* stop fighting. And that was precisely what I was going to do. Because Sasha was right. I would never be cutthroat enough to make it in fashion. Especially not if cutthroat meant lying and cheating and stealing.

"I can't do this anymore, Chase. I'm so tired of her. I'm tired of pouring so much energy and time and *hope* into a job that has literally given me nothing in return."

"Don't say that. It gave you me."

I managed a half-smile, then reached up and cupped my hand around his cheek. "That's true. And I wouldn't trade that for anything. But . . ."

"Enough is enough?" he finished for me.

"Enough is enough," I agreed.

Chase didn't leave my side while I quickly gathered the few personal items I had on my desk, shoving them haphazardly into my fortunately oversized purse. A scarf slipped off the back of my chair and fell to the floor, and Chase picked it up. "I don't like to see you giving up," he said. "You might have lost the battle, Dani, but—"

I held up a hand, cutting him off. "If you tell me I can still win the war I'm going to kick you in the shins."

He draped the scarf around my neck. "But maybe you still can. It might take a little time, but we'll think of something." He glanced over his shoulder, lowering his voice. "That woman is building a glass castle. Remember, she still has to launch an entire line of wedding gowns—now, without you. Eventually, someone important will see her for who she truly is. Lying can only get you so far."

"I appreciate your optimism, but she's sleeping

with the boss, Chase. She can lie all she wants, and no one will stop her."

His shoulders slumped, but he perked right back up, shaking away his doubt. "No. Truth has to prevail eventually. I'll talk to the other designers. Sasha may be in Alicio's bed, but if enough of us are on your side, well, he can't exactly run the company without us."

He was sweet to try. But I was a nobody. And in a place like New York City, there was *always* another nobody ready to take your place the second you lost your footing. Chase cared because he was my friend. But everyone else? They wouldn't think of me again the minute I was out the door, which meant they definitely wouldn't go up against the boss's bride-to-be for my sake.

I was halfway across the design floor, aiming for the elevator, my burgeoning purse over my shoulder, my coat draped over my arm, when I ran into Sasha. I stopped in front of her and the room around us grew silent, all eyes turned toward us.

"I am so sorry to see you go, Dani," Sasha said. She reached out and adjusted my scarf, her perfectly manicured fuchsia nails a nauseating contrast against the deep, winter-green. "Of course, I understand these things happen, and like I said"—her voice grew louder, like she wanted to make sure the entire office could hear her—"the minute you need a recommendation, you let me know. You know I have nothing but the kindest things to say about your work as an *assistant*."

I clenched my jaw. In a move almost bolder than when I'd quit in the first place, I shoved past her, ramming her with my bag. "Go to hell, Sasha."

"Do you really have to leave?" Paige sat on the end of my bed while I pulled things out of my bureau, shoving them haphazardly into the suitcases and boxes lining the floor against the wall. "You know Chase would let you crash on his couch. At least until you find another job."

I shook my head. "I can't do that to Chase and Darius." It was possible I was running away. But I'd tell my made-up truths as long as I could if it meant not having to face my real ones. And my made-up truths were this: Our lease was up at the end of the month. I could not afford to renew a lease and live in New York without a job. With Paige mostly moved out already—bouncing between Reese's place and her nannying job—it didn't make sense for her to renew the lease without me. Moving *out* was the only option, which actually fit my needs perfectly. Because *leaving* was all I felt like doing. "Another job as what, a secretary? No way."

She rolled her eyes. "You're being so stubborn

about this. LeFranc is not the only designer in town. You could find another job in fashion."

Maybe she was right. But LeFranc had been my dream. And with that dream completely shattered and ground into powder, it was hard to think about working anywhere else. Not when I'd come so close. "You know I don't have the cash to stay, Paige. I have two hundred dollars in my savings account. Even if I did manage to find a job and a cheaper place, there's no way I could cover a security deposit and first month's rent."

"But I could help," Paige said. "Go in for the first couple of months until you can find another roommate."

"You're sweet to offer, but you know that doesn't make any sense. You're getting married in less than three months. You need to save as much cash as you can. And you're basically living at Reese's now anyway. There's no reason to keep this place."

Paige collapsed onto the bed, pulling me down beside her and weaving my arm through hers. "I could call my dad. I wouldn't even have to tell him it was for you. I can fake a reason to need a few thousand dollars. You know he'd send it." She propped herself up on her elbow, shooting me a pointed look. "Or you could just ask your parents. Why haven't we discussed that option yet?"

"No. Absolutely not. If I ask my parents for

cash, they'll freak out and panic and race home from Europe to save me. Which is exactly what I don't need. And we can't ask your parents because they'll tell *my* parents. I don't want anybody's help, Paige. This was my dream. My choice. That means it's my failure, too. I have to own it."

"You haven't failed, Dani. It's just a little setback."

I shrugged, pulling her back down so we lay side by side again. I leaned my head onto her shoulder. "Maybe. But either way, a break might be good for me. I miss Charleston. Going home could be good."

"Except you aren't going home. You're going to Isaac's. That's totally different."

I'd actually checked the availability on my parents' house to see if it was vacant, but it was booked solid until Christmas. At least Isaac had a house big enough to accommodate me. At least, I hoped he did. He did have five roommates. "Isaac's will just be a place to sleep. Charleston is home. The beach is home. I need that right now."

We lay there silently for a few moments until Paige asked, "How are you going to face him, Dani?" She didn't have to explain that she was asking about Alex.

My head started pounding, a nauseating *thump thump* reverberating in my ears and behind my eyes. Showing up on Isaac's doorstep was going to be hard enough. He'd probably howl with laughter, but he'd eventually be nice. But Alex? How would I ever admit that all along, he'd been right about Sasha?

"I have no idea," I finally answered. "He's too good to say *I told you so,* which is almost worse."

"You still haven't called Isaac yet, have you?"

I pulled a pillow from behind me and slid it over my face.

"Dani. You have to call him. You can't just show up."

"Why not? I actually think my odds are better if I do. I mean, he can't refuse me if I'm standing on his porch with a suitcase."

"Yes, he totally can. And that would be a lot more embarrassing."

"He wouldn't do it. He's my brother. Even if all he can offer is a couch, he can't leave me out in the cold."

"Especially as ferocious as the winters are in Charleston. You'd definitely freeze to death."

I rolled my eyes. "Shut up."

"Want to know why *I* think you won't call him?"

I peeked an eye out from behind the pillow. "Why?"

She sat up, pulling the pillow off my face and holding it in her lap, her legs crossed under her.

She cleared her throat. "Even though you doubt whether or not *Isaac* will let you move in, you feel one hundred percent confident that Alex will not let him turn you out. He will advocate for you no matter what. And that makes you happy, because *Alex,* but also angry and annoyed and frustrated, because *Alex.* Alex who is still firmly on your hate list and therefore not able to do anything nice for you. Or be in any place where he might try to further convince you that he's actually very sorry for hurting you so thoroughly because, again, hate list. You pointed out the fact that he was actually right about Sasha and you were wrong but knowing it doesn't make it burn any less, so that's still an issue. To make things even *more* complicated, a part of you wants to go to Isaac's because Alex is there and you still, maybe, a tiny bit love him. If you call and ask and Isaac says no? Then there's no possibility of an Alex and Dani future. And you like the idea of a possibility."

I sat up. "Are you seriously some sort of a crazy-pants, mind-reading genie?"

She grinned. "I am exactly that. At least when it comes to you."

I sighed. "I don't know about all the Alex and Dani future stuff. That . . . feels like too much for my heart to process. But you're right that he will make Isaac be nice to me."

"Yes. Yes, he will," Paige said.

"And I will have to tell him the truth about Sasha."

"Yes. Yes, you will."

I groaned. "I hate Sasha."

"Oh, me too. Maybe even more than you do."

I was lucky that was all Paige had to say about Sasha. She'd handled the theft of her wedding dress better than I'd expected.

"Hey, before we start packing again, I need to tell you something." She sounded serious enough, I started to worry.

"Okay."

She winced. "My mom made me buy a back-up dress."

I froze. "A what?"

"Please don't be mad. I had every faith in your ability to make me a dress, but Mom wasn't so sure. The last time I was in Charleston, we went shopping and I bought another dress. Just in case."

It maybe shouldn't have stung so badly. It wasn't Paige's idea. But after all I'd been through, it felt like one emotional blow too many.

"Wow."

"It was long before you finished yours, Dani. And it isn't half as pretty, I promise. Nothing is as gorgeous as that dress. I'm only telling you now because I don't want you to have to worry about making me another one."

I *was* worried about making her another one.

I'd been counting yards of fabric and lace and cataloging pearl buttons all afternoon trying to see if I had enough to duplicate the first dress. I didn't, not by a long shot. And since the lace I'd used had been a vintage remnant, the likelihood of finding the same pattern was slim. If I had access to LeFranc's resources, I could probably find someone to duplicate it, but that would take weeks. And dollars. And connections I no longer had. But that didn't mean I couldn't make it again with different lace. "I have to at least try."

"I know you *could* make me another dress, and I love you for that," Paige said. "But I kind of feel like you're going to have your hands full these next few months. I want you to focus on figuring your stuff out. If that means I don't get a dress, I don't want you to worry. Plus, it's my fault we lost the dress in the first place. If I hadn't foisted it on Sasha, we might not be in this mess."

I dropped back down onto the bed with a huff. She was right. As much as I wanted to do it, remaking her wedding dress really couldn't be at the top of my priority list. At least not higher than *Find a place to live and a way to support myself.* I reached over and grabbed Paige's hand. "You're a good friend, Paige."

"I am not. I'm the one that got you in this mess in the first place. I have no right to be mad."

I squeezed her fingers. "You looked stunning in that dress. I'll never forget how perfect it was."

"Me neither." She sighed.

"I still hate your mom."

"She never should have doubted you," Paige said. "Come on. Buck up. You've got lots to pack before tomorrow morning."

"How about you do it for me?" I whimpered. I sounded like a toddler, but I was past caring. And Paige would love me anyway.

"Eight in the morning, right? Is that when Chase is coming with the trailer?" Classic Paige. She was nothing if not unfailingly optimistic. She always had been. Which was why she was so good at counteracting my tendency to wallow in my bad moods. Forward motion, she always said. Just keep moving forward and eventually you'll get somewhere.

I let her pull me off the bed. "Yeah. I guess Darius says there's room in his mom's driveway, so it can stay there for a couple of weeks until Chase can drive it down."

"He's really looking out for you, isn't he?"

I nodded. "He's also a good friend."

Paige put her hands on her hips and surveyed the room. "You do shoes, I do sweaters?"

I groaned. "Fine. But we're getting gelato when we're done."

Chapter Sixteen

Alex

Dani and Isaac's childhood home was in a community just north of the city. Wide sidewalks and large, looming oaks gave the neighborhood an idyllic feel that was entirely different from downtown. History was nice, but so was space. And houses less than two hundred years old.

"Is all this land yours?" I asked Isaac as he unlocked the front door of the home.

He looked over his shoulder. "Yeah. All the way back to the river. It's not much—just over an acre—but that's more than you'll find in most neighborhoods around here."

I stifled a laugh. "Did you know that in Manhattan, there's an average of one hundred and thirteen people per acre?"

"What? Like, living there?"

I nodded, following him inside as he flipped on the lights in the entryway. "We're spoiled down here in the South."

Isaac grinned. "You don't have to convince me."

"The contractor should be here any minute, but I want to go out to the garage. I think there's another box of records I never moved."

"How could there possibly be any records on the entire planet you don't already have stored in the dining room?"

"There's maybe a few left. Want to help me look?"

"I could. Or I could stay here and wait for the contractor."

He shrugged. "Okay. The bathroom in question is the first door on the left at the top of the stairs if you want to show him where to go. I'll be back in a minute."

I strolled through the first floor of the house, looking for any signs of Dani, but everything personal must have been packed up and put away. Made sense with vacationers in and out so frequently, but I still felt a twinge of disappointment. Not one I would admit to out loud. But it was there, nonetheless.

The sound of boots on the front porch pulled me back to the front door where I let the contractor in and pointed him in the direction of the upstairs bathroom and the leaking roof. After, I went searching for Isaac. The garage was just off the kitchen, so he was easy to find.

"Did you find anything?"

He looked up and grinned, holding up an old fruit crate. "Springsteen, The Eagles, Steely Dan." Isaac pulled an album out of the crate with both hands. "What?! It's here! I thought I lost this thing in the move." He turned the album to face me. "It's an original release of Red Renegade's first album. I can't believe it's been here all this time."

I paused at an open box pushed up against the wall, my eye caught by a shiny gold tag I would recognize anywhere. I pulled a navy handbag out of the box, the LeFranc label clear on the left corner of the bag. In the box, there were others, all different sizes and colors. And *all* LeFranc. "Did Dani ever tell you she's got a good friend who's the nephew of Red Renegade's lead singer?"

Isaac paused. "What?"

"Darius. She works with his husband at LeFranc."

Isaac hefted the crate and crossed to where I stood. "Ohhh, you found Dani's stash." He looked over my shoulder. "I swear she took more than this with her when she went to New York. I'm surprised she had so many to leave behind."

"Are they all LeFranc?" It was an impressive collection.

"The girl had a homing beacon to help her find them. Every thrift store, pawnshop, garage sale, whatever. If there was a LeFranc bag on the premises, she'd find it. But seriously. He's legit related to Reggie Fletcher? *The* Reggie Fletcher?"

"By marriage, I think? On his mother's side? But yes. I remember we were at Chase and

Darius's apartment watching a movie once and he stopped by on his way to London to give Darius the keys to his car. Did she *only* collect LeFranc?" I repeated. "No other designers?"

Isaac's eyes were wide. "Don't change the subject. You were actually in the same room with Reggie Fletcher? Did you talk to him?"

I dropped the handbag back into the box and pushed my hands into my pockets, suddenly surprised that Dani had never mentioned the encounter to Isaac. She had to know how much Isaac idolized him. "Just introductions. Nothing monumental."

He shook his head, leading me out of the garage. "*Anything* would be monumental. Dani was there, too? I can't believe she didn't tell me. Or take a selfie with him. Or get his autograph." He turned around, excitement in his eyes. "Do you think she could still get me his autograph? Seriously. I'm going to kill her for not mentioning this. I could send her my albums, except, no, I'd never risk putting them in the mail. Maybe we could drive them up there. Are you up for a road trip?"

Huh. Maybe I *did* understand why Dani hadn't mentioned it. Fortunately, the contractor showed up in the kitchen to go over his estimates with Isaac, so I never had to actually commit to a road trip. I knew Isaac well enough to know he wouldn't forget about the possibility of the plan, but his mind was busy enough he likely wouldn't get around to bringing it up again for at least a week or more. That was plenty of time for me to text Dani and warn her.

I could also text Darius, but we hadn't chatted in a while. In the breakup, Dani had kept our closest friends.

I thought back on the collection of LeFranc bags sitting out in the garage. Dani had always spoken highly of LeFranc and had been open with me about her desire to design for the company, but clearly, the dream had roots.

Deep ones.

Chapter Seventeen

Dani

$14.23. That's all I had left over after a one-way flight from La Guardia to Charleston, twenty-five dollars to check my baggage, and a bagel—the only food I'd eaten in thirty-six hours—on my way out of the airport. Which was tricky. Because the cab ride to my brother's front door totaled $23.50.

I dug through my purse, banking on the fifty-dollar bill I kept tucked away in the side zipper pocket. I hated to spend it. The bill was symbolic for me in a lot of ways, but desperate times called for desperate measures.

The cash wasn't there. I checked the opposite pocket, the one without a zipper where my sunglasses lived, then every other pocket in my purse. It didn't make any sense. I had *hoped* the cab ride would come in under fourteen dollars, but I'd climbed into the cab knowing that if it didn't, I'd still be covered. Because my fifty-dollar-bill was always in my purse, an ever-stalwart symbol of my survival, a talisman I'd grown to equate with my success in the city. My father had given it to me the morning I'd left for New York to attend design school. *In case there's an emergency,* he'd told me.

I still didn't know what kind of an emergency could ever be solved with fifty dollars alone, though I guessed the mess I was sitting in probably qualified. Only, the cash wasn't there. For years I'd hung onto it with a certain religious zeal. I lived paycheck to paycheck. I budgeted. I paid my bills and scraped together the extra to buy fabric or lace-covered buttons or a new pair of Gingher knife-edged sewing shears. But I always took comfort in knowing that I had that fifty dollars socked away. Ready to feed me or buy off a criminal or pay cab fare if I ever wound up in a not-so-safe part of town and didn't want to walk to the subway.

I sank back onto the faded upholstery of the cab's back seat. Fitting that now, in the middle of my abject humiliation, the very moment most defined by my failure as a New York designer, my talisman was gone.

"I'm sure I've got something," I said to the driver.

"You got a credit card? I take them all. VISA, Mastercard, American Express . . ."

Of course I had a credit card. But living in the city wasn't cheap. Especially when all your friends made more money than you did and constantly invited you to go to this restaurant or that club. My credit limit wasn't that high—intentional self-preservation—but I still managed to keep the balance hovering right around the maxed-out mark. When I'd tried to use it at the airport to buy something better than a bagel, it had been declined.

Verifying one last time that my purse wasn't hiding anything but a coupon for a free manicure and a receipt for Chinese take-out, I resigned myself to my inevitable fate, willing myself to accept how much pride I would have to swallow in the next five minutes.

"Give me a minute, okay? I can get the cash inside."

The driver shot me a look over his shoulder, then pulled out his cell phone. "Fine, but I'm leaving the meter running."

I paused on the sidewalk and stared up at Isaac's house. Suddenly I wished I'd given more credence to Paige's advice. She'd told me I should have called first, but in the end, I'd opted not to. Maybe there was a tiny smidgen of avoidance in my reasoning, but mostly, I just knew my brother. He'd have a harder time refusing me if I was literally stranded on his doorstep.

A light, drizzly rain started to fall so I hurried across the sidewalk, pausing outside the hospitality door that led onto Isaac's front porch. As a kid, I'd taken numerous walking tours through downtown Charleston, mostly with classes from school, to study the architecture and history of the city. I'd loved the crazy huge porches of the single houses. The porches didn't face the street but sat perpendicular to the sidewalk. So the home's front door—the hospitality door—actually just led onto the porch. When people felt like company, they could open up the door and welcome people onto their porch. When they didn't, the door stayed closed and locked.

I braced myself, fully expecting the hospitality door to be locked, but to my relief, the door swung open. I ducked onto the porch—the rain was falling heavier—and crossed to the main entrance.

It wasn't hard to remember what the internet had told me Isaac's house was worth. With less than twenty bucks to my name, even just standing outside the front door was a burn to my ego.

I glanced back down the driveway to the cab still idling on the street. It was maybe a better option than going inside. Isaac was inside. Even worse, Alex was probably inside too. Frustratingly enough, he'd taken up more than his fair share of my thoughts over the past twelve hours. Nothing like powering through the biggest failure of your work life by facing down rejection in your personal life.

Paige's voice echoed in my head. *Buck up,* she would tell me. I squared my shoulders and before I could lose my nerve, pounded my fist on the front door. Before I'd even sounded a third knock, the door swung open.

Alex.

Alex in jeans and a t-shirt. Hair all mussed and loose. Face unshaven.

The man was gorgeous. He froze when he saw me. "Dani."

I smiled weakly. "Hi."

"What are you doing here?"

Inwardly, I groaned. Could he sound any less excited? "Is Isaac home?"

"Alex, dude. Close the door. It's cold." I heard Isaac's voice before I saw him appear over Alex's shoulder. "Dandi? What are you doing here?"

Great. Warm welcome all around. "It's a long story. And I'd love to tell you, but I'm sort of . . ." I looked back at the street. "Can I borrow twenty bucks?"

Isaac followed my gaze. "Are you seriously asking me to pay your cab fare?"

"I wouldn't ask if I didn't have to. Please? I'll explain everything, I promise, but he's still running the meter and—" Before I could even finish my sentence, Isaac turned and stalked back into the house. "Seriously? Isaac!"

"Maybe he's getting you the cash?" Alex said, his voice more hopeful than I felt.

"Probably not."

Alex drew his eyebrows together in question. "Did you guys fight about something?"

"No," I quickly answered. "Or, I don't know. I might have offended him the last time we texted."

"Right. When you asked him about his little charity thing. I remember."

My cheeks flamed red. Were they that close? That I should start worrying about Alex reading *all* of my texts to my brother?

"That's not what I meant. I really did want to know how things were going. It just came out wrong." A few weeks before everything had gone down with Sasha, I'd made a genuine attempt to reach out to Isaac and see how things were. But the tension between us. The sarcasm and the snark and the constant needling. It was *hard* to undo all that history. Even when I tried, I still wasn't great at filtering it all out.

I pressed my forehead into my palm. "This has been a very long day."

Alex touched my elbow. "Hey. Go find your brother. I'll take care of the cab."

The tenderness took me by surprise and sent all kinds of feelings sparking through my chest. But no. This was Alex. The last thing I needed was charity from *him*. I shook my head no. "No, no. Don't do that. I'll go after Isaac and—"

"And if he gives you the money, you can pay me back. It's not a problem."

Before I could object again, he ducked into the rain and hurried toward the cab.

Reluctantly, I stepped into the house, following the sound of Isaac's voice to the kitchen. He was on the phone, so I waited in the doorway while he finished his call. He pushed his phone into his pocket then folded his arms across his chest. "If you came all this way for Alex, you can't have him back."

Well, *that* wasn't what I'd expected. "Um, what?"

"I saw the way you two looked at each other when we were in New York. Clearly there's still something going on between you, but you can't have him. He's happy here. He doesn't need to move back to New York."

"Isaac. I'm not here for Alex."

"He's the best thing that ever happened to me, Dani." Isaac pressed on like he didn't even hear me. "You can't have him. Also he's dating someone. And he likes her. A lot."

"Likes who?" Alex stepped into the kitchen behind me, sliding my suitcases up against the wall.

I looked from Alex to Isaac, then back to Alex again. I didn't even know where to start. Alex was dating someone? The thought settled in my stomach like a pile of river rock. Cold and hard and heavy. "Um," I waved my hand in Alex's general direction. "Isaac thinks we're . . ." I paused. "He thinks I'm here to see you."

Alex wiped raindrops off his forehead and the tip of his nose. "Oh. Are you?"

Had he seriously just asked me that? I scoffed. "Of course not."

"So you don't have any plans to lure him back to New York with your weird girl magic?" Isaac said.

Alex chuckled. Possibly just at Isaac. But it also felt like maybe he was laughing at the idea of me luring him anywhere.

"Even if I did," I said, "I'm pretty sure it wouldn't work."

Alex shot me a sideways glance, but he didn't disagree.

"Oh." Isaac reached for a bag of chips sitting on the counter and ripped it open. For how ancient the outside of the house looked—all historically appropriate and such—the inside was full of modern, clean lines. The kitchen was light and open, the appliances new, the countertops a shiny white marbled granite. It took me a minute to figure out what felt off about the room, but then it clicked. It was clean. *Really* clean. For a house full of bachelors, that didn't seem right. "So why *are* you here then?" Isaac asked.

My eyes darted to Alex. "It's kind of a long story."

Apparently, it was all the hint Alex needed. "I'll, uh, sorry. I'll be in the next room." I watched as he disappeared through the kitchen doorway.

As soon as he was gone, I glared at my brother. "Seriously? What was all that? Weird girl magic?" I crossed the kitchen and reached for the bag of chips. I was going on a bagel, after all. The second he'd opened the bag, the smell of the salt and oil had made my mouth water and my stomach rumble. Isaac pulled it out of my reach before I could get any.

"What else was I supposed to think?" he said. "You haven't been home since before Mom and Dad left."

"That's not . . ." Okay, so it was true. But traveling was expensive—today had proven that, if nothing else—and our parents had been out of the country themselves for nearly a year. It wasn't as if I'd been intentionally missing cozy Christmas dinners and Thanksgiving meals where everyone sat around and lamented my absence. There hadn't been much to come home to. "Fine. But still. What was with all that stuff about Alex? Can you please share the chips? I'm starving."

He rolled his eyes, then dropped them on the counter, nudging them my direction. He shrugged. "I thought with all your history and crap, you were . . . I don't know. He's been pre-occupied lately. And he's asked about you a billion times. I thought maybe you were getting back together."

He'd asked about me? Why had he asked about me? "I haven't talked to him since you were both in New York," I said, my tone flat. "And I thought you said he was dating someone."

Isaac raised his eyebrows but bless him, he

seemed to know better than to ask why I sounded so disappointed. He waved away my question. "He went out with Jasmine Cooper. You remember her? But only once. It was nothing. You still need money for the cab?"

I shook my head. "Alex paid for it."

"Sweet. So why are you broke?"

I took a deep breath, buying time with a handful of chips. Deliciously incredible, best-I'd-ever-eaten chips. "That's a funny story."

I expected sarcasm. Some sort of slanderous rebuke about my wannabe socialite lifestyle, or my pandering for attention from New York City's fashion gatekeepers. Instead, he just stood there, a concerned look on his face. "Let's hear it."

I crossed the kitchen to where a roll of paper towels sat in the corner and ripped one off. I wiped the chip grease off my fingers then folded the square into thirds, creasing it over and over without looking up. I had to tell him. I *needed* to tell him. I couldn't exactly ask for help if he didn't know what was going on.

I swallowed and finally looked up, meeting his gaze. "I lost my job."

"What? Why?"

"It's a long story, and not one I feel like telling right now, but I basically lost everything I've been working toward for the past four years. My dream job, my dream apartment. It's all gone.

And I'm pretty sure there's nothing I can do to get it back."

"Wow," Isaac said. "Do Mom and Dad know?"

I shook my head. "Not yet. And I don't want to tell them. Not until I've figured out what's next. I don't want them to feel like they have to come home and help me."

"I'm sorry, Dani. That really sucks."

The sincerity in his voice—and the fact that he'd called me Dani instead of Dandi—almost made me want to cry. Momentum had been carrying me forward the past few days, but so many emotions were close to the surface. Sympathy from my brother showed me just how fragile I really was.

He walked over and put his hands on my shoulders. "Maybe it's a good thing. A chance to start out on your own. You're finally free, you know?"

"But that's just it. I don't *want* to be free. I wanted to design for LeFranc and now I never will. I'm not ready to celebrate."

His jaw tightened. "Whatever. You're so much better than LeFranc."

"Please don't lecture me right now, okay? I need a place to stay."

He froze. "Oh. So you want to stay here?"

"I don't really know where else I'd go. I mean, Mom and Dad's house is obviously out, and I don't have the money to find a place on my own."

"You couldn't have stayed in New York? With a friend?"

In truth, I'd worked hard to convince myself leaving was my only option. But I hadn't tried very hard to stay in New York. I couldn't have stayed with Paige. All those reasons why we had to give up our apartment were perfectly valid. But I really *could* have slept on Chase and Darius's couch for a few weeks until I found another job and earned enough of a paycheck to find a new place, and a new roommate. But staying had felt impossible. I hated that it did, that I wasn't stronger. But my ego felt irreparably bruised, battered to the point that I couldn't even imagine walking into another fashion house and asking for a job. Especially since there was no way in hell I would ever ask Sasha for an actual recommendation.

"I couldn't stay in New York," I said. My voice broke on the last word and I pressed my lips together, willing myself not to cry.

"Couldn't? Or wouldn't?" Isaac folded his arms across his chest.

"Please, Isaac? I needed to get away for a little while."

"Why not ask Mom and Dad for some money? You know they'd help you."

"I don't want their money," I said, an edge to my voice I hadn't expected. "I can fix this. I just need a little bit of time to get back on my feet."

He seemed to study my face for what felt like an eternity before his features softened and he leaned on the counter. "I wish I could help, Dani, but I don't even have a spare room," Isaac said. "There's a couch in the living room, but there are six dudes in this house, awake at all hours of the night. The living room is almost never empty."

He turned and stalked into the dining room, or what I thought was supposed to be the dining room. He'd turned his into a music room. A huge stereo system and large shelves covered the wall, filled entirely with row after row of vinyl—a record collection Isaac had started when we were thirteen after he'd found his first vintage Beatles album at old Ms. Landry's yard sale at the end of the cul-de-sac. "Where else am I supposed to go?" I asked him. "I literally have nowhere else to turn."

Isaac sifted through a stack of records, pulled one out, then dropped it back onto the pile. He turned to face me. "I genuinely wish I could say yes, Dandi. I just don't think it would be comfortable for anybody. You wouldn't have any privacy."

"Please don't call me Dandi. And I don't care if I don't have privacy. It's temporary. You won't even know I'm here. Truly, it'll just be for a month or so. Enough time for me to save some money and figure out what I'm going to do next."

"I'll put you up in a hotel for a couple of

weeks. Long enough for you to figure stuff out."

I sniffed. A *hotel?* "I can't let you do that. I could never pay you back."

"What about the bedroom above the studio?"

Isaac and I turned to see Alex standing in the doorway. "Sorry. I couldn't help but overhear. I don't want to make it my business, but there is an empty bedroom above the studio."

"The studio?" I looked to Isaac for clarification.

"The kitchen house out back," he said. "We converted it into a recording studio a few months ago. It's where we do all of our filming."

"I don't mind sleeping above the studio," I said, hope blossoming in my chest.

"It's just an empty room," Isaac said.

"It isn't empty. The old red couch that used to be on set, the one you just replaced?" Alex said. "Tyler and Vinnie moved it up there." He looked at me. "The room even has its own bathroom."

"That sounds amazing. A couch and a bathroom are legitimately all I need."

Isaac stood quietly for what felt like an interminable amount of time. With his arms folded across his chest, his chin resting on his hand, he looked just like my dad. Watching him stand there brought on a wave of homesickness so strong, it nearly bowled me over. People had always said it—how much Isaac favored Dad. I knew them both too well to really see it. But I saw it then. And nearly cried for how it made me feel.

All I'd ever done growing up was dream of leaving Charleston. Leaving my family. Making my way in the vast world on my own. It wasn't that I didn't love them. That they weren't supportive. They were. The world they lived in had just been too small for my dreams.

But now, I wanted back in. I *needed* to be around the people in the world who gave me a sense of permanence. I would have preferred my parents, but Isaac was the next best thing. Even if he didn't want to be.

A few seconds more and Isaac nodded his head as if he'd come to some sort of decision. "Okay. Here's the deal. Take it or leave it," he said. "You can have the room above the studio, but instead of rent, you'll provide dinner three or four times a week for all of us. Everyone that lives here. Something you actually cook. No fast food. We eat too much of that already. I'll pay for the groceries, but you have to do all the planning and shopping. All of it. In exchange, I let you live here for free."

I frowned but willed the discouragement away. It could be worse. At least he hadn't asked me to do all the cleaning, too.

Plus, I'd secured myself a place to sleep rent-free, and a place to pee in private. As far as I'd fallen, that felt like something to celebrate. "Okay, deal," I said. "But I'm not taking requests. You have to eat whatever I feel like making."

"Fine. But nothing vegetarian," Isaac said. "We eat meat."

I rolled my eyes. "Want to bang your fist against your chest and grunt a few times, too?"

"If that's what it takes, Dandelion. Carnivores," Isaac said. "Don't forget it."

Chapter Eighteen

Alex

I led Dani across the patio and through the garden to the kitchen house at the back of the property. Many of the homes in the historic district expanded the main house to reincorporate the kitchen houses, once city ordinances no longer required the kitchens to be separate structures, but some still stood separate.

"1807," I said, as we approached the door.

"What?" Dani asked.

"That's when this house was built. 1807."

"Wow. Is that older than your house?"

"Much older. Well, sort of. The original Randall house was built in 1797, but it was lost to fire in 1861. I guess they weren't able to rebuild until 1870, so the house now isn't all that old."

"Right. 150 years isn't old at all."

I grinned over my shoulder. "It's all relative in a city like this."

"I'd like to see your house sometime."

I paused and turned around, pushing my hands into the back pockets of my jeans. "Really?"

Pink crept up her cheeks. "Is that weird? I don't mean anything by it. Just, for the history, you know?"

I nodded. She had to mean the house's history, but the first thing that came to mind was *our* history. "Yeah. Sure. I'd love to show you."

I turned and faced forward again, pushing open the studio door. Dani was tense, obviously uncomfortable in my presence, but we were at least talking. That had to be a step in the right direction.

I pulled Dani's suitcases into the room then stepped aside so she could follow me in. "Do you see there, on the right? Just hit that first light switch."

She flipped the switch and the room flooded with light. Her eyes went wide. "Wow."

I followed her gaze as she took in the cameras, the lights, the full set of *Random I.*

"So this is where the magic happens." She tugged at her hair, damp and slightly frizzed from the rain, like she wanted to pull it into submission, then settled for tucking it behind her ears.

I couldn't decide if the hint of something in her voice was sarcasm or actual awe. Sarcasm wouldn't have surprised me; she'd never made her disdain for Isaac's profession a secret. Still, the studio was impressive. For her to be dismissive felt cruel, even for her.

Even after a year of dating Dani and another year of working with Isaac, I still wasn't sure I understood their relationship. Sometimes it seemed like they were almost getting along, but the bad blood clearly ran deep and boiled up to the surface at the most random moments. At the same time, there was a ferocity to them both, to the way they spoke about each other. They definitely cared and would do anything, if it truly came down to it, to protect the other. But getting them to interact as *friends* was nearly impossible.

"What's down there?" Dani asked, motioning down the hallway.

"That's the chop shop. Where they do all the editing and mixing and all those other production words I don't know anything about."

"Hey Isaac, is that you?" a voice called down the hall. Tyler appeared seconds later. "Oh, sorry. I thought you were—" his words trailed off when he looked from me to Dani, his smile stretching wide across his face.

"Dandelion?" He quickly crossed to where she stood and pulled her into a hug. "It's so good to see you!"

I tensed, suddenly uncomfortable for reasons I wasn't willing to ponder. Stupid emotions.

Dani ended Tyler's hug with a playful shove. "Tyler Fernley, you know I'll take you down if you keep calling me that."

So Tyler must have been the one friend whom Dani and Isaac had actually shared. I felt like he'd told me as much once, but I still wasn't great at keeping all the roommates and their different backstories straight. The fact they were all so alike only complicated things. They all had distinct jobs, handling everything from the sound and lighting, to the final mixing and the social media, but I still wasn't confident I could match the right man with the right job.

Tyler looked from me to Dani, then to Dani's suitcase. "Are you staying a while?" he asked her.

"My parents are still in Europe," she said with a shrug. "So here's the next best thing, I guess."

"Right on, right on," Tyler said. "Well, welcome. You're taking the room upstairs?"

She nodded.

"Good to know." Tyler shot me a knowing look. "I'll be sure to tell Mushroom he can't use the couch for naps anymore."

Dani looked like the thought might make her cry. I couldn't say I blamed her. The idea of someone named Mushroom taking naps on my bed made *me* want to cry.

Tyler turned his attention back to me. "Hey, have you seen Isaac? I need him to look over the final edit before I upload this morning's episode."

"Last I saw him, he was in the kitchen on his phone."

"Got it. Thanks." Tyler looked back at Dani. "The rest of the guys are in the chop shop," he said. "You want to say hello?"

She turned and followed Tyler down the hall. I

trailed behind, leaning against the door frame of the small space. It was so filled with equipment—computers and video screens and soundboards—I wondered how they all fit without bumping into each other, but they all seemed to have their own corner.

Tyler handled the introductions. "You remember Vinnie and Mushroom," he said.

They waved and Dani offered them a weak smile. "Hi, guys."

"And that over there is Steven," Tyler said. "Actually, you might recognize him from the Daily News Drop on the show. He's on camera with Isaac a lot."

"Sure. It's nice to meet you. I'm Isaac's sister, Dani."

"But you can call her Chef Dani," Isaac said, barreling past me into the room. "She's a little down on her luck right now so she's going to earn her keep cooking for us."

"Down on your luck?" Tyler asked. "What's up?" He gave Dani a concerned look that made my jaw tense. I forced myself to relax. I was *not* jealous of Tyler, no matter how my emotions decided to react.

Dani looked from Isaac to Tyler, then to the rest of the men in the room; all their eyes were trained on her.

I slipped out of the room and pulled out my phone, scrolling to find Dani in my contact list.

As soon as she popped up, I called her number.

Seconds later, her phone started to ring. I listened as she started rummaging through her purse. "Sorry, I was expecting a call. I should . . . I should take this. Bye, guys."

She stepped into the hallway just as she pulled out her phone. She looked at the screen, then looked up, then back to her phone again, her face awash with relief. "Thank you," she whispered, dropping her phone back into her bag.

"Don't mention it."

She followed me up the narrow stairway and down a long hallway into a single bedroom that comprised the upstairs. I flipped the light, disappointed to see just how dismal the room actually appeared. It was completely bare, nothing but the red couch pushed into the corner and a row of boxes stacked to the left of the door. Only one window graced the room—a narrow transom that ran across the top of the far wall. "This feels really depressing," I said. "I'm almost sorry I suggested it."

She made a derisive noise. "So then I'd be where? Back on the street? Trust me. As tired as I am, I'd sleep just about anywhere right now."

I wheeled her suitcases across the floor and lined them against the wall, to the right of the couch. She needed a table. And a chair. A lamp and a rug for the floor. But then, if we were going to go that far, she needed a *bed* instead of a dingy sofa. There had to be some things sitting around Isaac's that could be moved into her room. I made a mental note to take a look when I went back to the main house. "I'll see if I can find you some blankets, at least. And a spare pillow." Even if it meant bringing her something from my own room, I could at least do that much.

"That would be great." She sank onto the couch, settling back into the cushions. "At least it's comfortable," she said. "I left all my stuff back in New York. It's sitting in a trailer at Mirna's house. Chase is going to drive it down for me in a few weeks."

"Darius's mom, Mirna?" I asked.

"Yeah. She actually told me to tell you hello."

"How's she doing?"

Dani smiled, the first genuine smile I'd seen since she'd arrived. "She's officially in remission. Chase and Darius are still trying to figure out how to pay for everything, but the cancer is gone, which makes it all feel worth it, I guess."

Chase and Darius and Mirna felt like part of another life, a separate life, with a version of myself far removed from the person I'd been for the past year. But Chase and Darius, Paige and Reese—they had mattered in a real way. A pang of guilt settled into my gut. When I'd walked out on Dani, I'd walked out on them all.

"I wish I'd done a better job of staying in touch," I said softly.

"Why didn't you?" Dani asked. There was an edge of defensiveness to her tone, but this time, I didn't think her malice had anything to do with the hurt I'd caused *her*. She really was just thinking about her friends, which somehow made the guilt feel even heavier.

"I don't know. It felt easier at the time. They still had *you*. And I knew they'd listen to your side of the story. I guess I felt like you deserved to keep them as friends more than I did. And I didn't want them to have to choose sides."

"But they cared about you, too. You literally just vanished. I mean, you and Darius used to text all the time."

"I know. You're right," I said. "I should have done better."

She shrugged. "It's not too late. I think they'd all be happy to hear from you." She hesitated. "Maybe not Paige. She's still pretty heavily 'Team Dani' at this point. But the others? You should reach out."

The idea of reconnecting with pieces of my New York life was surprisingly welcome. Intimidating as hell, but not impossible. The past year hadn't exactly been easy; I'd covered everything from anger to self-pity to quiet introspection and had only recently started to feel like I had a reasonable hold on my emotions. Realizing I felt ready to reach out to any part of my former life felt like no small victory. "You don't think it would be weird? For you, I mean?"

She rolled her eyes. "Weirder than living in my brother's studio while my ex-boyfriend lives with him in the big house and works as his business manager? We're so far into weird territory, I think I can handle sharing friends."

I chuckled softly. "Thank you for saying so. I do miss everyone."

"Then reach out," she said. "I think it's a good idea. And you can tell them all I said so."

"Thanks, Dani," I said. "I mean it."

I had so many questions. Why had she left? What had happened at work? But the peace between us felt so fragile, I couldn't risk ruining it.

She offered a small smile. "So how are things with the Compassion Experiment? Is it all coming together like you hoped?"

"I think so," I said. "The event planner is making it pretty easy, though I do feel like I'm constantly fielding phone calls, answering one question or another. But it's pulling together. The biggest challenge we face is finding a closing act."

"Did you ever hear from Red Renegade? Didn't you tell me you reached out to their agent?"

I nodded. "I never heard from them. I think Isaac has accepted it was never going to happen, but he still wants something musical; I'm not sure who he thinks we'll be able to book only two months out."

"Did you text Darius? I'm sure he'd reach out to his uncle for you."

I looked at my hands. I'd thought about texting Darius. Multiple times. "I . . . no."

Her face softened. "You didn't think you could."

"It felt wrong to text him for something I needed when I *haven't* for anything else. I didn't even text him on his birthday."

"Chase took good care of him on his birthday. I promise."

"Still."

"Maybe I can try," Dani said. "I'll text Darius and ask him."

I held her gaze. "You'd do that?"

"I mean, I don't expect it to work, but sure. Darius will be straight with us about whether or not he thinks it's an option. I don't know. It can't hurt, right?"

"If you wouldn't mind trying, that would be amazing." I stood there, in between her and the door, wondering if there was anything else I should say.

She leaned her head back against the cushions and closed her eyes. She looked *sad*. Broken.

I hadn't heard everything she'd said to Isaac about why she was in Charleston. I really had tried to give them their privacy. But she was here.

213

With suitcases. And Isaac had said she was down on her luck which could only mean one thing.

I took a step forward and lowered myself down beside her. "Dani, do you want to talk about what happened? I know I'm probably not your first choice, but I'm happy to listen if you need it."

She opened her eyes. "I probably *should* talk about it." She pressed the heels of her hands into her eyes. "But honestly . . ."

"You don't want to talk about it with *me?*"

"That's just it. There probably isn't anyone who would understand quite as well as you, which is frustrating. Because you're you, and I really didn't want you to be right. But you were. Sasha is a lying, cheating, conniving woman, and I'm so angry that I fell for her lies. That I believed her for so long. She cost me everything. My career. My life in New York. *Everything.*"

I tightened my hands into fists, wishing I could punch out the anger surging in my chest. I wasn't surprised, but I'd always hoped Dani would manage to escape LeFranc relatively unscathed. Well, that wasn't entirely true. For a while, I'd hoped she'd go down in flames with the rest of them. Time, at least, had dulled the sting of her choosing LeFranc over me, enough that I felt bad for her present circumstances. But that didn't mean there wasn't a tiny part of me that still wanted to say I told you so.

"I'm really sorry, Dani."

She rolled her eyes. "I'm sure you are. It's fine if you want to say I told you so."

I winced, not happy that she'd hit so close to the mark. "I don't want to say I told you so," I said, happy I sounded like I meant it. "For your sake, I would have much preferred to be wrong about Sasha."

She shook her head and breathed out a tiny laugh. "I don't believe that's true, Alex."

I didn't say anything. What was there to even say?

She reached over and patted my knee. "Listen. We have to get along for the next couple of months." She motioned to the room around her. "Obviously this isn't a permanent solution for me. Let's just agree not to talk about how everything went down between us. I'll cook for the seven dwarves and then as soon as I can afford it, I'll be out of everyone's way."

Her words were dismissive, condescending, but laced with a measure of hurt that made her seem vulnerable, even in her anger. It was as if she longed to be comforted but would prickle at the first touch if anyone actually offered that comfort. Maybe she would just prickle if *I* offered her comfort.

Also, dwarves?

It wasn't how I wanted to leave things. But if I pushed the conversation, I might end up saying something I would regret. I didn't want to leave things like *that,* either. I clapped my hands against my knees. "Fine."

"Fine," she said back.

"Fine," I repeated again. Not surprisingly, as I stood to leave Dani in the pathetic, empty room, nothing actually *felt* fine.

Three weeks in, I didn't want to admit to myself how much I was *trying* to be wherever Dani was. Particularly when considering how gutted being around her actually made me feel. It hadn't been easy to get over her. She wouldn't believe me saying so; I'm sure she thought since I was the one who had walked away, I'd felt little and had recovered quickly. But leaving had killed me. Even knowing that I'd had to do it. At least at Isaac's, there had been plenty to distract me, to keep my mind off how miserable I felt. Then time had done its work and dulled the constant ache.

But now I couldn't escape her. I saw her every day.

Worse, I wanted to see her.

I stopped working at the desk in my bedroom and instead opted for the kitchen table where I might run into her. I ate three meals a day out of Isaac's kitchen, cutting back on the lunches out that had become part of my regular routine. If Isaac or any of the other guys noticed my sudden eagerness to always be around, they kept their mouths shut. Fortunately, Dani had no baseline for my previous behavior so she couldn't know I'd never spent quite so much time at home.

Admittedly, *home* had an entirely different meaning now that Dani was around. The house was actually beginning to feel like one. There were new throw pillows in the living room and a rug in the entryway. She'd hung a seasonal wreath on the front door and had a row of hooks installed in the hall where everyone put their coats. New dinnerware showed up in the kitchen. She was even planning a Thanksgiving dinner for us.

I wasn't the only one appreciating her presence. The rest of the guys, except Isaac of course, were clearly mesmerized by her. Running her errands, completing odd jobs at her request—it was Mushroom who had installed the hooks in the hall—and just generally behaving with a little more decorum. They were all showering more frequently and wearing clothes that actually looked clean.

Observing the shift in behavior would probably qualify as a fascinating study for any anthropologist. I was just grateful everyone smelled better.

As for Dani and Isaac, they danced around each other in a careful choreography; they were kind and courteous, but their interactions were safely surface level. It couldn't last, I was sure, but I did hope that when one of them finally cracked, it would be a positive change and not one that brought the whole, fragile set-up crashing down around all of us.

I leaned back onto my bed and scrolled through old photos on my phone—old photos that had become newly familiar since running into Dani at Java Jean's two months before.

Every time I looked at the images, I was struck again by how different and far away my New York life felt. I stopped on a shot of Dani and me, arms around each other. I wore a designer suit, Dani a dress I remembered she'd made herself. She looked killer in it; she always did when she wore her own stuff. We held glasses of champagne in our hands and had huge smiles on our faces. I couldn't remember anything else about that particular night. There were so many nights just like it, they had all blended together. Nameless clubs, private parties, fashion events we'd only ever had tickets to because of who my stepfather was.

It had always thrilled Dani to go. Even after she got the job at LeFranc, her role as an administrative assistant hadn't warranted exclusive invitations. Only I could provide those. It had been a heady feeling, in the early months, to realize I could give her access to the world she found so captivating. I had been her golden ticket. And I'd relished making her happy.

In my weakest moments, I wondered if that's all our relationship had ever been. But it made Dani too shallow for me to think so. Regardless of the choices she'd made, and the way things had ended, I couldn't ignore the parts of our relationship that had been really good. Even since she'd moved to Charleston, though she'd mostly avoided me at first, I'd occasionally catch her in the kitchen, and we'd fall into talking about one thing or another in the same easy way we always had before. Finishing each other's sentences, laughing together. Even now, there was still a compatibility to the way we interacted that went far beyond just going places together. It had only been stronger before we'd broken up.

Still, there was something different about Charleston Dani. She was more laid back, less intense. Less ambitious. Not that ambition was a bad thing, but Dani had been so focused on her career, it had colored everything. I'd spent enough time competing with the LeFrancs for my mother's attention. It had killed me to fight the same battle with Dani. But it felt like Charleston Dani had finally ripped off the rose-colored glasses she'd worn when looking at anything fashion—anything LeFranc—and was seeing life in a different, more natural light. Whenever I felt the pull—because I *did* feel it—I had to wonder if this version of her would last. If given the chance, would she jump back into the world

219

she'd left behind? The answer to that question mattered because it was a world I didn't want to be a part of.

I scrolled to another photo, this one of Dani in her Chelsea apartment, leaning back against the headboard of her bed. Her blonde hair was loose and wavy, and the neck of her oversized sweatshirt had slipped down onto her arm, revealing a smooth stretch of neck and shoulder that made heat rise in my body. I remembered that morning, the time we'd spent lounging, talking. We'd stayed in all day, ordered take-out, watched ridiculous television for hours. The next photo was the same day, same setting. Only in this photo, Dani was sitting up, a playful smile on her face. She held up a small whiteboard, a marker tossed to the side. The words on the whiteboard read: *Just for the record, I said "I love you" first,* followed by the date.

"I'm just saying," she'd said, "one day we'll be happy we preserved this moment. Our grand-children will look back through our photos and feel inspired that their grandmother had been bold enough to say it first."

"I think they'll be too shocked by how sexy their grandmother once was to even care who said I love you first," I had countered.

"Are you saying I won't still be sexy when I'm a grandma?" Dani had asked.

I'd grabbed her then, ignoring her squeals as I

tossed her back onto the bed, pinning her arms above her head. I'd leaned in close, my nose inches from hers. "You might have said it first, but I hope that doesn't diminish how much I mean it when I say it back."

A knock sounded behind me on my open bedroom door. "Hey, Alex?"

I jumped at the sound of Dani's voice, closing out my photos and tossing my phone onto the bed. I sat up. "Hi. What's up?"

She eyed me curiously. Had she seen what I was looking at? "Dinner's ready," she said. "You okay?"

"Sure. Of course. I'm . . ." I swallowed. "Everything's fine." I followed her to the kitchen where the rest of the guys were already seated at the table. Isaac had something pulled up on his phone, and everyone leaned over, watching the tiny screen. Dani moved to the cabinet and pulled out six plates then started dishing up the first one.

Something didn't sit right. It was bad enough she'd been put in this position; serving a house full of men in order to earn her keep felt archaic in a way that made me cringe. But that was between her and her brother. Still, she'd only agreed to cook. She didn't need to serve everyone. Wait on us like we were at some restaurant.

"Hey, Dani?"

She turned around, a full plate in hand. There was a smudge of something on her cheek that I hadn't noticed before. Spaghetti sauce, maybe? I crossed the kitchen to where she stood and motioned to the plate she held. "Here. This one is yours. You don't have to serve the rest of us."

"It's not a big deal," she said.

"But it is," I said. "Don't condition them to think this is how it should be. You doing all the work while they sit around. You cooked. That's all you agreed to do. They can fix their own plates. *And* do the dishes."

She huffed. "I'll believe that when I see it."

"They'll learn," I told her. "I'll make sure of it." I scooted behind her and nudged her toward the table. "Come on. Go sit." I followed behind her, worried that someone at the table might say something when she sat with her own food before anyone else had a plate.

To my surprise and relief, no one did. The conversation paused momentarily, everyone seemed to internalize what was happening, and then Isaac stood and went to fix himself a plate, the others following closely behind. Maybe there was actual hope for them after all.

I watched Dani a moment longer, and something familiar surged in my chest. Something . . . protective? It wasn't quite the right word. Dani was strong and independent and didn't need protecting. At least not in her brother's house. But the look on her face said she was grateful to be sitting, not serving, and it made me happy that

I'd had a small part in that. And *that's* what felt familiar. The desire to make her happy. Which made sense since I'd dedicated almost a year of my life to that singular pursuit.

Dani mostly stayed to herself during dinner, which was probably smart. Whenever the other guys were around, Isaac tended to amplify his teasing. Dani could hardly say anything at all without him turning it into a joke.

"Hey Dani, you going for a run in the morning?" Isaac asked his sister.

She studied him a long moment, probably trying to see if he was setting a trap. "I'm planning on it. Why?" she finally answered.

"Oh, I don't know." Isaac shot me a look I didn't understand. "I was just curious. No reason, really."

"Do you want to come with me?" Dani asked, hesitation in her voice.

"What? No," Isaac said. "You know I don't run unless someone's chasing me."

"I, uh," Steven said. He cleared his throat. "I was thinking I might go with you. If, you know, you don't care or anything."

This time, Dani's eyes flicked to me before she looked back at Steven. How had I become everyone's emotional barometer? "Oh. Okay," Dani said. "I guess that's fine."

Was Steven interested in Dani? Not that I was surprised. She was beautiful and smart and all the things any man would find captivating. But the idea still didn't sit right in my brain. Wasn't there some sort of bro-code that kept any of Isaac's roommates from dating his sister?

Realization washed over me and my stomach tightened. Acknowledging just how much I wanted Dani to be happy, and how much I *didn't* want Steven to run with her in the morning, felt like a giant step toward the cliff I'd been hovering around for weeks. The image of her on her bed, whiteboard in hand, *I love you* scrawled across the front, flashed through my mind. It shouldn't matter, and yet it *really, really* did. I had fallen for her once. Hard and fast and completely. I didn't want to watch her fall for someone else. More importantly, how was I going to be around her on a daily basis, eat her food, listen to the sound of her laugh or catch the scent of vanilla on her hair and not fall again myself?

I'd had my reasons for ending things. Good ones. But watching her, itching to touch her, if even just to wipe the smudge of sauce off her cheek, made me wish I could forget why I'd left in the first place.

While I finished up the dishes, Isaac came back into the kitchen. "So tomorrow morning, while Dani is running with Steven, I need you to help me out. You busy?"

I placed the plate I was holding back into the sink and grabbed a dishtowel. "You finish the dishes and I'll help you out in the morning."

He hesitated a moment before moving to the sink and picking up the discarded dish. "Hasn't Dani been doing the dishes?"

"It's the twenty-first century, Isaac. She shouldn't *have* to do the dishes. She's cooking for us. This is the least we can do."

"Fine. I'm sorry. I'm helping. And don't make it sound like I don't care about her. That's what I need your help with in the morning."

I raised an eyebrow and he gave me a sheepish grin.

"I bought her some furniture. They're going to deliver it tomorrow morning while she's out on her run. Help me set it up?"

Chapter Nineteen

Dani

Steven was waiting for me in the garden when I went out for my run. The newness of his sneakers and the headband he wore across his forehead both screamed beginner, but I was hardly in a position to judge. I was much less an athlete than I was someone who appreciated the head-clearing therapy running proved to be.

"Good morning," Steven said, pulling one ankle up behind him in a quad stretch.

"Hi," I said. I pulled out my headphones but then hesitated. Steven didn't have any. Would it be rude for me to wear mine? It's not like we'd be taking a leisurely stroll around the battery. We were going to be running. No way I could talk and breathe and run all at the same time. Not without hyperventilating. "I hope you don't mind," I said, holding up the earbuds. "I figure we won't be able to talk much anyway, right?"

"Oh, yeah, sure," Steven said. "I totally get it."

Still, I could see the hesitation in his eyes. So he *did* want to talk. The realization made me nervous. I hadn't known Steven very long and had spent very little time with him one-on-one, but the energy around him buzzed with a certain *something* that made me fairly certain he wanted to ask me out.

I walked up the narrow path that led around the house and to the sidewalk, wondering if there was a way I could head him off. Earbuds would only protect me for so long. We hit the sidewalk and turned toward the water. A cool breeze blew off the Ashley and Cooper rivers that wrapped around the city before converging in the bay and flowing out to the open ocean. The air held a slight chill, but it was still pleasant, even for the early hour. Could I claim I was still on the rebound? Nursing wounds from my last breakup? It occurred to me that I didn't even know if the other guys knew that Alex and I had ever been a thing. Isaac might have told them, but knowing Isaac, I doubted it had ever come up. For all his faults, Isaac was maybe the least prone to gossip of anyone I knew. Celebrity news held zero appeal. Even stuff pertaining to people he actually knew personally didn't interest him. He was much more a live-and-let-live kind of guy. I'd always admired that about him.

Either way, it felt weird to tell Steven I was still getting over my ex when my ex was one of his roommates. I picked up my pace. Maybe I was wrong, and Steven really did just want the exercise?

Four blocks in, it didn't matter either way. I'd

almost forgotten Steven was behind me. With the breeze on my face and the music in my ears and the endorphins pumping through my veins, the weight of everything I'd been feeling lifted, even just temporarily, and I felt like I was going to be okay.

We followed Church Street past St. Philip's Anglican Church and the Dock Street Theatre. We took a left on Broad, staying straight until we hit East Bay. We ran by the old tavern across from Rainbow Row, the one with the hatch in the floor that led down to the underground tunnels beneath the city, then carefully cut across South Adger's Wharf—the cobblestones were pretty to look at but had broken ankle written all over them—to the path that would lead up to Waterfront Park.

With only an occasional glance to make sure Steven hadn't fallen too far behind, my mind mostly stayed on Alex. To his credit, he was obviously doing a lot to make me more comfortable. But there was still so much we weren't saying to each other.

Except, something had happened the night before when he'd insisted that I sit down with my food instead of serving everyone else. He'd stayed true to his word and remained in the kitchen long enough to make sure all the guys had helped clean up, making it clear it was their responsibility, *not* mine. A couple of times throughout the night, I'd caught Alex looking at me, something in his eyes reminding me of when there was a *we*.

If I let myself forget how much he'd hurt me when he'd left New York, it was easy to remember how much I'd loved him *before* he left. And that felt dangerous. Treacherous. But also, a little *thrilling*. And that was the scariest realization of all.

I slowed to a stop in front of the massive pineapple fountain in the center of the park. In the spring or summer, I might have skipped Waterfront to avoid all the tourists. But in early-November, the place was nearly deserted. I glanced over my shoulder. Steven was a few paces back and he stopped as soon as he saw me, leaning over to prop his hands on his knees. Poor guy. We weren't running that fast, but we'd maybe gone a little far without a break for someone who wasn't in running shape.

I motioned to a bench to the right of the fountain and he hobbled over, dropping down beside me. "You okay?" I asked.

He nodded but didn't speak, holding up a finger while he caught his breath. Finally, he managed a smile. "And to think, we still have to run back to the house."

"We can take a break for a few minutes if you want," I said.

He leaned forward, dropping his head between

his knees. "Ugh. You might have to bring the car back for me."

I laughed. "Come on. Sit up. Enjoy the view. You'll be fine."

It *was* a view. The morning sun was low on the horizon, reflecting off the still water of the bay. Seagulls flew overhead, black dots against a spread of fluffy clouds in the deep blue sky. I breathed in, letting the serene setting calm my nerves and whisper peace into my soul. The water always did that for me, the beach, especially. I'd already made the trip out to Sullivan's Island multiple times since arriving home. Luckily, Isaac had been pretty easy about loaning me his car.

Steven sucked in another deep breath. "Okay. I think I'm maybe okay now."

I chuckled. "You don't run much, do you?"

"Not unless I'm running to the fridge for another drink, no."

Just then, a group of cadets from the Citadel ran by, their breathing labored and heavy, their pace probably double what ours had been.

"It could be worse," I said to Steven. "You could have been trying to keep up with those guys."

Steven shook his head. "No joke."

He stared at the cadets as they ran away, the silence stretching long between us.

But then Steven sat up, his posture stiffened,

and he turned to me with obvious intention. "Is there something going on between you and Alex?" he blurted.

That . . . was not what I'd been expecting. "Um, what?"

"Sorry. I was just thinking I'd like to ask you to dinner. But I didn't want to if something was going on between you two."

Why would he think there was something going on between me and Alex? Had Alex said something? Done something? Or had I? Was I being too obvious? Staring at him too much? Was he staring at me? Even as my brain raced through the possibilities, I realized how ridiculous they were. Did I *want* Alex to be staring at me? It was like my life was one giant game of Hot or Cold. One minute I hated him with my entire soul. The next, I was feeling the feels, trying not to swoon over some charming thing he'd said or done.

"Sorry," Steven said. "Was it wrong to ask? You've got this—" He raised a finger and motioned to the deep crease between my brows. "So serious."

I relaxed my face. "I was just thinking. Why did you think there was something going on with me and Alex?"

"Because he watches your every move," Steven said. "And he nearly punched Mushroom when he said something about your—"

I held up my hands. "Please don't finish that sentence. I don't want to know."

Steven shrugged. "He seems into you. And I'm not that guy that's going to try and infringe on that. If there's something there, I completely respect it."

"Why didn't you ask *him* this question?"

Steven didn't even miss a beat. "Because I'm strangely and inexplicably intimidated by the dapper businessman with his fancy car and cuff links. I mean, I know he's a nice guy. But . . ." He shrugged. "You felt a little more approachable."

I shot Steven a look. "The dapper businessman? Is that really how you guys see him?"

"Oh, come on. Southern accent aside, you don't think he seems like he walked out of a Jane Austen novel? He's just so polished."

"Wait, wait. You read Jane Austen?"

Steven rolled his eyes. "Why do women always ask that? I studied British Lit in grad school. I've read Austen, Bronte, Wolfe, Eliot. Why is everyone so surprised?"

"Steven. You co-host a YouTube show that devoted an entire episode to the flavor profiles of toothpaste-filled donuts."

He paused. "Fine. Fair point."

I shook my head. Steven's graduate degree was definitely worth another conversation, but he *had* asked me on a date. And he deserved an answer.

"Alex and I are friends," I said. I forced myself

to meet Steven's gaze. "But I can't have dinner with you."

"Okay," he said slowly. "Can I ask why not?"

"It's complicated. We *are* just friends, me and Alex. But, there's history there. We were a thing, and now we're . . . And I'm just not in a place mentally, you know? Where I can think about dating or, anything, really. I have a lot to figure out."

"So you're the ex that—*oh.*"

"Oh, what?" I asked. Had Alex talked about me?

"Nothing. Don't worry about it," Steven said. "Thanks for being honest with me."

I smiled but didn't say anything, struggling to let go of what he'd meant.

"Do you think you and Alex will get back together?" he asked, taking me by surprise.

"What? No." Even I could hear the uncertainty in my voice.

Steven laughed. "Wow. Way to convince me."

A blush crept up my cheeks. "It's not that easy. We're just so different, you know? And . . ." My words trailed off. Why was I telling him any of this anyway? "Like I said. It's complicated."

"Yeah, you already said that," Steven said. "You guys clearly have something going on though. Everybody senses it. Maybe you need to stop thinking about it and see what can happen. Just jump in. Buck the plan, ignore the outline, trust your gut, and take life as it comes."

"Wow. That was a lot of clichés in one sentence."

He grinned. "Things only become clichés because people say them all the time. And if people say things all the time, it must be because they work. Take it from me. As a guy who ended up doing the exact opposite of what he'd always planned for himself, sometimes you have to embrace the unexpected."

I was pretty sure Steven was only referencing my relationship, or lack of relationship, with Alex, but I wondered if his sage advice couldn't also be applied to my work life. I'd clung to the idea of working for LeFranc for so long. Even since I'd left, I'd had a hard time imagining a future in fashion without the LeFranc name giving me confidence. But maybe it was time I let go of my LeFranc dreams. I'd walked away from my LeFranc job, yes. But as I watched a pelican swoop down and scoop a fish out of the bay, I realized with startling clarity that I still hadn't let go of my dreams. And I'd never move forward if I couldn't well and truly cut myself free.

"You okay?" Steven asked with a warm smile.

I liked Steven. He was completely unexpected. And funny. And he had an adorable dimple in his left cheek that showed up when he smiled big. In a different life, a life where I wasn't completely hung up on the fact that Steven said Alex stared at me all the time, I would have said yes to dinner. "Yeah. Just thinking."

"Want to think and run?" he asked. He stood from the bench and offered me a hand, giving me a reassuring squeeze when I slipped my fingers into his.

After my run, I climbed the stairs to my bedroom above the studio and flipped on the light. I froze. My room was totally different. The red couch was gone; in its place, there was a bed. An actual bed with sheets and pillows and a fluffy duvet. There was an end table with a lamp, and a dresser against the wall, and a chair by the window.

I stood in the middle of the room and turned around in amazement. I'd only been gone an hour. I sank down onto the bed—a bed!—my heart tight in my chest. It had to have been Alex. He was the only one who would have thought to do something this nice. Curse the man. He was making it really hard for me to stay mad at him.

I paused at the top of the stairs. Was that his point? Was he trying to fix things between us?

If he was, did I want the same thing?

I found Alex in the kitchen. Without a word, I crossed to where he stood at the counter and wrapped my arms around his neck, pulling him into a hug. The closeness nearly did me in, kicking my senses into a hyperaware state. His scent was familiar, amazing, bone-melting. And his touch. It was like every nerve ending in my body was suddenly on high alert, so that I could instantly identify every single part of me that was in contact with any part of him. The stretch of my arm across his neck and shoulder. My cheek against his chest. It was heady, intoxicating, in the best possible way. He hesitated at first, then slowly raised one arm, wrapping it loosely around my back.

"Thank you," I said softly, as I pulled away.

Alex furrowed his brow in confusion. "For what?"

"For my room," I said. "It's really nice."

Alex's face didn't change. "Dani, it wasn't me."

My shoulders fell, heat rising in my cheeks. If it wasn't him, then that hug was way out of line. I took a step backward, putting some much-needed distance between us, but clung to my conviction a moment longer. "The bed. The table. Everything. It wasn't you?"

He quickly shook his head. "I didn't have anything to do with it."

I took a giant step back. "Then who did?"

He shrugged, almost dismissively. "Maybe you should look around a little more."

I ran back to the studio and climbed the stairs two at a time to look at the furniture again. It was all new, stuff I'd never seen. But there, on the top of the dresser, was a stack of books I'd somehow missed before. I crossed the room and ran my hand across the spines. They were mine. Books from my old bedroom, probably boxed up and stored in the garage before Mom and Dad had left for Europe.

"Do you like it?"

I spun around.

Isaac stood sheepishly in the doorway.

"You did this for me?"

He ran his fingers through his hair. "I guess, when I saw how much time you were spending up here, I just figured . . ." His words bled into each other, tumbling out one after the other. "I realize the guys are probably hard to be around all the time and you've been a good sport about it and the food has been really good the past few weeks and I guess, just, I wanted to say thank you. It's actually been nice having you around."

Tears welled up. It was the nicest thing Isaac had ever done for me. And the nicest thing he'd ever *said* to me. What had gotten into him? I crossed the room and hugged him tightly.

"Thank you," I said, with a sniff. "I don't even know what to say."

"I wasn't sure if you had furniture and stuff in New York; at first I thought I could bring it all down, but then I called Paige and she said your place up there had been furnished and so there wasn't much to move, so I figured I'd buy new stuff." He pressed the heel of his hand into his eye. I recognized the gesture from when we were kids. He was nervous. "I'm not much of a designer, but the lady at the furniture store said she thought this would work for a girl. Oh, and sorry about Steven," he added at the end. "I hope he didn't pester you too much."

"Wait, *you* told Steven to go running with me? He tried to ask me out!"

Isaac's face fell. "He did? I told him to keep you out of the house for a while, not to hit on you! You didn't say yes, did you? Please tell me you didn't say yes."

I narrowed my eyes. "I didn't. But why would it matter if I did? Am I not good enough for your co-star?"

Isaac balked. "What? No! Dani, he's not good enough for you."

"He has a master's degree in British literature," I said, my voice all smug-like.

"Yeah, and he uses that master's degree to bait all kinds of women he brings back to the house in excessive numbers. He's nice on the surface, and he's great on camera, but the dude's a total player."

Oh. Well then.

It kinda made me happy to hear Isaac being all big-brother-like and protective.

We stood there a moment longer until I reached up and gave him another hug. "Thank you for the bedroom," I said. "It's perfect."

He took my hand and led me to the bed where he sat, his hands propped up on his knees. He took a deep breath. "I can tell you've been sad, Dani."

I sat beside him, wondering where this was going. This version of Isaac was foreign territory.

"I don't know everything that happened in New York," he continued, "and I won't pretend to understand fashion or how important it is to you. But if a place is toxic?" He shrugged. "It's a good thing to move on. I know it stinks that moving on meant coming here, having to live with—" He made a sweeping motion with his hands to the studio below us and out toward the main house. "But you're going to be okay." He looked at me, right in the eyes. "You'll get through it. And if I've learned anything about Alex in the year we've been working together? It's that you can totally trust that guy. He's honest to his very core, Dani. If something were to happen between the two of you? I wouldn't be telling you you're too good for him."

"So, what, he's too good for me?" I said, a grin on my lips.

"Absolutely," Isaac said. "But he's got all kinds of money. If he's willing to support your fabric habit, I think you ought to grab on and not let go."

I rolled my eyes and elbowed him in the gut. "I

can support my own fabric habit, thank you very much."

"Right. Which is why you're living here. Because you're rolling in all kinds of cash to blow on fabric."

I scooted back on the bed and grabbed a throw pillow, pulling it onto my lap. "Don't remind me."

"Why don't you try designing on your own, Dani? You know you're good enough."

"I don't know that," I said. "I've never sold anything. I love you for saying so, but it's nearly impossible to break into the fashion industry alone."

"It's definitely impossible if you don't try."

"I *did* try. I went to New York—"

"You went to New York because you wanted to work for LeFranc," Isaac said, cutting me off. "That's different. You've never tried designing on your own."

I shook my head, my fingers playing with the edging on the pillow in my lap. "It's more complicated than that."

Isaac stood. "Nah. It isn't. You just have to go for it."

He was at the door before I finally spoke. "Like you?"

He turned back, his hand resting on the door jamb. "I knew what I wanted, Dani. And I knew I wouldn't find it getting a normal education, working for some cookie-cutter company some-where."

My phone buzzed from where I'd dropped it on the dresser, pulling my attention away from Isaac. He crossed the room and grabbed it, tossing it to me before heading back toward the door.

I glanced at the screen long enough to see a text from Chase. His message was brief—he'd only reached out to check on me—so I turned off the screen and dropped the phone face down on my bed. I looked at my brother one more time. "Isaac, thank you. I don't think I've been very fair to you."

"Well, no," he said with a grin. "But I don't always make it easy, do I?"

Late that night, well after midnight, nestled into the covers of my very own beautiful bed, I called Mom. I'd eventually texted, letting her know I'd moved back to Charleston and was staying with Isaac, but I'd spared her all the gory details of what had happened at LeFranc and with Paige's dress. Now that I'd been home long enough to feel settled, she more than deserved an update.

I caught her in the middle of her early morning walk along the banks of the Rhone in some remote French village. "It's perfect, Dani. You'd love it here. It's our favorite place by far."

I half-wondered if my parents would ever return home. They'd saved long and well for their retirement, but they'd only planned on a year abroad. I wouldn't be surprised if a year turned into two, or more. It might take grandchildren to actually get them back in the states. After a few more minutes of chit-chat, I launched into an explanation of everything I'd been through. I spared no detail as I talked through Sasha's betrayal, and Paige's dress, and Alex, and my sudden move back home, finally ending with Isaac and his totally unexpected room renovation.

"Wow," Mom said when I finished my tale. "That's some story."

"Tell me about it," I said. "But seriously, Mom. I have no idea what got into Isaac. It was so unlike him."

"What do you mean unlike him? That sounds just like something your brother would do."

I scoffed. "No, it doesn't. Calling me Dandelion and hiding all my hairbands in the back of the toilet sounds like something he would do."

Mom laughed. "He was ten when that happened, Dani. Cut him some slack."

"It was just so out of the blue," I said. "We haven't gotten along in forever, and all of a sudden he's doing this huge nice thing for me. I mean, it's amazing. I'm grateful. I just didn't expect it."

"Dani," Mom said. "Permission to speak freely?"

I shifted, pulling my knees up close to my chest.

If I said yes, she wouldn't hold back. "Fine, go," I finally consented.

"You are the most driven woman I know," Mom said. "Single-minded. Focused. Determined."

I braced myself. The *but* was coming.

"But sometimes that single-minded dedication inhibits your ability to see other people."

My shoulders tensed. "What do you mean?"

"I mean, your brother has always had a heart the size of Fort Sumter." My heart squeezed at the *Mom*-expression I'd frequently claimed as my own. "He's been taking care of people since he was tiny. Sitting with the kid on the bus that no one else would sit with. Making people laugh. Making people feel included. You've never been very good at seeing that about him. You see an MIT dropout. I see a man who has created an entire online empire based around the notion that random acts of kindness can change the world."

I rolled my eyes. "His show is all about him, Mom. It's YouTube. They're all that way."

Mom cleared her throat. "When was the last time you watched his show?"

I didn't answer.

"Give your brother the credit he deserves, Dani. He had to swallow a lot of pride to reach out to you in this way. You've hurt him with your doubting and scoffing and condescension."

"That's not fair," I finally said. "Maybe that's what he tells you, but then when he's around *me*, most of the time he's constantly making fun of me, cracking jokes, calling me Dandelion. He's not always nice, Mom. Not to me."

"Maybe not. But is it possible the jokes are a part of his defense mechanism? He's so desperate for you to be proud of him."

I huffed a sigh. "I am proud!"

"Have you ever told him that?"

"It's not like he's spent a ton of time being proud of me," I said defensively. "He's just as critical of my career choice as I am of his."

"He's never been critical of what you do; he's been critical of LeFranc. There's a difference."

She had a point there. "Yeah. I've seen some of that since coming home. Did you know he has a picture of my prom dress on his phone?"

Mom chuckled. "That dress was something else."

"That dress was horrible."

"You were sixteen."

"And I thought I was the stuff, too. I was so proud of that dress."

"Isaac was proud of that dress. Do you remember all the time he spent ironing the seams for you?"

I closed my eyes. "And then when my sewing machine broke, he pinned the zipper for me while I fixed my hair."

Mom chuckled. "You were hand-stitching that zipper in seconds before your date showed up."

"I had forgotten how much he helped me that day."

"It might do you some good to remember, Dani. I know his jokes can hurt, but he loves you."

"I know. Thanks, Mom."

"How has it been with Alex around?"

I sighed. "It's fine, I guess. On the surface, anyway. But being around him so much reminds me of all the things I loved about him. That part's hard."

"Do you still love him?"

I pulled the blankets up closer, noting the softness of the sheets. Isaac hadn't skimped. "Sometimes I think I do. But I can't stop remembering how desperate I felt after he left. When I think of the messages I sent him, the voicemails, it's embarrassing. And all that time he was down here with Isaac, ignoring everything I sent."

"Why would you feel embarrassed?" Mom asked. "You think he was seeing your messages and judging you? Laughing at you?"

"No," I said quickly. "Except, maybe yes. Otherwise, he would have responded."

"Dani, if thirty years of marriage has taught me anything, it's that everything isn't always about me. Sometimes your father will go silent and I'll assume it's because I've said something or done something that made him mad. And every once in a while, it *does* have something to do with me. But you know why he's usually silent?"

"Why?"

"Because he's frustrated with *himself*. He's processing, internalizing. Don't be so quick to assume that Alex's silence only had to do with *your* actions. He was surely going through something too."

"Yeah, I guess that's true."

"Have you talked about it yet?"

I shifted, pulling the covers closer to my chin. "Not really. I mean, he apologized, which is good. I'm just having a hard time understanding why he had to run away." I thought of the explanation he'd offered—that he legally couldn't talk to me. Surely whatever legal order he was under hadn't demanded wordless abandonment.

"People make mistakes, Dani."

"Yeah, I know." I thought about our hug in the kitchen this afternoon and a fresh wave of embarrassment swept over me. It had felt amazing in the moment, but thinking back, I wasn't so sure about it. It had taken Alex a long time to hug me back and when he had, it had only been halfway. I'd probably made him so uncomfortable.

"Hang in there, sweetie," Mom said. "It'll all work out."

"Tell Dad I said hi," I told her. "And I love you both."

With Mom's advice fresh in my brain, I keyed

out a message to Alex. *I'm sorry if I made things weird with the hug.*

His response came through only seconds later. *The hug was nice. I didn't mind.*

My heart rate spiked as I read his words. Nice? What did that mean? Feeling bold, I typed out, *Steven asked me out. But not until he asked me if there was something going on between me and you.*

Oh, he texted back. *Okay.*

I told him no. Why did I feel like I needed to explain? *To the date,* I quickly amended. *Also to the thing about us.*

Okay, Alex texted again.

I pressed my phone to my forehead. Why had I even started this conversation? I chewed on my lip as I considered what to say next. My hands trembled as I keyed out my next message. *I think I'm ready to talk.*

Right now? About . . . us?

I closed my eyes. He thought there was an us? *About LeFranc.*

Right. That makes more sense.

So he didn't think there was an us.

I breathed out a sigh. I needed to sleep. *Tomorrow is good. Or just, soon.*

Okay, he texted back. *Goodnight, Dani.*

Goodnight.

Chapter Twenty

Alex

It wasn't that I wasn't excited about the Compassion Experiment. The entire event was turning into something bigger, more impressive than anything I'd imagined. But I couldn't wait for the thing to be over. It felt as though every day brought additional problems, small details I'd forgotten about, phone calls from the other sponsors asking questions that only I knew how to answer. I hardly had enough hours in the day. Isaac and the rest of the team were as helpful as they could be, but they still had a daily show to write, film and produce. We were all stretched thin.

I listened as Rizzo went on and on about his expectations for the actual Christmas Eve event— food he wanted to see, the number of VIP passes he expected to receive. If nothing else, the man had firmly cemented my appreciation for Isaac's charitable heart. Rizzo still seemed incapable of grasping the actual reason for the entire event. "I hear you, Rizzo," I said through clenched teeth. "But I'm not making any promises. I can assure you, everything about the food and the décor will meet your satisfaction. We've hired the best there is to handle it."

Dani walked into the living room, mail in her hand, and held up a few letters that must have been for me. I held up the phone, and she motioned down the hall toward my room. I nodded, sure she'd just drop them on my desk. We still hadn't had the conversation she'd alluded to the night before. Time and privacy were scarce.

A few minutes later, when I finally ended the call with Rizzo, Dani still hadn't returned.

I dropped my phone into my pocket and moved down the hallway, pausing when I reached the doorway of my room. Dani stood at my desk, Sasha's wedding invitation in her hand.

"Hi," I said softly.

She spun around, dropping the invitation back onto the desk.

"Hi. Sorry. I just . . ." She tucked a lock of hair behind her ear. "Sorry. I shouldn't have snooped. I saw it sitting there and curiosity got the best of me."

I walked over to the desk and touched the invitation with a single finger, spinning it so it faced me. "I'm honestly surprised they sent me one."

She sank down onto my bed, her shoulders slumped. "Are you going to go?" she asked, without looking up.

"I wasn't planning on it. I don't think they truly want me there." The thought occurred to me that *she* might want to attend. Fashion was her world, after all, and the wedding was sure to be one of the biggest events in fashion in quite some time. "Do you want to go? I mean, I would go. If you wanted me to take you."

She scoffed and I winced at the sound, though I shouldn't have been surprised. Attending a destination wedding in the Florida Keys with your ex probably didn't sound like a picnic.

"I'm touched that you'd be willing to do something so horrible for my benefit, but I don't want to go," Dani said softly. "I couldn't bear to see it. To see *her*."

I sat next to her, landing closer than I'd intended. I expected her to shift aside, making room, but she didn't move. Our arms touched, the warmth of her cutting through the sleeve of my shirt and reaching my skin. I swallowed, intensely aware of how close she was. Everything about her felt familiar. The smell of her hair, the way it tumbled down her shoulders, even the rhythm of her breathing felt like something I recognized. Like all the time we'd spent in each other's arms had somehow left a permanent imprint of her on my consciousness. I closed my eyes, remembering the lazy afternoons we'd spend lounging around, the way I'd trail my fingers over her shoulder before wrapping a curl of her hair around my finger, pulling it straight before watching it bounce back into place. She'd always swatted my hand away, claiming the more I touched her hair the frizzier it would get. But I'd rarely been able to stop myself.

"You said you wanted to talk, right?"

She nodded her head just slightly.

"Is now a good time?"

She looked my way, bringing her face only inches from mine.

I willed the images of her out of my mind and focused on what Dani needed. She needed a friend. Someone to listen. "What happened at LeFranc?" I asked softly. "Why did you leave?"

She sighed, looking up at the ceiling before bringing her gaze back to me.

I couldn't push her for details. I was curious for sure, and maybe even half-hoped that Dani's departure had something to do with Sasha's criminal activity. I still dreamed of confronting Alicio with the truth I *knew* was hidden somewhere inside his company. Sasha was a thief and a liar and maybe Dani could help me prove that.

But I couldn't make her leaving LeFranc about me. That wasn't fair.

"You don't have to tell me if you don't want to," I added. I willed my voice to remain even, neutral.

"I *should* tell you," she said, shaking her head. "It's just embarrassing. I should have seen what was happening and I didn't. I literally walked right into her trap."

"Dani, Sasha is very good at manipulating people. Whatever happened, it wasn't your fault. You shouldn't feel—"

"I made a wedding dress for Paige," she said, cutting me off. "It's the most beautiful thing I've ever made, and it was perfect."

She pulled out her phone and opened up a picture, handing it over for me to see. It was a photo of Sasha in what I assumed was the wedding dress Dani had made.

"Chase sent that to me yesterday. She just showed it to the design team. It's the first in the Sasha Wellington Collection, LeFranc's debut line of wedding gowns. That's the one she plans to wear at her wedding."

"Except you made it," I said.

She nodded. "For Paige. Sasha saw it and promised that if I let her have it, she'd make me lead designer on her new team. I thought she just wanted it to be a part of the line, that she for sure already had her own dress designed, but I was wrong. I caught her *wearing* the dress, having it altered to fit *her.* She stole it. And she never had any intention of letting me design with her. It was a lie just so she could get her hands on the dress."

I cursed, familiar frustration welling up inside. The woman was rotten from the inside out. "She can't really get away with it, can she? Surely someone would believe you if you came forward and told them what happened."

"Why would anyone believe me? Sasha's a powerful woman. She threatened to ruin my name in the industry, and she could, too. Negative feedback from LeFranc? There's not a designer in all of New York that would hire me with that on my resume."

I hated to admit it, but she was right. Sasha really did have that kind of influence. Not that she deserved it.

"What about Paige? Can you make her the dress again?"

She shook her head. "I can't. It would cost me hundreds of dollars to buy the lace and fabric I would need. Plus, where would I work? All my sewing stuff is still in a trailer parked at Mirna's house in Brooklyn. What's more, I'm pretty sure if I made the same dress, Sasha would find a way to sue me for stealing her idea."

"Paige is just one person. How would Sasha even know that Paige wore the same dress?"

"That's just it. Paige's mother is a Pinckney. You know what that means around here. Debutante balls, big society events, private schools, yacht parties, all of it. Her mother has already hired Southern Royalty magazine to come and photograph the wedding. I mean, I can't know for sure Sasha would do anything, but I'm not sure I'm willing to risk everything to find out."

"That probably would have been some nice

publicity for a new designer. Paige wearing your dress."

Dani only shook her head and let out a disheartened laugh. "Yeah. It would have been." She shrugged her shoulders. "It doesn't matter. Paige's mom made her buy a back-up dress anyway." She looked at me. "Great that she had so much confidence in me, right?"

"I bet Paige loved the dress you made," I said.

Dani offered a small smile, almost enough to lift the frown lines creasing her forehead. "Yeah. She really did."

The smallest seed of a plan took root in my mind. It was ridiculous. And probably wouldn't work. But just maybe . . . "Did she love your dress more than the back-up dress?"

"I don't know why it matters, but yes. I'm pretty sure she loved it even more."

I reached over and grabbed Dani's hands, pulling her up so we stood facing each other beside the bed. "I think I have a plan."

Her eyes narrowed. "A plan for what?"

"I have an invitation to the wedding," I said as if that were explanation enough.

"And?" she prompted.

"And I can bring a date."

Her narrowed eyes turned into a frown. "What are you getting at?"

"Let's go to the wedding. Me and you. Let's go get Paige's dress."

Dani's eyes went wide. "What? Like, steal it?"

"It's not stealing if what you're taking already belongs to you."

She remained silent for a few moments, as if considering my plan, then shook her head. "No. It would never work. They'll have security at the wedding and I'm not exactly Sasha's favorite person right now. I'd never get close enough."

"That's where I come in," I said. "I'm not technically still family, but they're getting married at Alicio's house in the Keys. I know that house. If Alicio still uses the same security firm he always has, I'll know people there. And I *was* officially invited to the wedding. They can't stop me from going home. I have a room there. Full of things that belong to me. I have a right to show up."

"Getting into the house and getting close to Sasha are two entirely different things. Even if we manage to pull it off, if I steal the dress, she'll know it was me. What's going to keep her from going public with the theft? I'm not too naive to still care what Alicio thinks of me, and I absolutely don't care what Sasha thinks, but I would like to eventually work again. Everyone who is anyone in fashion will be at that wedding. I can't afford to trash my name, even for Paige's dress."

She made a very valid point. If all we did was steal the dress, it wouldn't be enough. There had to be a way to simultaneously incriminate and expose Sasha, which I couldn't do because I didn't have the evidence.

I paced around the room. *I* didn't have the evidence, but maybe Dani did. She'd been Sasha's assistant which meant she was probably the one who had handled Sasha's expense account—managed statements, filed receipts, sent validating documents to accounting.

I could ask. I could ask, and we could find out the truth and I could give it all to Alicio.

But he'd made the consequences clear.

Keep digging, break the cease and desist, and I'd be cut off. My Ivy League education had cost more than four hundred thousand dollars. That was a lot of student loan debt to suddenly inherit.

But truth was truth.

And Dani was hurting.

And I still cared about that.

I didn't want to, but I did.

"Dani, were you the one who handled Sasha's expense account?"

She looked at me funny but then nodded. "Sure."

"What did that entail?"

She wrinkled her brow. "I sent statements of her account with attached receipts to accounting once a month."

"So you had access to her actual account?"

She looked at me quizzically but answered anyway. "Yes."

"Do you think you *still* have access?"

Her expression clouded. "I doubt it. The system required me to change my password monthly. Even if Sasha didn't have all of my credentials erased manually, it's been long enough, it would have already required a password reset."

I grumbled under my breath. "What about your email? Can you still access it? The messages you sent to accounting would still be in your sent messages, yes?"

She frowned and shook her head. "They would be, but I can't access my email anymore. I tried a few days ago. It didn't work." Nervous energy radiated off of her in waves. "But," she said, her voice full of sudden excitement. She pulled out her phone and started swiping.

"What?" I asked, my voice impatient.

She shook her head, a gesture willing me to wait a moment longer. Then she looked up, a smile stretched wide across her face, and handed me her phone. "My computer at work kept crashing. The hard drive was faulty or something and I kept losing files. So tech support set up an account in the cloud where things were automatically backed up. It wasn't standard protocol, so when HR erased me from the system, they probably didn't know to wipe this."

I looked at her phone, quickly scrolling down. Dozens and dozens of files were listed, purchase orders, design specs, but I immediately picked out a handful labeled with some variation of monthly statement. It was exactly the information I could have used a year ago when I was trying to incriminate Sasha, but that didn't matter anymore. I had it now. Matched with the screenshots I'd saved before I left, it might be enough.

"Can I access this from my laptop?" I asked Dani.

She shrugged. "Sure. I can text you the password."

"Perfect."

She wrung her hands. "Do you think it'll be enough?"

"I don't know. I think so, but I'm following hunches here. I could dig in and find out that I was wrong, and Sasha's only crime is being a first-class jerk. But if I'm right, I should be able to find the proof in these statements."

"What exactly do you think she was doing?" Dani asked. "I mean, what is it you're trying to prove?"

I only hesitated a moment. It wouldn't take *that* long to pay for my education. "Company expenditures took a huge climb when Sasha came on board. It was a subtle increase at first, but then over time, the increases became more noticeable. The increases were all categorized as design development. I tried to access the information needed to break down the expenditures further, to see where they were coming from and which designer was responsible for them, but I was shut down and told to back off. I became insistent, called for an internal audit—"

"And then you left." She interrupted me, finishing my sentence.

I looked up and met her gaze, hurt still visible in her eyes. I nodded. "That's when I left."

"Because you thought Sasha was stealing from the company and I refused to believe Sasha was anything but my one-way ticket to my dreams."

We sat in silence, thousands of unspoken words hanging in the air between us. It still hurt to think about those painful days right after I left LeFranc.

"Alex, why didn't you tell me?"

I moved to the desk, flipping through the letters Dani had left. "I wanted to," I said, my back to her. I turned around and crossed my arms across my chest. "But I couldn't tell you specifics. You were still so loyal to Sasha. I couldn't risk her finding out I was suspicious for fear of her destroying any proof of her activities. To be fair, Dani, you were pretty defensive when I implied *anything* negative about Sasha. I don't think you would have taken the details kindly."

She bit her lip. There were so many emotions behind her eyes, but she didn't say anything.

"Once I left, I *couldn't* say anything because of

the cease and desist. They threatened legal action. I had no choice but to back down, especially since I couldn't prove anything."

"Except . . ." She paused. "You just did say something."

I offered her a small smile. "You don't work for her anymore. And you possibly just gave me the proof I need to convince Alicio she's been stealing from him."

"It's still a risk though, right? For you, personally?"

I couldn't lie, not when she'd asked me so plainly. "I haven't been financially dependent on Alicio since I graduated, but he has threatened to retroactively charge me for my very expensive education that he paid for."

Dani shook her head. "That's a lot of money, Alex. You can't take that on for me."

"But I would, Dani. In a minute, I would." The fire in my gut raged fierce enough, the words I'd spoken had to be true; it was not lost on me that I'd just committed to do the very thing I *hadn't* been willing to do before.

I'd been a coward. And it was time to make it right. "Also, it's the right thing to do. Someone needs to stop her. And I might be the only person who can."

"Alex, when did your mom die?"

It wasn't a question I expected. "Why?"

"What year? You were still in school, right?"

"I was almost finished, but yes. She died just after Thanksgiving. Five years ago."

Her face fell. "So Sasha met Alicio *before* your mom died?"

"I'm not sure," I said, feeling suddenly agitated. "I've always suspected—she appeared in his life so soon after Mom was gone—but I don't have any way to know for sure. Why?"

Dani bit her bottom lip the same way she'd used to when we'd played Scrabble and she'd known she had a word that was going to score big. She'd always tried to play it cool, but she had a terrible poker face. When she knew something—anything—I'd always been able to tell with one look.

"Nothing. I was just curious."

"Dani. Just tell me."

She closed her eyes for a moment before locking her gaze with mine. "Sasha told me right before I quit that she and Alicio were going away for the weekend to celebrate the five-year anniversary of when they first had dinner. That was three months ago, which means—"

"Alicio was sleeping with Sasha while Mom was in the hospital." I dropped into my desk chair and took a deep breath. "Wow." It was hardly an adequate response, but it was all I could manage. Something fierce and hot roiled inside me; anger at Alicio for cheating on my mother when she was sick, anger at Sasha for taking husbands and money and dresses and ideas without even thinking about the consequences. I had to stop her. For Dani, but for my mom, too.

Dani reached out and curled her hands over my arms, squeezing them gently. "I'm sorry, Alex."

She dropped her hands, but I wished she'd left them there. I felt untethered, and the contact had felt a little like a lifeline I didn't know I needed until it was gone.

"About your mom, but also . . ." She looked up, sorrow in her eyes. "I should have listened to you. I'm sorry I didn't." She wrapped her arms around herself and I squelched the desire to reach out and give her a hug. We'd had a pretty profound twenty minutes. I didn't want to push my luck.

"What do we do now?" she asked.

I willed conviction into my voice. "Do the research, find the evidence, take it to the wedding, steal a dress, and expose Sasha as a thief."

"You just made that sound really easy."

"It won't be easy, but—"

"Wait," Dani said, cutting me off. "When is the wedding again?"

"New Year's Eve."

"So we'll be finished with the Compassion Experiment by then. That's good."

"And we will have plenty of time to fly home and then make it to Islamorada."

"Isla-where?" Isaac asked from the bedroom doorway. "Sounds tropical. Can I come?"

Dani gave him a quick rundown of everything we'd been discussing. When she got to the part about stealing the wedding dress back, Isaac whooped and hollered like a kid who'd just won a video game tournament. "A legit wedding dress heist. I am so coming with you to Florida. Please tell me you'll let me put this on the air."

"Absolutely not," Dani and I said in tandem. Even the tone we used was identical.

Isaac rolled his eyes. "Come on. Not even highlights? After the fact? And only if everything works just as it should?"

"There's too much at stake, Isaac," Dani said. "My career. Alex's relationship with his stepdad. You can come if you want, but cameras have to stay off."

I wasn't sure *relationship* was the right word for what I had with Alicio. But what Dani said was still true. Odds were against anyone in attendance at a LeFranc wedding also watching Isaac's YouTube channel, but we couldn't be too careful. If I found what I hoped to find, I'd be making some pretty hefty criminal accusations that would likely land Sasha in jail. This was about much more than a wedding dress.

"Fine," Isaac said. "No cameras. But you have to at least let me drive the getaway car."

This time, Dani rolled *her* eyes. "Oh my word.

Are you seriously twelve years old?" Isaac moved behind us and put an arm around each of our necks, pulling us into an awkward three-way hug. "New Year's in the Florida Keys," he said with a grin. "This is going to be so much fun."

Later, a text came in from Dani containing the password to access the cloud files I needed. *This is awkward,* the text read. *But I'm afraid to change it in case I get locked out and we can't get back in. The password is AL3XmyLuV.*

Chapter Twenty-One

Dani

I stood at the back of Isaac's studio watching him wrap up the last of his filming. Mom's words echoed through my head. It was hard for me to believe that Isaac actually cared about my approval. But Alex had said he did, and so had Mom, two people I trusted.

So I stood in the back. I watched. And much to my surprise, I laughed *a lot.*

Isaac sat behind a large desk next to Steven, an array of vegan food spread out in front of them. The point of the episode was to taste test vegan foods against their traditional counterparts. Vegan hamburgers. Vegan bacon. Vegan milk. It wasn't groundbreaking material; there were probably a hundred YouTube videos that attempted the very same thing. But his commentary was roll-on-the-floor funny. I'd always known he was a performer. He'd been showboating his way through life since we'd first learned how to talk. But seeing it translate into an actual job—a thing that people watched and liked and reacted to? It was pretty eye-opening.

Suddenly inspired by a new sense of appreciation, I pulled out my phone and texted Darius.

Hey. Any word back from your uncle? We're nearly out of time.

I slipped the phone back into my pocket but pulled it out again almost immediately to answer a call from Chase. I stepped outside to answer the call but made sure to make eye contact with Isaac before I did. I wanted him to see me standing there. To see me laughing. To see that I appreciated what he did. Mom had been right. I'd never given him enough credit.

"Hey, are you close?" I said to Chase, pulling the studio door closed behind me.

"I'm here," Chase said. "At least, I think I am. Is there a driveway where you want me to put this trailer, or should I park in the street?"

"No, pull into the driveway. I had everyone else move so there was room for you." I cut through the garden and down the narrow alleyway separating Isaac's house from the neighbor's, hitting the driveway right as Chase cut the ignition. He jumped out of his car and I barreled into him for a hug.

"You're here!" I said. "How was the drive?"

"So long," he said. "You better get me to the ocean by nightfall, so I feel like all that time in the car was worth it."

"Did someone say ocean?" Darius stepped out from behind the trailer. "Sign me up for that."

"Darius! You came, too?"

He pulled me into a giant hug. I always forgot

how giant of a man Darius was until he hugged me. It literally felt like I disappeared into his arms.

"For Thanksgiving dinner with you? Don't you know it."

"Truly? What about your mom?"

"My sister flew in from Chicago to be with her," Darius said. "She's staying until next week so I'm all yours."

"Don't let him fool you," Chase said, slipping an arm around Darius's waist. "When I told him you were cooking a Thanksgiving meal for you, *and* Alex, *and* Isaac, all at the same table, he wasn't about to miss those fireworks."

Darius shot Chase a wide-eyed look. "That is not what I said." He looked back at me. "You know we're here for you, Dani. No matter what."

I smiled. "I know. And I love you for it. You're going to be nice to him though, right?"

Chase motioned like he was cleaning out his ears. "I'm sorry, what was that? It sounded like you were expressing concern over whether or not we planned to be *nice* to Alex Randall."

"I know. Shocking. I guess seeing him again has maybe made me realize it doesn't have to be all or nothing. And you guys were his friends, too."

Darius wiped a fake tear from his eye. "Chase, our baby girl is growing up."

I rolled my eyes. "Seriously. You guys are the worst."

Darius grinned. "Alex actually texted me the other day. We've been chatting back and forth. It's cool."

Chase pouted. "What? He texted you but not me? Why are you always everyone's favorite?"

"Raw charisma, baby," Darius said. "Raw charisma."

"Speaking of texts, I just texted you," I said, motioning to Darius. "Have you heard back from your uncle?"

Darius grimaced. "About that. I *did* hear back, but I'm not sure you're going to be on board with Reggie's reply."

"What? Why? Doesn't he just need to say yes or no?"

"Oh!" Chase said. "I almost forgot! There's actually another surprise for you in the car."

Darius motioned to the car with his head. "Go ahead. I'll fill you in later."

"What is it?" I asked, peering around Chase's shoulder toward the car.

"Go open up the passenger side door and see for yourself," he said with a wide grin.

I ran around Chase's car and pulled open the door. Paige flung her arms out wide and smiled. "Surprise!"

"Paige!" I pulled her out of the car and into a hug. "What are you doing here?"

"Languishing in the car, apparently." She shot Chase a dour look.

He mouthed a silent sorry in her direction.

"Are you here for Thanksgiving, too?" I asked her.

"I'm here until the wedding," she said. "Mom's been pestering me to come and help her finalize all the plans anyway, and without work to keep me in the city, I figured, why not?"

"What will Reese do without you?" I asked, not that I really cared. Reese was getting her for life. I was thrilled to have my best friend all to myself for another month.

"Oh, he'll be fine. It's what, seven weeks until the wedding? Plus, he's coming down for Christmas and I'm sure I'll fly back up to New York at least once." She took my hands, squeezing them in her own. "Now. How are you? How are things with Alex?"

I raised my shoulders in a shrug. "Good, I think? Weird. Awkward. Sometimes I think it's getting easier to be around him as a friend, but then he'll walk through the room and I won't be able to focus on anything other than how good he looks in a pair of jeans."

"That man looks good in anything he puts on," Chase said.

"I agree," Darius added, coming up behind us. "Some people just wear clothes well and he is definitely one of those people."

"Unfortunately, that does very little to assist my efforts to get over the man," I said.

Chase pursed his lips. "Yeah. That would be tough. I vote you forget getting over him and get back together."

"Hold up," Paige said. "I'm not ready to vote for that yet."

"Has she been texting you the updates of what's been happening down here? He's clearly still in love with her."

"Then why did he leave?" Paige asked with a smirk.

Chase rolled his eyes. "You're right. Real people don't make mistakes. I'm sure Reese has never done anything stupid in *your* relationship."

"Uh, nothing that compares to—"

"Hey, hold up," Darius said, cutting Paige off. "Dani asked us not to choose sides, remember? What we want is for both Dani *and* Alex to be happy. Whatever that means, whether they are together or apart. Right?"

"Right," they both mumbled.

"Thank you." I looked at my three closest friends and almost cried for seeing them all together. "It really is so amazing to have you all here."

Darius leaned over and pulled me into a half hug, kissing the side of my head. "You know we got you, D."

Paige's phone dinged with a text and she pulled

it from her bag and glanced at the screen. "That's my mom. She'll be here any second to get me." She looked my way. "I'm doing the family thing for Thanksgiving, but early next week, we're meeting with the caterer. I guess there's something they want to change on the menu, and they need me to approve. Want to come?"

"Of course. Text me the details. I wouldn't miss it for the world."

As soon as Paige was safely stowed in her mom's luxury SUV, I turned to Chase. "Please tell me you didn't tell her about stealing the dress back."

"What do you take me for?" Chase said. "You told me not to tell, so I didn't tell."

"Coming down for Thanksgiving was a great cover," Darius said. "She didn't question the trip at all."

I breathed a sigh of relief. "I just don't want her to get her hopes up."

"She doesn't know," Chase said. "I promise."

I motioned toward the trailer they'd hauled across six states. "Any idea how close my fabric bins are toward the front?"

"I have no idea, but I refuse to unpack a single thing from that trailer until you've taken me to the beach. Didn't we already talk about this?" Chase said.

"Oh come on," I said. "Just one quick peek? I'm pretty sure I have a stretch of ivory satin that's going to be perfect for Sasha's replacement dress."

Chase propped a hand on his hip and shook his head. "Girl, you are pure evil."

"Don't act like you don't love it," Darius said.

"Of course I love it," Chase agreed. "I feel like I've been dropped into the middle of a Danny Ocean movie. I wouldn't miss this for anything."

Darius helped me open the back of the trailer. I paused and stared at the entirety of my New York life crammed into a six-by-twelve-foot box. *So sad.* I heaved a sigh, willing the sadness away. Dwelling on the unfairness of everything that had happened wasn't going to help. I shifted around a couple of boxes, stacking them next to the giant armoire—the only furniture in my old apartment that had actually been *mine*—and reached for a bin of fabric.

If I was going to steal Paige's dress back, I had to have a replacement I could swap it for. I could have bought something benign and harmless from a local shop, but that didn't feel nearly as fun. I wanted to make something that Sasha, in all of her conniving glory, really deserved. And that meant I needed my stuff.

Three bins later, I found what I was looking for. The ivory was perfect; perfect weight, just enough sheen. I held up the fabric. "This is it."

Chase looked over my shoulder. "I thought you wanted to make something hideous."

I shook my head. "No, it can't be hideous. At least, not obviously so. Then she wouldn't wear it. I need to make something convincing enough for her to actually go through with wearing it. I mean, she'll be desperate. She won't have another dress on hand. But still. I want the awful of the dress to be a little more nuanced."

"So, you mean, *not* awful to the David's Bridal crowd, but *definitely* awful to anyone in high fashion?"

I clutched the ivory fabric to my chest. "Exactly."

Isaac and Alex came out and helped haul the essentials up to my bedroom above the studio. Darius and Chase each gave Alex a hug and the three of them spoke for a minute or two before they picked up any boxes. Seeing them there, standing on the sidewalk, hands shoved in pockets like true men, I was filled with a sort of . . . longing. We'd been good together, the group of us. I missed that.

There was barely enough room to work once we'd unloaded all my stuff, but we managed to fit a card table for my sewing machine, my dress form, and a stack of plastic bins full of notions— lace and buttons and anything else I might need—into the tiny space. It wasn't ideal, but it would have to do.

"Any progress?" I asked Alex. He lingered in the doorway while Isaac took Chase and

Darius to the main house to show them around. Ultimately, there wasn't a reason to even make a dress if Alex didn't think he could mount enough evidence against Sasha. Because without it, I wouldn't risk crashing the wedding, not when Sasha wouldn't hesitate to ruin my future in designing.

"I think I'm getting closer," Alex said, though the doubt in his voice betrayed him. "I'm trying to look for patterns. Similar amounts, similar dates. I don't know. I think I'll get there."

"I've been thinking back through my time there trying to remember anything that seemed suspicious," I said. "The only thing I can come up with is this one fabric dealer she always worked with. His name was something different. Solomon something?"

Alex nodded. "Solomon Rivers. I've seen his name on the statements. He was a fabric dealer?"

"That's what she told me. A wholesaler. She was very protective of their relationship. I don't think any of the other designers ever worked with him, and I definitely didn't ever see him at the office."

"As a Senior Designer, that would be typical, right? Didn't she handle most of the buying?"

"She did less than everyone else, but she was involved enough, it didn't seem unusual for her to have a specific relationship with a whole-saler. At least not from my side of things. I can ask Chase for his opinion if that would help."

"Do you remember ever seeing statements of what she purchased from him?"

"That's just it. There never were any. No receipts. That's what made me ask about him. Because it was my job to catalog the receipts. She said Solomon sent them straight to Accounting so I didn't need to worry about them."

"Sounds fishy," Alex said.

"Let me text Chase and ask him what he knows," I said. I keyed out a message, asking him to come up to my room before he and Darius left for their hotel.

A few minutes later, he dropped onto the chair that had replaced the red couch and leaned his head back. Poor guy. He'd been on the road for almost twelve hours. He was probably exhausted.

"Have you ever heard of a fabric wholesaler named Solomon Rivers?" I asked him.

He furrowed his brow. "Solomon? No. Never."

"Sasha did a lot of ordering from him. I actually think most of our fabric came through him. You're sure it doesn't sound familiar?"

Chase looked at me like I'd stolen the only pecan pie at the end of Thanksgiving dinner. "The last two years we've worked almost exclusively with Phoenix and Finn. Their agent, Carmella, you remember her, right?"

I shook my head no, but that wasn't surprising. Sasha kept me pretty far removed from the design side of her job. Well, except when she was stealing *my* designs, but that was a moot point.

"So you never saw or met with this Solomon Rivers guy?" Alex asked.

"Never," Chase said. "What kind of a name is that anyway?"

"Maybe a made-up one," Alex said. "Do you have any memory of working with fabric that didn't come from Phoenix and Finn?"

"No," Chase said. "Well, possibly here and there. Sample pieces an individual designer would bring in. But even those things would be taken to Carmella, in hopes that she could provide us with something similar when it came time to buy for a new collection. As long as I've been at LeFranc, Carmella has handled our wholesale account. I'm sure about that."

"So what we need is proof that Solomon Rivers isn't a fabric wholesaler or a dealer of any kind," I said. "If we can prove that, then we can prove that all those charges Sasha made over the past however many months were fraudulent, right?" I looked at Alex. "Can you do that?"

I glanced at Chase. He sat perfectly still, his lips pulled into a tight line across his face. I'd explained everything when I'd called him; he knew he didn't have to be involved unless he wanted to be. I didn't have anything to lose, really. I'd already lost my job at LeFranc and left New York. But Chase did.

"I don't know," Alex said. "I'm suddenly wishing I'd taken that class on forensic accounting when I had the chance." He moved to the door. "If Solomon Rivers is incorporated, then the location of their headquarters, the president of the LLC, general contact information, that's all publicly accessible information on file with the state."

"What if it's registered overseas?" Chase said. "That's what people do, right? If they embezzle money, they store it in offshore accounts to avoid taxes?"

I raised an eyebrow in Chase's direction.

He shrugged "What? I watch a lot of movies."

"Let me do some research," Alex said. "I think I might know someone who can help. My friend, Angelica, *did* specialize in forensic accounting. I think she'll at least be able to point me in the right direction."

I raised my arms into a shrug, motioning to the room around me. "And in the meantime?" I asked.

"Oh, start sewing," Alex said. "This woman is going down."

As soon as we heard the studio door close, Chase leaned in. "Okay. All jokes aside? I need to know what's going on between you two."

I huffed a laugh. "What does it look like?"

"Uh, it looks like he's going to a lot of effort to help you steal back a wedding dress."

"It's not about that for him," I said. "This is his family we're talking about. It's personal."

Chase crossed his arms. "Stepfamily."

"Still."

Chase just looked at me, doubt written all over his face.

"Why is it so hard for you to imagine two people working together to reach the same goal for different reasons?"

"Maybe I could if we were talking about any other two people. But the two of you were in love less than a year ago. I think I'm justified in saying that complicates things."

"It's been more than a year," I said. "A year and . . . four months."

Chase rolled his eyes. "But who's counting, right?"

"I know. It's weird. But it's like we've landed in this strange middle ground where we're polite and courteous and we get along. We just don't talk about anything that happened."

Chase huffed. "But that's not sustainable. Eventually, stuff will come up."

"What else is there to say?" I countered. "He apologized in New York."

"But you're still mad," Chase said.

I stared at my hands. Mad wasn't the right word. "I'm scared," I finally said. "I feel like I barely came out of the fog a few months ago. It was worse than just getting over a broken heart. It was getting over it without any sense of closure. I finally feel okay again. I don't know if I can risk opening my heart to him again."

"I know, sweetie," Chase said. "But you're still standing, even after all that. And now there's this man who is so good in so many ways. And it might be worth recognizing—at least acknowledging that it's a possibility—he's doing this big thing because he still cares about you."

I pressed the heels of my hands into my eye sockets. "Don't say that. I can't think about that right now."

"You know what Mark Twain said about denial?" Chase asked. "It ain't just a river in Egypt."

I shook my head. "It's not about being in denial. It feels like I just got the dam built, you know? My feelings for Alex are contained, safe, walled up. If you mess with that wall right now? It's not like a little bit might trickle out. It's all or nothing. The whole dam will break, and I can't deal with a deluge. I'm afraid it will break me for good."

Chase stood and crossed the tiny room to where I sat at my makeshift sewing station. He pulled me to my feet and wrapped me in a hug. "Okay," he said softly. "I get it. I won't push."

I gave his shoulders a quick squeeze and draped

my measuring tape over his shoulders. "Ready to make an ugly dress?"

"Absolutely not. I'm ready to go to the beach. We can start the ugly dress tomorrow."

"What is it with you and the beach? It's November. It's not even warm enough to be at the beach."

"It was sixty-five degrees when we pulled up this afternoon," Chase said, indignant. "That's plenty warm enough. I didn't say I wanted to *swim*."

"But it's forty degrees now. And windy. I promise it isn't as magical as you think this time of year."

He tossed my measuring tape back at my head. "You're a terrible buzzkill, you know that, right?"

I grinned. "What if we compromise and go get seafood for dinner?"

"Ohhh, I'm intrigued. All of us?"

I shrugged. "Sure. But you're buying. I'm totally broke."

Chase rolled his eyes. "I miss the days when Alex was making enough money to buy us all dinner, all the time. How much does your brother pay him anyway?"

"I doubt it's half as much as he made at LeFranc, but he doesn't seem to care."

"Yeah, I've picked up on that. He seems happy here," Chase said. "Different, but happy. It's like Alex 2.0."

I couldn't tell Chase how much I agreed with him; if I did, I was pretty sure he'd pick up on the hope in my voice—the hope I'd just tried really hard to convince Chase didn't even exist.

Chapter Twenty-Two
Alex

I'd never really loved Thanksgiving. Since I lived with my dad full time, I'd always spent holidays with Mom and Alicio. Thanksgiving at the LeFranc house had always looked like it belonged in a magazine. Everything looked perfect, right down to the coordinating outfits Mom made us wear to dinner. The meals had been extravagant, prepared by a kitchen full of personal chefs I always felt sorry for because wouldn't they rather have been cooking a Thanksgiving meal for their own families?

Once a photographer from *ELITE* Fashion had come to dinner and taken a photograph of Alicio at the head of the table, a cashmere scarf loosely draped around his neck, the glistening, perfectly browned turkey displayed on the table before him. In the photo that made the magazine, he held my mother's hand. Though he stared at the camera, smiling broadly, she stared at him, warmth and affection in her gaze. In the foreground, two boys in matching sweaters sat on either side of the happy couple. I had taken my sweater off before dinner, claiming the wool made my neck itch. That was the reason my mother gave later, after the magazine had gone to press with the third son cropped out of the shot. My lack of a sweater.

Dani and I had spent one Thanksgiving together in New York, the only time I actually remembered liking the holiday. It had been the six of us. Chase and Darius, Paige and Reese, me and Dani. Reese and Dani had done most of the cooking; Darius baked all the pies. I'd felt mostly useless—I didn't know the first thing about basting a turkey—but there was something magical about watching from the sidelines, seeing the meal come together from the efforts of the people I'd grown to care most about in the world.

That Thanksgiving felt like a lifetime ago.

The scene in Isaac's kitchen wasn't all that different, though Reese had been replaced with Isaac as sous chef. When Dani had asked for an assistant, he'd been quick to volunteer before anyone else even had the opportunity. The gesture had clearly surprised Dani, but I could have predicted Isaac's willingness. He had been intentional in his effort to be closer to his sister lately. Things weren't perfect between them, but they were both trying, which went a long way toward creating a happy holiday atmosphere as they prepared the meal.

Darius, of course, had agreed for a second time to take care of dessert. Which left me and Chase and the rest of the guys watching football in the living room.

"Hey, can we get a hand in here?" Dani called from the kitchen.

Chase moved to stand up, but I reached out my arm and stopped him. "I'll go."

He raised an eyebrow, the expression in his eyes telling me he knew exactly why I was eager to be in the kitchen. I shrugged my shoulders, but I couldn't exactly contradict him. I'd found a hundred different reasons already to pass through the kitchen, all of them completely unnecessary except for the fact that they brought me closer to Dani. I wasn't ready to admit what it meant that I still felt so drawn to her, or worse, what it meant that I was finally giving in. But I wasn't idiot enough to try and deny it either.

I rounded the corner into the kitchen, and Dani smiled. Had her eyes lit up when she'd seen it was me? She and Isaac stood holding the large roasting pan full of turkey between them. "We didn't exactly plan ahead," Dani said. "Can you clear a space on the counter?"

I shifted Darius's pies to the edge of the island and moved a package of celery and a bag of carrots back into the fridge. "Where's Darius?"

"He had to go buy more butter for the mashed potatoes," Isaac said. "Apparently, we underestimated just how many pies he intended to make."

"I should have warned you," Chase said from the doorway. "Even when it's just the two of us and his mom, he makes at least two pies per person. The man feels strongly about his dessert."

"Two pies per person," Isaac said. "I think this is a tradition we should try and implement when Mom and Dad come home."

"If they ever come home," Dani said with a laugh. "I did not anticipate them loving Europe this much."

"They'll come home eventually," Isaac said. "I mean, sooner or later one of us will get married or have a kid. They're bound to come back for something like that."

At once, Dani's gaze flew to mine. The conversation we'd once had about children popped into my head. We'd been walking in Central Park after attending a fashion gala at the Met a couple of months before we'd broken up. We'd just passed the zoo, where some sort of children's charity event had been taking place. "Do you want kids?" Dani had asked bluntly, looping her arm through mine.

"I do," I'd said, hardly taking time to think about my answer. "I'd like them to come with blonde curly hair and bright blue eyes." I'd stopped walking then, and turned her to face me, slipping my arms around the small of her back. "Just like their mother."

She'd closed her eyes and I'd wondered for

a moment if I'd spoken too plainly, too boldly. "What about you?" I whispered. "Do you want kids?"

She'd smiled then, her cheeks full of new color. "Yeah. Twins might be fun. But I'm kind of partial to brown eyes." She'd pulled herself closer to me, reaching up on tiptoe to kiss me just beside my left eye. Her lips trailed a row of kisses down to my earlobe, and then across my jawline until she found my lips. Her hands moved to my cheeks and she'd kissed me right there in front of a homeless woman, a hotdog vendor, and a pair of teenagers who appeared to be high on something, but not so high to keep them from whistling at us when the kiss didn't stop. We'd kissed so many times in our relationship. Every day. But there was an unexpected tenderness to that moment that I wouldn't ever forget.

"One of each then," I had said when she'd finally pulled away, my voice thick with emotion.

"It's a plan," she'd whispered back.

"Yo, Dani, we carving this bird or what?" Isaac said.

Dani gave her head a little shake, turning her eyes back to Isaac. Had she been remembering the same conversation? "No. I mean, yes. Just not yet. It has to rest first." She pressed a hand to her forehead and closed her eyes. "I think I, um . . . I'll be right back." She pulled her apron off and draped it over a kitchen chair before sliding into the garden through the back door.

"What was that all about?" Isaac asked, looking to me.

I shrugged. "She's probably just too warm from all the cooking." I moved to the fridge and pulled out a bottle of water. "Maybe I'll see if she needs this."

"You better let me," Chase said, showing up in the kitchen and reaching for the bottle. "I have a feeling you are not the man Dani needs to see right now if the goal is to cool her down."

"Wait, what?" Isaac said. He watched Chase leave then turned his gaze on me. "Is something going on with you and Dani?"

"No," I said quickly.

He narrowed his eyes like he didn't believe my response.

"No," I said again. "Nothing has happened."

"But you want it to?"

I forced out a breath. "I don't know. Possibly?" I sank onto a barstool and dropped my head into my hands. "But after what happened, I'm not sure it matters. I don't think she'll have me."

Before Isaac responded, Darius pushed into the room and dropped a grocery bag full of butter onto the counter. He looked from me to Isaac, and then back to me again. "Did I miss something?"

"Just Alex admitting that he never stopped loving Dani. Did you remember to get some heavy cream?"

"Isaac, please," I said, shooting a glance over my shoulder at the back door.

"She's still in the garden with Chase," Darius said. "You're cool." He sat beside me on a neighboring stool. "Is it true?"

"I don't know. And that's all I said earlier. I don't know how I feel. Or how she feels."

Darius nodded his head. "You know, you're different now. So is Dani. You never know. Maybe different is what you both need."

"You're talking as if I didn't make a monumental mistake. There are no guarantees here. Even if I did, hypothetically, want us to get back together, she likely won't forgive me. I'm not sure I would if she'd done the same thing to me."

Isaac leaned on the counter across from where Darius and I sat. "There are two sides to every coin, man. I was here those first few months after you left. You can't tell me she didn't do any damage to you. Any other employer would have fired you for all the moping around you did."

I shook my head. "I was a coward."

"And she had tunnel vision," Darius said. "We all saw it."

Isaac scoffed. "What? Dani focused? Driven to the point of madness? Narrow-minded and determined to reach her goal? Never."

"Like I said," Darius said, reaching out and placing his arm across my back. "You've both changed in the past year. Never say never, you know?"

After dinner, I stood in the kitchen alone doing dishes, happy to have something to focus on outside of my earlier conversation with Isaac and Darius. It wasn't as though I hadn't considered the possibility of Dani and me getting back together before. But I'd worked really hard not to let myself dwell on the possibility. Not when she was still committed to her LeFranc dream job. And not when I was positive that even if that one obstacle were out of the way, she likely still wouldn't forgive me.

I wanted to believe I had changed, that we both had. But I wasn't sure it was enough.

"Hey Alex, you got a minute?"

Dani appeared beside me, her eyes wide with excitement. She slipped a hand over my forearm. "Come here. I need to show you something."

I turned off the water and dried my hands, tossing a dish towel over my shoulder as I followed her into Isaac's music room. She pulled out her cell phone and tapped on the screen a few times before handing it over. I stared at the screen, noting a New York number at the top, no contact name attached.

Band said yes, the text read. *But jackets needed for each of us, not just me.*

I looked up at Dani. "I don't understand."

"That's a text from Reggie Fletcher. Red

Renegade will play at the Compassion Experiment."

"You're serious? I thought Darius said he wouldn't do it."

"He did, but I had to try. And I mean, it did take a little convincing, but he agreed. He's going to do it."

"What's this part about needing jackets?" I asked.

"That was part of the convincing I had to do. You remember that time we were over at Reggie's with Darius, when he and Chase were pet sitting?"

"Right. The weird miniature poodle dogs, right?"

"Right. And then Reggie came home early and we were all sort of lounging around in his living room like we lived there?"

"He loved your jacket," I said, picking up the story. "The leather one. With the red stripe down the sleeve."

She nodded. "He wants one. And I guess now he wants them all to have one."

"Matching jackets? That feels a little more nineties boy band than it does Red Renegade."

"Who cares? If they're willing to appear, I'll make them matching tutus if they want them."

"It's amazing that they're willing, but that jacket took you a long time. You handstitched most of it, didn't you? Also, don't celebrities have access to designers? Surely someone would want to put their name on a band like Red Renegade, even if just for one YouTube performance."

A flit of something passed over Dani's face. Was it disappointment? "Maybe *I'm* the designer who wants to put her name on a band like Red Renegade."

"Oh. Of course. Dani, that isn't, I didn't mean—"

"I know you didn't. I know what you meant. But Red Renegade hasn't had a hit in twenty-five years. They aren't really on the map for anyone else, at least not any other designers looking for publicity. I'm probably the best they can do. Aside from that, I want to do this." She shrugged. "For Isaac."

Chapter Twenty-Three

Dani

I hauled the heaviest bin of fabric into the back of the SUV Paige borrowed from her mom, then scooted it to the side, making room for Paige to slide the smaller bin in beside it. Paige and I had a mile-long list of wedding stuff to tackle, but first, a design boutique on King Street had agreed to look at my stash and purchase the lot of it if they liked what they saw. Hopefully, that would give me more than enough cash to special order the leather I would need for Red Renegade's jackets, and still have some left over to catch up on some overdue bills.

"I have no idea how you're saying goodbye to all this fabric," Chase said, coming up behind us, a certain solemnity to his voice.

"Please don't make me talk about it," I said. I pushed my hands into my back pockets.

"I still don't understand why you won't let Alex pay for the leather. He could even write it off as a business expense," Paige said.

"But this isn't Alex's thing. I *need* to do this for Isaac. He's been good to me the past couple of months. I need to do this on my own."

Paige nodded, but Chase shook his head.

"Honey, I doubt Alex would ever tell Isaac who actually paid for the leather. Isaac might not even realize the band is wearing jackets. He's going to be so completely mind-blown that you got Reggie Fletcher into the building in the first place, I'm not sure anything else will matter."

"Maybe not. But it matters to me."

Chase pulled me into a hug. "You really are too good for LeFranc, you know that, right?"

I laughed softly into his shoulder. "It's funny," I said, pulling away. "I feel so different about LeFranc now. The dream isn't quite so shiny anymore. I mean, except for you. I loved everything about working with you."

Chase placed his hand on my cheek. "I know, darling. I know."

Darius walked down the drive toward the car, his and Chase's bags slung over his shoulder.

"I wish you didn't have to leave," I said, giving Chase another hug. "The week has gone by too fast."

"Stupid adult responsibilities," Chase said. "I'm glad we got most of that horrid dress made while I was here."

I smiled. "All I need to do is sew the sequins on. Now I just hope something actually comes of it."

"Trust Alex," Chase said. "He's working hard. I'm sure he'll find what he's looking for."

Darius draped his arms around us both. "Let's

hope what he finds doesn't put *you* out of a job, too," he said, looking pointedly at Chase.

I froze. "Oh my gosh. I hadn't even thought of that. Do you think it could?"

Chase shot Darius a warning look. "I think it doesn't matter even if it does. I'll be fine. I'm resilient. And hello, have you seen me? New York fashion will never not love this."

I smiled, but Chase's reassurance did little to settle my uneasiness. There really was so much on the line.

"If Sasha really is a crook," Chase said, clearly sensing I wasn't convinced, "I don't want to work with her either. You're doing the right thing. Trust that. It'll all work out."

I nodded. "You guys are good to me."

"Have you thought about what happens next?" Darius asked. "After the wedding? Will you come back to New York?"

"Of course she'll go back to New York," Paige said. "Fashion is in New York."

I almost agreed with her, but somehow, the words wouldn't come. It was as though in the back of my mind, without me even realizing it had happened, a new reality had coalesced into something that felt more like *me* than New York ever had.

Spanish moss and cobblestone. Beach walks, shrimp and grits, open-air markets. Warm winters, hotter summers. Ocean breezes as I walked to work—a tiny design studio at the end of King Street with my name above the door.

Evenings hanging out with my brother.

Nights with Alex.

A longing that I'd never felt before swelled within me, nearly bringing tears to my eyes. I was homesick for a life I'd never even lived. But I wanted it. It still felt fragile. Dangerously fragile. But it was there, and it was real. As quickly as I acknowledged the existence of possibility, fear swept in, clutching my insides with vigor. Staying in Charleston would be abandoning so much. I'd dreamed of LeFranc because I'd dreamed of being the best. Of being a designer that people talked about, knew about, aspired to work with. I'd dreamed of runway shows and pulsing stage lights, of recognition and acclaim. I'd dreamed of being the best and I'd always told myself I wouldn't settle for anything less. I wasn't sure I could let all of that go.

"I don't know," I finally said, meaning every word. "I guess we'll wait and see."

Paige pulled her keys out and glanced at her watch. "You ready? We've got a lot to accomplish today."

I nodded but paused before getting in the car when Alex joined us on the street to say goodbye to Chase and Darius. He gave them each a hug, lingering a moment longer with Darius, almost like he was whispering something to him. Darius quickly nodded, confirming my suspicion, then gave him an encouraging pat on the back.

"Ohhh, secret somethings whispered between them," Chase said to me. "Know what that was about?"

"I don't have a clue," I said. "You?"

"No, but Darius will tell me eventually. He always does." Chase nudged my shoulder with his. "You're going to be okay, Dani."

I smiled. "I know. I'll see you at the wedding?"

"God help us," Chase said. "I hope you do."

Chapter Twenty-Four

Alex

2:43 a.m. I stared at my phone, bleary-eyed, and tried to figure out why my alarm was going off at such a stupid hour. But then I realized it wasn't an alarm. My phone was *ringing.* I propped myself up on my elbow and answered the call.

"Hello?" I was impressed at how *not asleep* I sounded.

"Alex, it's Angelica. Did I wake you?"

I hesitated just long enough.

"Oh, I did, didn't I? Sorry about that. I'm in London. I didn't think about the time difference until I'd already dialed."

"It's no problem," I said. "I'm glad you called. What's in London?"

"We brought the kids over to meet their grand-parents," Angelica said. "We're driving up to Cambridge in the morning."

I smiled. I hadn't seen Angelica since grad school. Except for an occasional interaction on social media, we'd lost touch after graduation. Imagining her married, the mother of a toddler and a newborn, was crazy. We weren't actually old enough for that, were we? Families. Kids. A slight twinge of jealousy welled up, taking me by surprise.

"How's the new baby?" I asked.

"Exhausting. But adorable as ever. At least she is now that we're no longer on a transatlantic flight."

"I bet."

"So I have news," Angelica said. "I've been through everything you sent over, and I think you're right. The evidence definitely points to embezzlement. I called in a few favors with a friend of mine—he's a private investigator—and get this. Solomon Rivers *is* a real person."

My heart sank. I had really hoped he was a made-up entity to cover Sasha's trail.

I swore under my breath.

"No, no, don't be disappointed," Angelica said. "This is actually better. He *is* a real person, but he doesn't have anything to do with fashion. He lives with his mother in Blue Springs, Alabama."

"Alabama?" I asked, cautiously.

"Yes. In the same town where the one and only Sasha Wellington grew up."

I sat all the way up, my heart rate climbing.

"Here's where it gets good," Angelica said. "Eleven years ago, Sasha Wellington had her name legally changed. From Sally Mabel Rivers. Solomon Rivers is her younger brother."

"Wow."

"So the LLC under Rivers' name is legit, licensed in the state of Alabama, but the cash is all in a bank in Brazil."

I swallowed. "How much?" I knew how much I'd tracked through her fake purchases, but I had a hunch she was colluding with someone else—someone in accounting who was willing to turn a blind eye—which meant money could have been siphoned out in multiple ways.

"Just over twelve million dollars," Angelica said.

The number nearly knocked the wind out of me. "Is there enough evidence to convict?" I asked.

Angelica hesitated. "I think so. There's a definite paper trail if you know what you're looking for, but my hunch is that she has someone working with her, covering things up on the accounting side. Otherwise, LeFranc would have caught her by now."

"Thanks for your help, Angelica. I owe you one."

"Don't worry about it. I'll give you a call when we're back in the states. I've heard Charleston is lovely. Maybe we'll come down for a visit."

We said our goodbyes and then, almost immediately, an email from Angelica popped up in my inbox, a summary of everything we'd talked about on the phone, complete with corroborating evidence. I chuckled when I looked over Sasha's petition for a name change. Sally Mabel. I never would have guessed.

Suddenly I didn't want to wait to tell Dani what

I'd learned. It was after 3 AM, but I didn't care. If it were me, I'd consider the news worth waking up for. I threw on a t-shirt and crept silently through the house. The November chill bit into my bare arms and legs as I crossed the garden to the studio door. Charleston had mild winters for the most part, but a front had come through and it was *frigid* outside. Inside the studio, I rubbed my hands up my arms in an effort to chase away the chill, then moved to the stairs.

Crouching beside Dani's bed, I suddenly thought better of my impromptu outing. She was sleeping so peacefully. Surely the news would keep until morning. But then, I was already there. If I didn't wake her up then I'd snuck all the way up to her room to watch her sleep, which felt worse than waking her up. I was excited; I wasn't a creep.

I reached out, gently nudging her shoulder. "Dani," I whispered. "Dani, wake up."

She opened her eyes, and jumped back, scrambling backward on her bed. I realized, belatedly, that in the darkness, she probably couldn't see who I was. I was just a dark shadow looming over her.

"Dani, don't freak out. It's Alex," I hurriedly said. "It's just me."

She reached over and turned on the lamp beside her bed. "Geez, Alex, you scared me half to death. What's wrong? Is everything okay?"

"Sorry. It was dumb to wake you. Everything's fine."

"Oh." She sat all the way up, then reached up and took down her hair. It had been piled high on top of her head and I watched, mesmerized as the blonde curls fell onto her shoulders. She ran her fingers across her scalp a few times and rubbed her eyes. She was just trying to wake up, and I was staring like an idiot. But how could I not? She was stunning.

"So did you want to hang out?" she said. "Or . . .?"

"Oh. Sorry. No. I, um, I have news."

She glanced at the clock on her nightstand and stifled a yawn. "It better be good."

"Do I need to give you a minute to wake up?"

She scrubbed her hands across her face one more time. "No, I'm good. Fully awake."

I sat on the side of her bed and launched into the information I'd learned from Angelica, explaining everything as best I could. I'd have to forward her the email, so she could see all the evidence for herself, but for now, it was incredibly vindicating just to know, to say the truth out loud.

"Sally Mabel?" Dani repeated. "I never saw that coming."

"I wonder how long it took to train the Alabama Southern out of her voice," I said.

"No kidding," Dani said. "I have a good ear

for it, and I never caught even a shadow of a Southern accent from her."

"The dress is ready, right?" I asked her.

She nodded. "I finished it right after Chase left. I had to so I could focus on the jackets."

I looked to the small sewing table she'd been using the past couple of weeks. Three of the four leather jackets for Red Renegade hung on a rack in the corner. "They look good."

"Thanks. I'm a little worried about fit. I mean, I had the band go into the Mood on Thirty-Seventh Street so my friend, Harper, could measure them for me, and I trust her measurements. But it's not quite the same as seeing them in person, myself, you know?"

"I'm sure they'll be perfect."

"So I guess it'll be a big couple of weeks," Dani said, settling back against the headboard.

"Right. The Compassion Experiment and then Florida a week later. I'll start working on our travel arrangements tomorrow."

"Don't forget about Paige's wedding the week after that."

"Right. Your week *will* be busy. How's all of that going?"

She shrugged and rolled her eyes. "It's been a little crazy. Paige's mom is super committed to making sure the wedding is worthy of Charleston's finest. She and Paige argued for ten minutes yesterday because the napkins arrived, and Ms. Perry doesn't think they're the exact shade of cream they need to be."

"Sounds . . . fun?"

"If anything, it's helped me realize what I *won't* care about if I ever end up getting married."

"Like napkin colors?"

"Absolutely not."

Dani stilled, the humor and lightness of the moment quickly transforming into something much more serious. She kept her eyes down for a moment before she reached out and touched my arm, her fingers resting lightly just above my wrist. "I know you have a lot on the line here. Thank you for everything you're doing. For helping me."

I twisted my hand, closing my fingers over top of hers, and held her hand, my thumb rubbing slow circles across her knuckles.

She looked up and met my gaze, her expression showing surprise, but she didn't pull her hand away.

"I'm happy to help," I said softly. I swallowed, craving her in a way I hadn't experienced in over a year.

I tugged her hand toward me, a gentle invitation, and she leaned forward. Our foreheads touched and I moved my free hand to her face, cradling her cheek. "Dani," I whispered softly.

Her breath hitched and then she gasped just before a tear slid onto my fingers.

She was crying?

She tilted her head up, closing the fraction of space between us and pressed her lips against mine. Fire ignited inside me, overwhelming my senses until every heartbeat echoed the sound of her name. I couldn't get close enough, couldn't breathe in enough of her, touch enough of her. When she pulled away, breaking the kiss only seconds after it started, I stilled. Her shoulders dropped and her eyes closed, and I knew, immediately, what was coming.

"I can't, Alex." She reached up and took my hand, still touching her cheek, and held it to her lips. She kissed my palm then dropped my hand and wiped at her tears. "I'm sorry."

I shook my head, my longing suddenly replaced with intense regret. We had only just begun to be friends again and I'd likely ruined everything. "Don't, Dani. It should be me apologizing. I shouldn't have—I'm sorry." I stood and moved to the doorway.

"Alex, wait."

I turned. She looked so small sitting alone in the middle of the large bed.

"It isn't that I don't want—"

"Dani, please," I said, cutting her off. "You don't owe me an explanation. It's all right."

She closed her eyes and shook her head, pulling her bottom lip into her teeth. Everything about her expression spoke of how much she didn't want to hurt me. But I realized with startling clarity how inevitable that hurt actually was. I'd never stopped loving her. And probably never would.

Once outside, I leaned against the studio door, letting the cold air wash over my skin. I pulled it into my lungs, a pitiful attempt to quell the fire Dani had ignited in my gut. I tried to tell myself it wouldn't ever work between us. We wanted different things, dreamed of different things. But my heart wouldn't be convinced; the only thing my heart wanted was her.

Chapter Twenty-Five

Dani

The flight to New York was mostly uneventful. The rest of the team wouldn't fly up until the following morning, but I'd wanted an extra day to deliver the custom jackets to Reggie and the rest of Red Renegade; the jackets were, in my not-so-humble estimation, freaking spectacular, so I'd convinced Alex to book me an earlier flight. Instead of sending me on my own, he'd booked flights for Isaac and himself as well, mentioning some important meeting with the venue people they needed to attend. I was pretty sure there wasn't actually a meeting, but I wasn't going to argue.

I leaned back into my first-class seat, a luxury Isaac had insisted on. "It's a business expense," he had said. "You're flying first class with the rest of us, end of story."

I'd caved on the New York tickets, but I'd put my foot down when Alex had tried to upgrade our tickets to Key West. Even though Isaac was coming along, he was only coming as an accomplice to *my* evil plan. No matter how he stretched it, he couldn't write off Florida as a business expense and there was no way I was paying for a first-class ticket. It had been hard enough letting him pay for my coach seat. The cash I'd had left over after buying the leather had been enough to cover a plane ticket, but I was so cash poor, I'd hated to spend it. Not if I wanted to keep my phone turned on and my credit cards in good standing. When Isaac had offered to loan me enough to cover my ticket, I'd relented.

The list of money I owed my brother kept getting longer and longer. But I would pay him back. Somehow, I would get through all this madness, find a new job, and figure out a way to pay him back.

My phone dinged from my bag, stashed under the seat in front of me, and I reached for it, remembering that I hadn't yet switched it to airplane mode. Before I did, I opened my messages. There was a new text from Chase.

Food for thought, the text read. *Sasha has hired and fired two assistants since you left. Seems like she can't find anyone as amazing as you.*

Ha. Maybe. Probably she just couldn't find anyone as gullible as me.

"What is it?" Alex said.

I turned the phone so he could read Chase's message. "From Chase," I said.

Alex's eyes passed over the phone, then he nodded. "Interesting. What do you think it means?"

I shrugged. "Probably nothing. It doesn't really change our plans."

"It does make you feel good though, right? You were good at your job. Apparently irreplaceable."

I stashed my phone back in my bag and turned toward the window. Talking about Sasha, thinking about my time at LeFranc left me uneasy. It hadn't been so hard in Charleston; I was removed enough that it had felt easier. Easier to breathe. Easier to forget. Now I was flying back to New York. To the city I'd dreamed of my entire life and then abandoned. I reminded myself that this trip wasn't about me, which helped, but only a little.

I said a silent prayer that our luggage wouldn't get lost somewhere between Charleston and La Guardia and took several deep breaths to try and settle my nerves. I generally loved flying. Was it Chase's text that had me feeling so off-kilter?

Alex shifted next to me, brushing up against my arm. I leaned into him, almost involuntarily, but then retreated back to the window. What was I doing? No, Chase's text wasn't the only thing messing with my head. Chase. Sasha. New York. Red Renegade. Alex. Paige. I leaned my head against the cool windowpane and closed my eyes. I was just shy of a complete mess.

The past week and a half leading up to the Compassion Experiment had been fraught with more tension and awkwardness than I'd ever experienced before. Alex had been polite, gentle, perfectly respectful. But it had almost made things worse. He was acting on the assumption that I had stopped the kiss and sent him away because I didn't *want* him. Which was the furthest thing from the truth. It had taken every ounce of my willpower not to scoot over and pull him right down beside me.

But wanting him physically wasn't the same thing as *needing* him. And as sure as I was that we still had chemistry, that I still cared about him, maybe even still loved him, I was too afraid to talk about it, too afraid of what loving him meant. Alex had made it clear he liked the Charleston version of himself much more than the New York version—that he'd never loved his life in the city.

If I decided to go back to New York, to find a new job, would he go with me? Or would loving him mean giving it up? The flicker of a dream I'd imagined once before passed through my mind—a Charleston version of my future self that had stirred so much longing. I looked over at Alex, wishing I had the courage to take his hand, admit what I was feeling, admit how terrifying it all was.

There were still too many questions, too many uncertainties tainting every one of my thoughts. I couldn't make sense of anything without immediately second-guessing my certainty and starting the whole vicious cycle of doubt all over again.

Of course, I couldn't overlook Alex's motives.

Darius had suggested that Alex was helping me get Paige's dress back because he still cared about me. But Alex's relationship with the LeFrancs was even more complex than his relationship with me. His need to prove to Alicio that he'd been right about Sasha all along was intense, too intense to assume this entire shenanigan was only a grand gesture of love. It had never been that simple.

I had to wait.

Get through the wedding.

See where everything fell after, well, after everything.

The venue was a large warehouse space in Brooklyn, with tall ceilings and huge windows and a great view of the Statue of Liberty. The decorations felt like Christmas, but not in the cheesy Hallmark movie kind of way. No poinsettia. No mistletoe or fake fireplaces. Instead, it was a little more modern, a little more dressed down.

The Christmas trees lining the stage were full of tiny white lights but didn't have any ornaments on them. They really only served as a backdrop for the words. Oversized posters filled the venue, all displaying quotes about kindness and love and reaching out to others.

Center stage, a huge wall of video screens displayed the Compassion Experiment logo and hashtag. Later, when the scavenger hunt was going on, the screens would show multiple live streams of the teams as they moved through the tasks on their list, racing to be the first one back to the party.

It was pretty incredible to see it all shaping up the way Isaac and Alex had envisioned. Pride swelled in my chest and tears filled my eyes. I suddenly understood the Isaac that *he'd* always wanted to be. He'd always been brilliant, but I'd been stupid to think he could only use that brilliance one way. For the first time in a very long time, I was genuinely, intensely proud of all that my brother had accomplished.

I crossed the street to the hotel where we'd stayed the past couple of nights and headed for the elevator. I pressed the button and waited, filling the time by pulling out my phone to make sure, for the billionth time, that the soundcheck with the band was going okay.

Yesterday afternoon Alex had kept Isaac busy long enough for me to grab an Uber and take the jackets to Reggie's apartment, where the entire band had gathered for a rehearsal. The jackets all fit as well as I had hoped, and they'd been genuinely pleased to receive them. Even so, I couldn't shake my worry that something might still go wrong. I wanted to surprise Isaac almost more than I wanted to get back Paige's dress. Something *couldn't* go wrong.

I'd ended up having to pull Vinnie and Tyler in on the surprise in order to make the soundcheck happen without Isaac finding out. On my own, I never would have gotten Isaac out of the venue long enough to get Red Renegade in. But then Vinnie had needed to buy some sort of splicing cable that the A/V company didn't have and had roped Isaac into going with him. His performance was practically Oscar-worthy.

Just before the elevator dinged, a text came in from Tyler letting me know that the band had completed their soundcheck and was sequestered in their private green room where they would remain until it was time for their performance. Isaac, he'd said, was on his way to the hotel to change. I breathed out a sigh. Everything was actually going according to plan.

After my late-night conversation with Mom when she'd challenged me to consider Isaac with a new perspective, I'd spent some time thinking about the things she'd said. It hadn't taken long for me to come up with my own list of the small ways I'd seen him bring joy to other people, his YouTube show notwithstanding. He was ridiculous in so many ways. And his fashion sense was completely nonexistent. And sometimes his inability to tone down the silliness left me completely exhausted. But I'd never given

Isaac enough credit. He deserved for tonight to be a win in every way it possibly could be.

The elevator doors dinged open as I slid my phone back into my purse. Alex stepped off the elevator.

"Hey," he said, the Southern lilt to his voice evident enough to turn the heads of the women waiting next to me.

"Hi. I'm just going up to change." I looked him up and down, trying not to dwell too long on his perfectly fitted suit or the intentional stubble lining his jawline. Maybe *that's* what had caught the attention of the women standing next to me. I swallowed. "You look really nice."

"Thanks. Is everything set with the band?"

I nodded. "Soundcheck is done and they're in the green room."

Alex smiled. "You did good, Dani."

"I'm still nervous. You don't think Isaac has figured it out, do you?"

"I'm positive he hasn't," Alex said. "I'm not proud of how many lies I've told to keep him in the dark, but he doesn't have a clue. He might be a little disappointed we don't actually have Harris Town booked, but I think he'll forgive me once he sees who *is* going to close the show."

The elevator had come and gone and then arrived again since we'd started talking. When the door slid open a second time, I stepped inside. "Going up," I said awkwardly. *Going up?*

I fought to keep a straight face despite my stupid comment.

Alex nodded. "I'll see you shortly." He held my gaze with an intensity that nearly made my knees weak until the doors closed, cutting me off from view.

A low moan escaped from somewhere behind me and I turned to find an older woman standing in the corner of the elevator, her handbag clutched to her chest. "To have a man look at me like that," she said when we made eye contact. "I'd hold on to him."

I managed a smile. I'd tried that once before. Was it possible I wanted to try again?

Chapter Twenty-Six

Alex

I didn't exactly have a reason to hang around the hotel lobby. And there were any number of things I could have done to keep busy across the street at the venue. But I had my phone on me. If anything were to go wrong, I'd know and could be there in a matter of seconds. That argument worked for a solid twenty minutes before I nearly caved, deciding I couldn't wait any longer before checking in with Isaac in person. But then the elevator doors dinged open and I'd never been so happy to have wasted twenty minutes playing Ball Blast on my phone.

Dani stepped off the elevator, wearing a red dress that both hugged and flowed at the same time, flattering her figure in an understated, classy way. I'd spent time enough around women who dressed in a way that begged for attention; that wasn't Dani. She exuded confidence, poise, elegance.

She smiled as she approached in a way that filled me with hope. She'd pushed me away, and I respected her need to do so. But maybe she wouldn't push me away forever. "You're still here," she said.

"Yes." I slipped my phone into my pocket. "I realized I hadn't yet defeated level one hundred and twelve on Ball Blast and it really felt important that I take care of that. Now. Here. In the lobby of this very elegant hotel."

She raised an eyebrow and I shrugged. "It seemed like an appropriate location for such an important task."

"I'm sure." Her eyes said she completely understood why I was still around, but they also said she didn't really mind it.

"You look beautiful."

Her eyes dropped to the floor, but only for a moment before she met my gaze head-on. I'd always loved that about her. She never shied away from a compliment. "Thank you. I thought the dress felt like Christmas."

"Ah, see? I had the same thought." I motioned to my red and green striped tie.

"I noticed that earlier," she said. "Very festive." She motioned to the front doors of the hotel. "Shall we?"

As we turned, we both froze, until Dani reached over and gripped my hand. Sasha and Alicio, as well as Gabriel and Victor, were directly in front of us, not ten yards away.

"What are they doing here?" Dani asked, her voice strangled and small.

"Having a family dinner, apparently." The restaurant in the hotel lobby was nice enough to warrant their patronage, but still. What were the odds?

Dani dropped my hand, and slipped an arm around my waist, turning me slightly so she could lean up on tiptoe and whisper in my ear. "We're together, all right? Dating again. Desperately in love. And we can't wait to see them at the wedding next week."

I leaned back and looked at her, a question in my eyes. "What? Why?"

She pressed her body against me, placing a small kiss just below my ear. "Trust me."

Sasha noticed us first. Her eyes narrowed before she slid an arm through Alicio's, pulling herself closer to him.

Dani tugged me forward. "Sasha," she said as we approached, a wide, genuine smile on her face. "It's so lovely to see you again." She let go of my arm and leaned forward, giving Sasha air kisses on either side of her face.

I pushed my hands into my pockets, nodding a brief acknowledgment to my stepfather, and brothers. Gabriel, at least, extended his hand. "How are you, Alex? Merry Christmas."

"Thanks. Same to you."

He looked over his shoulder at the rest of his family. "We didn't know you were in the city or we would have asked you to join us."

It wasn't true, but I appreciated that Gabriel would try and make me feel better anyway.

"That's all right. I'm working tonight, actually. We've got a thing across the street."

"Oh. Cool." He looked at Dani. "You're back together?"

I nodded, wishing I didn't have to lie to say yes. "Yeah. We are." Dani still spoke to Sasha, her expression warm, her body language open. What was she doing? "I'm bringing her to the wedding next week."

"You're coming to the wedding?" Victor said, suddenly joining the conversation.

Alicio turned as well, his eyes meeting mine.

"I *did* receive an invitation," I said hesitantly.

Alicio smiled tightly. "Of course. If you want to come, we'd love to have you."

"I think it's great that you're coming," Gabriel said, though his kindness did little to kill the tension that hung in the air around the rest of us.

Dani slipped her arm through mine. "Ready to go?" she whispered. She turned back to my stepfamily. "It's so good to see you all. Merry Christmas."

We pushed through the hotel lobby doors and moved toward the crosswalk at the corner. Dani gripped my hand so tightly, I almost couldn't feel my fingers, but I was glad of it. The pain kept me anchored against the waves of feeling washing over me. Anger. Resentment. Sadness.

I didn't want to be a part of the LeFranc family. I didn't like what they stood for. I didn't care for their lifestyle. And yet, seeing them all together like that, imagining my mother on Alicio's arm instead of Sasha? It burned worse than I wanted it to. They were the closest thing I had to family, even though they were the furthest thing from what a family actually should be. I stopped on the sidewalk, overwhelmed by a surge of loneliness so intense, I could hardly move.

Dani paused and turned to face me, nudging me toward the building behind us, out of the main path of the sidewalk. A sharp wind blew past and Dani drew in a breath, closing her eyes for a moment.

"You're not wearing a coat," I said.

She shook her head dismissively. "We're only walking across the street. I didn't think I'd need one." She gripped my arms, just above the elbows. "Are you okay?"

I nodded. The loneliness wasn't gone, but it was accompanied by a sense of resignation that at least made me feel like I could keep walking.

"You don't need them, Alex," Dani said.

My heart warmed that she'd sensed my feelings so easily, but her words didn't change the fact that some part of me still felt like I *did* need them. Or maybe it was just that I wanted them to need me.

"Come on," I said. Taking Dani's hand, I led us across the street and to the doors of the Compassion Experiment venue, where the bouncers had already started checking tickets and admitting the first guests. The bouncer closest to us waved us through. Inside, we crossed a large, open area, pausing at the foot of a wide set of stairs that led to the main event space.

"What did you say to Sasha?" I asked.

She grinned. "That I missed working for her, and that time away had made me realize what a wonderful opportunity she had given me."

I narrowed my eyes. "I had no idea you were such a good liar."

"It wasn't totally a lie," Dani said. "I do miss *some* things about working at LeFranc, and by forcing me to leave, she did give me other opportunities."

"That's true," I said, though I still wasn't sure I understood her motivation.

"And now, when we arrive at the wedding next week, it won't feel so out of the blue when I text Sasha and ask her if there is anything I can do for her. If she doesn't have a good assistant, she's probably going to need help."

"Which means it will be that much easier for you to swap out the dresses."

She grinned. "Exactly."

"I'm impressed. A little terrified, but definitely impressed."

We stopped at the top of the stairs. The venue was buzzing with energy, guests filling the tables and chairs scattered through the space.

Isaac stood on the stage doing a soundcheck.

"Is Isaac wearing a tie?" Dani asked.

"He looks good, doesn't he? I told him since he's the Master of Ceremonies, he had to wear one."

Dani shook her head. "The breadth of your influence never ceases to amaze me."

Everything progressed smoothly as the night went on, except for one scavenger hunt team that was down a team member because of the flu. But even that crisis only lasted a moment. Isaac held an impromptu trivia game on stage for anyone willing to join the team and gave the open spot to the last woman standing.

The man was quicker on his feet than anyone I knew.

The best part of the night was watching the video feeds of the teams, and all the acts of kindness they performed. Kids in hospitals opening presents. Unsuspecting grocery shoppers having their carts paid for in full. Free hugs. Isaac had managed to orchestrate an event that showed the very best of humanity.

Just past eleven, when all the teams had returned to the party, and the opening acts had finished their sets, I met Dani backstage. "Are you ready?" I whispered.

She gave me a slight nod before Mushroom materialized beside her and handed her a microphone. "The stage lights will be down when the band gets in place, and they'll stay down, except for one spotlight out front. When you see my cue, walk to that spot, turn on the microphone using the little button right here, and you'll be ready to roll."

Dani nodded. "Got it."

Moments later, I watched as she took center stage. Isaac, who had been distracted by Tyler long enough for Red Renegade to take the stage, reappeared at the sound of Dani's voice and immediately crossed to where I stood watching her. "What is she doing?" he asked.

I only smiled. "She's about to give you the greatest Christmas present you've ever gotten."

Chapter Twenty-Seven

Dani

Late Christmas morning, I still hadn't talked to Isaac. Not really, anyway. He'd given me a bone-crushing hug right after I'd walked off the stage, but then he'd been so wrapped up in hanging out with Red Renegade, taking pictures with Red Renegade, talking to Reggie Fletcher with unbridled enthusiasm, there hadn't been time for a conversation.

Not that I'd been expecting one. I'd made him happy; that was enough.

Yet, when he found me lounging in the hotel lobby, a cup of coffee in hand, my heart swelled even while a wave of nervousness washed over me. *Had* I made him happy? Did he recognize the gesture as the apology it was meant to be?

"Hey," he said, dropping into the chair across from me. "Where'd you get the coffee? I could use some."

I motioned to the far side of the lobby, where a small café sat nestled in the corner. "Over there. But here." I held out my cup. "This is my second one. You can finish it."

He took it, taking a long swallow before setting the cup down on the small table between us. "So last night," he said, leaning back in his chair.

"It was an amazing event, Isaac. You should be really proud."

He nodded. "We raised a lot of money. More than we expected. But that's not why I brought it up."

I smiled.

"I don't know how you pulled it off, Dani, but that . . . that was the greatest thing anyone has ever done for me."

"Darius helped too," I said.

"Did you make the jackets they were all wearing?"

I nodded. "It was the one thing they demanded in exchange for doing the event."

Isaac's eyes flashed with understanding. "That's why you sold all your fabric."

I winced. "I was hoping you wouldn't realize that had happened."

"Thank you. Truly. It—" He swallowed. "It means a lot."

"I'm sorry I was a jerk about your YouTube channel."

"I'm sorry for always calling you Dandelion."

I laughed. "No you're not."

He grinned. "Okay. I'm not. But I'll stop doing it anyway." He leaned forward and drained the last of the coffee. "So, what's going on with you and Alex?"

I groaned. "What, we're getting along now so I have to tell you everything?"

He shrugged. "Only if you want to. I'm just saying. The fact that *something* is going on is written all over both your faces. I'm hoping you'll figure it out so the rest of us don't have to keep tiptoeing around the subject. Just get together already so everything can go back to normal."

I leaned my head on the cushion behind me. "If only it were that easy."

"Are you thinking you might stay in Charleston?"

"I don't know. Maybe? I might have to. Next week might not work out the way we're all hoping."

"True." He nodded. "Well, if it matters, I think it'd be cool if you stayed." He ran a hand through his hair. "It's been nice having you around."

"You mean it's been nice—"

He cut me off. "Not just because of the food." He stood, moving behind me, and dropped a hand onto my shoulder.

I smiled and slid my hand over his.

"I'm getting another coffee," he said. "You want anything?"

I shook my head no and gave his hand a quick squeeze before letting him go.

Two days later, the seven of us sat around Isaac's living room in Charleston sorting through the accumulation of Christmas cards and fan mail that had arrived over the holidays. With all of us so focused on the Compassion Experiment, Isaac had fallen behind on reading it all. I was just impressed that he *did* read it all.

"Hey, listen to this one," Alex said from his place on the floor. "Dear Isaac. Thank you for the episode where you talked about saying something nice to one of our teachers. I made my history teacher cry which was weird, but also awesome. Sincerely, James. From San Bernardino, California."

"I like this one better," I said. "Dear Random I, I'd like to marry you. I know I'm too young right now, but if you wait for me, I'll grow up soon. Love, Avery Morris, age twelve. From Springfield, Illinois."

"This girl sent you stickers," Tyler said. "Of your face."

"What?" Isaac said. "Let me see."

Tyler handed them over. "I think she drew them."

"Dude. These are amazing. They're totally going on the air."

The doorbell rang and I jumped up. "That's probably Paige." I picked up my overnight bag from beside the couch.

"So let me get this straight," Mushroom said. "Her parents are giving her a fancy vacation house as a wedding gift, and you're holing up in the fanciest hotel in Charleston so they can move all the new fancy furniture in without Paige seeing it?"

"Ridiculous, right?"

"I think it's nice," Alex said, though he didn't look up from the card he held in his hand.

Tyler tossed a pillow at his head. "You would. You're used to that kind of money."

Alex grinned good-naturedly, deflecting the pillow with his arm. "Pretty sure you make more money than I do. I meant that I thought it was nice that Dani and Paige would get to spend some time together one last time before the wedding."

My stomach swirled as I thought about the wedding that would happen first, *before* Paige's wedding. I looked at Alex, waiting for him to finally meet my gaze. "I'll be back in time to pack for Islamorada."

He nodded, that indefinable *something* passing between us, gripping my gut and making me feel as though my life depended on me running to him and throwing myself into his arms.

I tightened my hand around the straps of my bag.

"Okay," he said.

I swallowed hard—what was wrong with me?—and willed my feet to move around the corner and into the entryway. I paused when I heard Tyler laughing. "Okay," he said in a sing-songy voice. "I'll miss you, Dani. I *loooove* you, Dani."

"Shut up," Alex said, followed by an indistinguishable grunt, then more laughter.

The doorbell rang again, startling me out of my stillness. I threw the front door open, but Paige wasn't behind it. Instead, a delivery man stood on the porch, three large boxes beside him. "Delivery for Danielle Bishop." He held out his tablet, asking for a signature. "Sign here."

"What is it?" I asked.

"I just deliver them, ma'am."

I nodded and thanked him before shifting the boxes one by one into the entryway. I pulled the tape off the first box and gasped. The box was filled with fabric. *My* fabric. I pulled out several yards of emerald green twill. I'd planned to make a pencil skirt out of it someday. Underneath, I found the calico chintz I'd been saving, confident it would be big again within a year or two, as well as the half-dozen yards of lavender satin I'd scored at a Mood flash sale. Movement caught my eye, and I looked up to find Isaac leaning against the wall in front of me.

"You did this?"

He shrugged. "I'm surprised they got here so quickly."

I shook my head. "You big jerk."

"It's not all of it. There were two pieces they'd already—wait. Did you just call me a jerk?"

I laughed, tears coming to my eyes. "Why can't I do something nice for you without you doing

328

something back? How am I ever going to even the score if you keep loaning me money and furnishing my bedroom and buying back all of my fabric?"

He crouched down next to the box, fingering the satin that sat draped across my lap. "That's just it. Sometimes it isn't about keeping score. You don't always have to be winning, Dani. Sometimes life really is just about being nice to people. About doing what you want, instead of what makes you first."

The doorbell rang again and we both looked up. "That probably *is* Paige," I said.

Isaac stood.

As I stood and put the fabric back in the box, shifting it so it sat to the side of the entryway, it felt as though a piece of something I'd long been missing clicked into place in my heart.

I didn't need New York.

I didn't need to *win* the fashion industry.

I really could just do something because it made me happy.

I paced from the window to the door, then back again inside my tiny hotel room on Islamorada. We were only five minutes away from the LeFranc summer estate which made everything feel real in a way it hadn't up to that point. We were *in* Florida. Committed. The thought made me jittery and uncomfortable. On what had to have been my five hundredth pass around the room, I gave up and grabbed my phone, my fingers hovering over Alex's name on my screen.

I can't sleep, I finally texted.

Alex replied immediately. *Me neither.*

TV?

It took a full minute for his response to come through. *Come on over.*

I grabbed my hoodie, tossing it on over my pajamas, and slipped on my flip-flops, trying not to think about why it had taken him so long to respond.

Alex was waiting at his open hotel-room door when I reached him. He backed into the room and held the door open for me, closing it once I was inside.

"Hi," he said.

"Hi."

Nervous energy had been pulsing through me all night as I'd stressed and worried about Sasha's wedding, but *this* nervous energy felt entirely different. Heat radiated off Alex's body and I itched to step closer, to breathe him in, to feel his solid warmth under my hands. I was tired of being angry. Tired of feeling hurt. Tired of being afraid and nervous and uncertain. But there was nothing uncertain about the man standing in front of me.

"Do you want—"

I lunged across the small space between us and cut his words off with a kiss.

He stepped back, obviously startled, but steadied himself quickly without breaking the kiss and wrapped his arms around my back. I took hold of his t-shirt, bunching it in my fists as I pulled him even closer. I tilted my head to the side and deepened the kiss, eliciting a whimpering moan from Alex that told me just how much he didn't mind my forwardness. My hands moved up to his face then slid into his hair.

There were no guarantees concerning the next forty-eight hours of my life. Things could go perfectly well, or they could completely explode in my face. Either outcome could have a significant impact on my future.

But none of that mattered. Not with Alex in front of me, not with his hands on my skin, his lips tracing kisses down the side of my neck.

"Dani, what are we doing?" he whispered.

I arched my neck, leaning it back toward his lips. "I don't know but I think we're really good at it."

He planted a kiss on the curve of my jaw, right below my ear just as a knock sounded on the door behind us.

We both froze, Alex's hands tightening around my arms.

"Alex? You still up?" Isaac said through the

door. "I'm going downstairs for a quick drink. You want to come?"

Alex cleared his throat. "I think I'm okay. Thanks though."

"You sure?"

I leaned my forehead against Alex's chest and smiled.

"Yep. I'm sure," Alex said, laughter in his voice.

"Cool. See you in the morning."

As soon as Isaac's footsteps retreated down the hall, I half-expected us to pick back up where we'd left off. But then Alex released my arms and took a faint step away from me, perching himself on the edge of the dresser.

I stood in silence waiting for him to say something, but he didn't even look up. My confidence fizzled. What had just happened? Everything had felt so right and then in a blink, it was wrong again. "So I guess I should get to bed?" I finally said, my voice soft.

Alex met my gaze. There was warmth there, but also a distance I couldn't quite define. He'd pulled away from me, and I had no idea why. "That's probably a good idea," he said gently. "We've got a big couple of days ahead of us."

"Right." I pressed my forehead into my hands, mortified to be so blatantly rejected. "Got it."

Alex sighed. "Dani—"

"It's fine. I get it. I was just feeling . . . and you

were always . . . but you're right. It's a big day tomorrow. We should focus."

Alex reached for my arm, tugging me toward him. He wrapped his arms around my back, and I settled in, resting my hands on his chest. "We were always good at this part," he said, sadness tinging his voice. "But it can't just be about that."

The logical part of my brain knew that he was right to stop things. We still needed to have a conversation about what was happening. About what it all meant. About New York and Charleston and what a potential future together would even look like. But standing in his arms just felt so good.

I tilted my head up, willing him to kiss me again. "What if this is what I want?"

His jaw tightened. "This? Right now? This *moment* is what you want? Or I'm what you want?" He released me a second time, this time walking clean to the other side of the room. "There's too much at stake for me to do *this,* without an answer to that question. I can't go through losing you again."

So this was the conversation we needed to have? Right here, at midnight in some random hotel room in the Florida Keys?

"What do you want, Dani?" Alex asked again.

"I don't know," I said, desperation filling my voice. "Is that what you want me to say? My entire world has been turned upside down the past few months. Everything I ever thought I wanted, everything I spent my entire life dreaming about, it's all different now. I can't just make sense of it all right now, here, because you ask me to."

"That's not what I said. You take all the time you need. I think I've been pretty good about giving you space when you've asked for it. We kissed a month ago, Dani, and then we never even talked about it. All I said was that I couldn't do this"—he motioned between us—"until you *do* figure out what you want." He ran a hand across his face. "No matter how much I want to."

I moved to the hotel room door but turned back, one hand resting on the doorknob. "What do *you* want, Alex?"

He didn't even hesitate. "I want you, Dani. You. Us. All of it. I never stopped wanting you."

The next morning, Alex knocked on my hotel room door just after ten. "Morning," he said. "You ready to go?"

I nodded, moving aside to let him into the room. "I think so. I didn't get much sleep last night."

His eyes spoke understanding, but he didn't bring up our conversation from the night before, not that I really wanted him to. There was too much riding on the success of our day for us to get waylaid by another heart-to-heart.

"I can't stop thinking about all the things that might go wrong."

He moved like he meant to touch my shoulder, but then his hand dropped, and he shoved it into his pocket. "It's all going to work out; I promise."

There was no way he could actually guarantee as much, but I appreciated his attempts to assure me anyway. "What if we just leave?" I said, yielding to my fear. "Paige has a dress she can wear next week. She doesn't need this one."

"Is that really the only reason we're here today?"

A part of me thought it actually *had* become my only reason. After my fabric-induced epiphany with Isaac before we left, I'd been feeling more and more sure that I didn't actually need a way back into fashion's good graces. But the look in Alex's eyes told me it wasn't *his* only reason. He needed to tell Alicio the truth about Sasha for personal, validating reasons, and I wasn't about to prevent him from seizing the opportunity. Sasha really *was* a criminal. If we had the means to stop her? There wasn't a good reason not to do so.

The plan was for me and Alex to head to the house that afternoon. Alex still had enough claim on the family, he assumed he'd have a place to stay in the house. He had a suite of rooms he'd always used in the past and since he *had* RSVP'd, he felt pretty sure they'd left his rooms empty for him. Taking me as his date was the easiest way to hide me in plain sight, so to speak, and gave me a legit reason to be sleeping under the same roof as the wedding dress. The fact that we'd run into his family on Christmas Eve and had appeared to be together only cemented the likelihood of my acceptance.

Isaac would be on standby, ready to shuttle the dress off the premises as quickly as I could sneak it away. He'd promised us early that morning that he had a plan for securing transportation that would get him onto the estate with ease, but Alex and I were both doubtful.

Alex's phone rang and he glanced down, answering the call then turning on the speaker. "Isaac? You're on speaker. Dani is here."

"Perfect. Go look out the window."

We looked at each other, wondering what Isaac was up to, then crossed the room and stepped out onto a small balcony. Below us in the parking lot, Isaac stood in front of a large van, a giant bouquet of flowers painted on the side.

"It's perfect, right?" he said. "I only had to pay the guy two hundred bucks to borrow it until tomorrow night."

I shook my head and laughed, but I was hardly surprised.

Alex echoed my thoughts. "I think your brother could convince the Pope to lend him his motorcade if it were truly necessary."

Minutes later, Isaac was back in the hotel room wearing a blue polo shirt, a florist's logo embroidered on the breast pocket.

"He gave you his shirt as well?" I asked.

"I had to trade him the one I was wearing," Isaac said. "No big deal."

The three of us went over the plan one more time.

"Once we arrive this evening," Alex said to Isaac, "we'll text you and let you know of any additional security measures that are in place at the house. At the very least, the gate will be guarded, but with the flower van and a claim of a last-minute delivery, you should be able to gain access."

"Wear a hat though," I said to Isaac. "And sunglasses. We can't risk someone recognizing you and wondering when *Random I* started moonlighting as a flower delivery guy."

"Got it," Isaac said. "So I wait for a briefing on security systems tonight, then tomorrow I hang out here until you give me the signal, I come to the house, you hand me the dress, then I whisk it away to a secure location."

He made it sound so easy. But there were five hundred variables we weren't sure about yet. And really wouldn't be sure about until we were in the house and had determined, one, how much welcome would be extended to Alex, and two, how easy it would be to get to the dress. Then

337

there was the matter of deciding *when* to make the swap. In the middle of the night? Right before the wedding, seconds before Sasha would be putting it on? Timing was essential.

If Chase's text was right, and my brief conversation with Sasha had been enough to plant the seed, my hope was that texting her and asking if I could assist her would be enough for her to let me in. It was risky. If Sasha thought too hard about it, she'd recognize the risks of letting me close. But I was banking on the size of her ego. She'd believed me when I told her I thought I'd made a mistake in leaving. She loved herself that much, she'd naturally believed I'd want to come back.

When I'd told Isaac of my plan, he'd rolled his eyes. "Oh, gross," he'd said. "I mean, it'll probably work, but gross."

There was always the possibility that she would say no, but my gut told me she wasn't going to.

"Meanwhile," Isaac continued, gesturing to Alex, "you'll talk to stepdaddy dearest and let him know who he's really about to marry."

"Do you think he'll actually go through with the wedding once he knows?" I asked.

"I hope not," Alex said. "I *really* hope not."

After saying goodbye to Isaac and getting an unexpected good luck hug, I followed Alex to a *really* nice BMW parked in the hotel parking lot. I paused on the sidewalk. "Is this *your* car?" I had been expecting a rental. I'd ridden with Isaac from the airport in Miami, Alex claiming he had a quick errand to run and would meet us at the hotel. From the looks of it, his errand involved a seventy-five-thousand-dollar luxury sedan.

Alex looked a little sheepish. "Yes?"

I didn't answer, not even attempting to hide the fact that my jaw was nearly touching the concrete.

"It lives at the summer house," he said. He hesitated and a flash of *something* flitted across his face. "I don't drive it much, but I figured I'd better pick it up before everything went down. I'm not sure how welcome I'll be after."

He popped the trunk and I placed my bag inside, then draped Sasha's replacement dress, safely tucked away in an opaque garment bag, across the top. It was a masterpiece, that dress. With Chase's help, it had pulled together beautifully. The silhouette of the dress was actually pretty elegant, but we'd glitzed it up with a layer of Las Vegas-style trashy that would have made Liberace proud. It was perfect. *Awful.* But perfect.

I climbed into the car, reveling in the butter-soft leather and finely finished interior. "So you've already been to the house? Do they know you're here?"

He shifted his weight. "No. The house has several garages. I had moved the car to the one farthest away from the main house. It's mostly used for lawn equipment. They'd probably forgotten it was even there."

Several *garages?* "What have you been driving in Charleston?" I asked. I couldn't actually remember what kind of car it was, though I'd ridden in it a few times when he'd taken me to the grocery store, and when we'd taken Chase to the beach.

"Oh. That's my *other* car."

I shot him a look. "Seriously?"

"I know it sounds ridiculous. And I've been meaning to sell one or the other."

"The other," I said emphatically. "Sell the other one and keep this one. It's beautiful."

"It was a graduation present from my mother," he said simply.

I looked over and noticed how tightly he gripped the steering wheel, his eyes hyperfocused on the road in front of him. Was that why he never drove it? Because it was a gift from his mom? Or maybe that was the reason he couldn't sell it? I suddenly felt, quite keenly, just how much Alex had kept hidden over the years. The realization felt a little like a punch to the gut. What hadn't he told me? Why had I never realized how hard working for Alicio must have been for him?

I let my mind wander back to the night we'd gone to see *Hamilton*. I'd kissed him in the theater, but it had been brief. Heartfelt, yes. But brief. But then, after the show, he'd kissed me on the stairs of my apartment building, and it had nearly been my undoing.

We'd stood hand in hand, me one step above him so that our faces were nearly level. "I loved watching you watch the show," he'd whispered softly. "It makes me happy to see you happy."

With sudden clarity, I reframed so many of our experiences in New York through that filter. Alex watching *me,* happy because I was happy. He'd smiled through the fashion shows and the galas, the highbrow parties in elite clubs. He'd used his influence to get us into places that I never would have had access to on my own. But never because it was truly what he felt passionate about. He'd done it for me. All of it.

"You okay?"

I looked up, heat flooding my cheeks as if, just by looking at me, Alex had been able to follow my train of thought. "I'm fine," I managed to squeak.

"We're almost there," he said.

"Right. Okay." I rubbed my hands together, willing my nerves to settle. "Let's do this."

Chapter Twenty-Eight

Alex

We pulled down the long, pebbled driveway that led to Alicio's home on the remote Florida island. He'd always called it the summer house, but I'd spent just as many of my summers growing up in Manhattan as I had lounging around the Keys. It was more like Alicio liked the *idea* of a summer home more than he did the actual use of one. Though I had to admit, it did make a great backdrop for a wedding.

Dani craned her neck, looking out the passenger window at the looming mansion. "Wow," she said. "It's beautiful."

We pulled to a stop just outside the front door and climbed out of the car. The house *was* beautiful. The kind of beautiful I appreciated. It had a more subdued grandeur than Alicio's home in Manhattan. Natural wood and stone, large windows, earth tones. It blended naturally into the lush landscape of the island, the beach just yards beyond the edge of the finely landscaped grounds. I should have wanted to go inside but I held back, feeling a familiar tension spreading through my shoulders and neck.

"You okay?" Dani said.

I forced a smile. She would hate knowing how uncomfortable I was. "Sure. You ready?"

We headed up the neatly manicured pathway to the front steps. We'd left our overnight bags in the car—best not to look too presumptuous when first arriving—so my hands were free. Free, and *trembling*. Before I could shove them into my pockets, Dani reached out and took one, squeezing it gently, before lacing her fingers with mine.

I glanced at her, catching her eye, and she smiled, just slightly. "You look like you could use a little steadying."

Without dropping Dani's hand, I rang the front bell. A long moment later, it swung open.

"Deliveries for the wedding are to be taken to the—Oh." Alicio's long-time housekeeper Elaine shot me a dour look. "Alexander. I didn't expect you," she said.

"Hello, Elaine." I offered her my best smile. She'd always liked me, but there was no telling how much the family's overall discontent with me had trickled down to those in their employ. "Can we come in?"

She backed up and opened the door wide, motioning us into the entryway.

"This is my girlfriend, Dani," I said, proud that I hadn't hesitated on the word *girlfriend*.

Dani reached out and shook Elaine's hand. "Hello," she said.

"How are you?" I asked. "I hope everything is going well for you."

She shrugged, crossing her arms across her chest. "Things are fine."

So I *was* on her bad list. Might as well get right to it then. "Right. Well, I was hoping we could use my old rooms tonight. Will that be a problem?"

She furrowed her brow. "You're staying? For the wedding?"

"Yes, of course," I said. "I did RSVP that I was coming. And I ran into the family last week in New York. They know to expect me."

"Oh. I saw that, but, well, it's just that Victor told me *not* to expect you."

"Because I didn't think he'd actually show." Victor descended the stairs and stopped in front of me, narrowing his eyes as he looked from me to Dani. Instinctively, I pulled her closer, putting an arm around her waist.

"You remember Dani," I said pointedly.

Victor looked her up and down in a way that made *me* uncomfortable. I could only imagine how it made Dani feel. "Right. So, an ex-employee, and an ex-stepbrother. Tell me why you're here again?"

"My mother didn't divorce Alicio, Victor, she *died*. It's not the same thing."

A shadow passed over Victor's eyes at the mention of my mother and he looked to the floor.

When he looked back up, his face had softened somehow. "I don't understand why you would even want to be here," he said. "*Because* of Mom. After what Sasha—" He shook his head.

"I'm not here for Sasha," I said. "But the rest of you are the only family I have. I came to support Alicio." It was the truth, though not in the way I'd implied. I *did* want to support Alicio. And telling him of Sasha's deceit was the very best way I could think to do it.

Elaine cleared her throat. "The pool house is free."

Victor nodded. "Fine. But you better not cause a scene. There are a lot of important people coming to this wedding."

"Should I add two more for the rehearsal dinner?" Elaine asked, her question aimed at Victor.

"That won't be necessary," I said before he had the chance to answer. "We've been traveling all day and don't want to impose on plans already made. We'll be fine seeing everyone at the wedding tomorrow." Traveling all day was a stretch. But attending the rehearsal dinner would be too dangerous for Dani. The less Sasha saw of her the better. At least until Dani was ready to make her move.

We were silent as I led Dani through the house and out the rear door, just beyond the kitchen. The back lawn and patio had been transformed into a wedding wonderland. Several large tents filled the space, their sides open and tied back. It looked as though the ceremony would take place in the smallest tent, while the other two were set up for the dinner and reception. Several workers were busy constructing the centerpieces on the tables. They looked like giant, leafless trees draped with cascading flowers and what looked, from a distance, like peacock feathers.

"Wow," I muttered under my breath.

"Oh, just wait," Dani said. "There's an actual peacock here somewhere."

I paused and looked her way. "Are you serious?"

"Absolutely serious. For the photographs. I had no idea there were people who rented out peacocks until Sasha asked me to find her one."

"Did you do a lot of the wedding planning?"

"Not too much. She had an actual wedding planner, Roberto somebody, so I just ended up with the overflow stuff. When she would get wild ideas and wanted to prove to Roberto they were possible."

"Like renting peacocks."

"Or having a pod of dolphins swimming in the cove behind the house."

"She didn't really ask for that," I said.

"Oh, she did," Dani responded. "I mean, it isn't happening. I called every Aquarium in Florida, the local university's marine biology program, and the coast guard and they all laughed at the request. Sasha sent me home early that day. Said I was too incompetent to spend another minute in her presence."

"Ouch."

Dani shrugged. "She apologized the next day and took me to lunch at The Vine. Which is generally how she operated. Impossible one minute, then incredibly nice the next. It was exhausting, trying to keep up."

"I'm surprised you made it as long as you did."

"In retrospect, I am too. Though I was so blinded by my own stupid ambition, maybe I'm not really surprised."

We reached the door to the pool house, nestled over on the left side of the grounds beyond a grove of palm trees. I paused, my hand resting on the knob. I thought about Dani's collection of LeFranc purses I'd seen in her garage. "I'm sorry you had to lose that."

Her expression softened. "Thanks, but I don't know that I *am* sorry anymore. In my head, LeFranc embodied everything I thought high fashion should be. It was above reproach. I think I let that blind devotion influence me too much. I spent all my time only thinking about what kind of designer LeFranc would want me to be."

"But that makes sense if you were trying to get a job designing for LeFranc."

"True." She hesitated, like she was afraid to say what came next.

I opened the door to the pool house and motioned her inside.

"But what if I don't want to design for somebody else? What if I want to design as me?" She paused and looked around, surprise filling her eyes. "Wow. This is the pool house? It's amazing."

"Wait until you see the view." I walked across the living room and opened the patio doors. The pool was a sparkling blue in the sunshine; just beyond it, the open water of the ocean shone a bright, brilliant turquoise.

Dani stared, her eyes wide. "This place is magical," she said. "You spent every summer here?"

The sea breeze lifted a strand of her blonde hair and tossed it across her cheek. I barely resisted the urge to brush it away before she reached up and tucked it behind her ear. "We spent more time in Manhattan," I said. "But yes. We were always here for at least a few weeks, maybe a month or so, every summer. Christmas was always here, and Thanksgiving when I came for that."

"I can't even imagine," Dani said. "I thought I was lucky growing up in Charleston, but this takes the beach to a whole new level."

I pushed my hands into my pockets, the safest

way to keep myself from touching her. "Hey," I said.

She turned to face me. "What?"

"I think you'd be great designing on your own."

She grinned. "Really?"

"Really."

There was so much more I wanted to say. To ask. Would she go back to New York to do it? Would she stay in Charleston? Did this version of her future have room for me in it?

She bit the side of her bottom lip and looked at me in a way that spoke of possibility. "It would be really risky," she finally said. "I might not make it. Especially if Sasha works against me."

"But you might. And you'll never know if you don't try."

She nodded, looking back out toward the ocean. "It's hard to let go, Alex. One minute I think I can do it, and then the next it's like I don't even know myself anymore and I just want things to be the way they were before, when I still believed designing for LeFranc was a possibility."

But what about me? What about us? The question pulsed through my brain, willing me to open my mouth and ask her.

I took a step backward. "I should get our bags from the car."

"Right," she said, pressing a hand to her stomach. "I'll just wait here if that's okay."

I left her staring into the Atlantic and headed

back to the front drive to move the car and get our bags. I'd wanted to ask her, but I couldn't do it. If I'd asked, she might have answered. And I still wasn't sure she was willing to give the only answer I wanted to hear.

Chapter Twenty-Nine

Dani

While Alex went to park the car and retrieve our bags—all but the wedding dress which we felt was probably better hidden in the trunk of his car—I wandered around the pool house. It was nicely decorated, comfortable, but not showy or gaudy in any way. Pictures of Alicio's sons filled the living room, snapshots from their youth of them swimming in the ocean behind the house, paddle boarding, surfing, eating ice cream on the small boardwalk that led down to the water from the house. Alex was conspicuously absent from all but a few photos. In those few, he never looked very comfortable; he seemed to be hovering on the fringes of the photos, in the frame, but not really *a part.*

But then, he hadn't been around nearly as much, only spending a few months out of the year with his mom and Alicio's family. Maybe that was enough to justify the disparity.

In the wide hallway that led to the bedroom, a large, family portrait hung across from an ornately framed mirror. Victor and Gabriel were maybe twelve and fourteen years old in the photo. They posed with their parents on the beach, the blue waves crashing behind them. Their father looked flawlessly tanned, not too different from the Alicio I'd caught glimpses of around the office, except that his hair was dark instead of the snow-white he now sported. He had his arm around Alex's mom, her hand resting loosely on Gabriel's shoulder. It was the perfect family photo, except Alex wasn't in it.

Sadness swelled inside as I thought of him coming home each summer, seeing the portrait, and countless others undoubtedly just like it. She was *his* mom, and yet, looking at the photo, you'd never know she had any other children.

A noise sounded behind me and I turned, attempting, and likely failing, to wipe the sadness from my face.

Alex followed my gaze back to the portrait.

"She was *your* mom," I said sadly. "How could she—"

"She did the best she could," Alex said, cutting me off. He stalked past me into the bedroom, dropping my overnight bag onto the fluffy duvet that lay across the bed. His hands now free, he shoved them into his pockets. "It was a glamorous life. I think she got swept up in it all. Plus, I chose to live with my father. I think a part of her always resented that choice."

"But still," I said. A part of me knew I should let it go. Stop pushing. But the injustice of Alex's position as an outsider in the family his own mother had been such a vital part of felt blatant. "Didn't she fight for you? How could she exclude you like this?"

"She did the best she could," he repeated. "And she did fight for me. For my education to be paid for, for the car, the job. She wanted me to be successful." There was a hollow note to his words that I couldn't help but notice. The words he *wasn't* saying almost told me more. Money, she had given him without question. But time? Attention? Acceptance? Had Alex ever gotten enough of that?

Suddenly, I understood on a deeper level why Alex had been so driven to discover Sasha's crimes. This was about so much more than a wedding dress. It was about *Alex* saving Alicio's company. He wasn't just seeking vindication. He was seeking acceptance.

Later that night, my thoughts kept returning to the family portrait in the hall.

What must it have felt like for Alex when he spoke out about troubles at LeFranc, and his girlfriend sided with the company rather than him? A knot formed in my stomach. He'd spent his entire life watching his mom choose the LeFrancs. When he'd come to me—the one person who should have been on his side no matter what—I'd defended Sasha. Told him multiple times he was overreacting.

I'd picked LeFranc. Just like his mom.

No wonder he'd left me.

I'd hurt him in the worst possible way.

It took hours for me to fall asleep. Twice I crossed the room, opening the bedroom door determined to wake Alex, who slept on the living room sofa, apologize, and tell him I finally understood why he'd left so abruptly. Both times I chickened out, closing the door and huffing back to bed. How would he react? Would he accept my apology? Would he trust me again? He'd said he never stopped wanting me. But I wanted him to *love* me. Because—Paige would be happy to hear me acknowledge she'd been right all along—I had never stopped loving him.

Early the next morning, I sat on the side of the pool, my feet swirling in the cool, blue water, and called Paige. Though it was not quite seven a.m., she answered on the first ring. I sighed with relief when I heard her voice. I no longer had the guarantee that she'd be up with the children since she'd officially given up her nannying job, but I'd hoped she would answer anyway. I needed the clarity only a conversation with Paige could bring.

"Dani! How are you? How's Florida?"

"Oh, good. I was afraid I'd woken you up."

"Nope. Just got back from a run. Are you avoiding my question? How's Florida?"

I'd told Paige I was simply attending the

wedding with Alex, that he felt obligated to go and try and make amends with his stepfather. She still had no idea we were attempting to get back her dress. "It's warm," I said. "And beautiful. Alicio's house is unbelievable. We're staying in the pool house and even just that is amazing."

"Have you seen Sasha yet?" Paige asked.

"No. But I promise to kick her in the shins for you when I do. How's wedding prep going?"

"Let's see. My job for today is to convince my mother she does *not,* eight days before the wedding, need to have the caterer add five different kinds of shrimp to the appetizer list. *Five,* Dani. Who needs five kinds of shrimp at one dinner?"

"A Pinckney, of course," I answered in an exaggerated Southern drawl.

"Yeah, yeah. So seriously. How has it been? How are you and Alex?" she asked.

I told her about the portrait I'd seen hanging outside of the pool house bedroom, as well as the chilly reception we'd received from Victor. "It all seems so clear now," I concluded. "When I saw that portrait with him not in it, everything that happened between us made a new kind of sense. I was never fair to him, Paige. I didn't mean to do it, but in his eyes, I chose LeFranc over him. It was the worst kind of betrayal."

"So what are you going to do about it?"

"I have to tell him how I feel. Convince him

that I recognize now that there's more to life than fashion. That I'm not willing to put my career over the people who are most important in my life."

"Do you think he still cares about you?" Paige asked gently. "I'm with you a hundred percent, Dani, but I don't want you to get hurt again."

"No, he does. He's . . . he's told me he does."

She squealed. "Then go get him! Find a way to tell him. The sooner, the better."

Three hours later, Alex and I leaned on the counter of the pool house kitchen and went over our plans for the day.

First, find Sasha. Ingratiate myself enough that she'll allow me to assist her until the wedding.

Second, find the right moment to swap out the dress, relying on Chase who, after arriving as the most obnoxiously early wedding guest ever, will rendezvous with Alex to get the replacement dress and bring it to me to facilitate the swap.

Finally, meet Isaac, on standby with the floral delivery van, at the back door with Paige's dress. Make sure Alex knows so that at the same time, he can find Alicio, tell him everything he discovered about Sasha/Sally Mabel Rivers, and provide proof of her embezzlement.

Timing was key.

If Sasha found out about the dress before Alex had the chance to talk to Alicio, it was possible she'd have a first-class tantrum and create so much of a distraction, Alicio would no longer listen to Alex. If Alicio heard of Sasha's deceit before the dress was safely off the premises, it might lead to a confrontation that would eliminate my access to both Sasha, *and* the dress. Alex and I would have to stay in constant communication to avoid both scenarios.

"You're nervous," Alex said, looking my way.

Ha. He had no idea. I was nervous enough about stealing a wedding dress, but the thing that had me really feeling queasy? Standing next to him. Feeling the warmth from his skin when my arm brushed against his, or the heat flood my cheeks when he held my gaze for an extra-long moment.

The words were hovering at the front of my mind.

I'm sorry I betrayed you.

I'm sorry I didn't listen to you.

I still love you.

But I couldn't say them. Not yet. Not here.

"Nervous, yes," I said. "But determined. Paige deserves to wear her dress."

"Do we have a contingency plan?" he asked. "If Sasha doesn't want to take you back?"

I chewed on my lower lip. "I guess I have to hope I'll at least get close enough to see where she's keeping the dress. Then hopefully I'll find a way to sneak back in and make the swap."

He reached over and closed his hand over

mine, giving it a quick squeeze. "Let's do this," he said. "I'm sure Sasha is up and beginning her preparations. I'll walk you over and point you in the right direction."

I stood, smoothing the fabric of my dress. It was Chase's creation this time—floral silk in shades of purple that fit and flowed in all the right places. He'd pulled the fabric out of my stash and made it while I was working on Sasha's replacement dress. I'd never had something custom made that I hadn't made myself; it was a treat to be the beneficiary of Chase's impeccable taste and skill.

Alex shrugged on his suit coat and I noticed, as always, that he was equally dressed to impress. His suit was a light gray, his tie a deep shade of purple that was a nice compliment to my dress. He reached for a tiny box that was sitting on the kitchen counter. I hadn't even noticed it until he grabbed it. "I almost forgot," he said, opening the box. "Isaac gave this to me yesterday in case you wanted to use it."

I leaned forward. I couldn't even see what it was he was holding up. It was the size of a pea, maybe? And made out of what looked like clear plastic. "What is it?"

"It's a Bluetooth headset," Alex said. "Just in case you need to call one of us without letting Sasha know."

He held out the device and I took it, careful not

to drop it. We'd never find the thing again if I did. "It's so tiny."

"I don't think they're available commercially yet. It was sent to Isaac for review. Here." He held out his hand. "Where's your phone? I'll pair it for you."

I pulled my phone out of my bag and unlocked it before handing it over, realizing a second too late that I maybe didn't want him to see the wallpaper on my home screen. Because it was *him*. Us. A photo of the two of us all wrapped up in each other's arms. We'd taken it the night after we'd seen *Hamilton*. The first night we'd kissed. The night I knew I'd fallen in love with him.

I should have changed the photo. Paige had insisted I'd never actually get over him if I didn't. But every time I'd pulled up my phone's settings and scrolled through my photos to pick something new, I hadn't been able to do it.

He took one look before his eyes darted back to mine. He held my gaze, his unspoken question hanging in the air between us.

I gave my head a small shake, my shoulders rising into a shrug. "I don't know," I said. "It's from the night we saw *Hamilton*. I guess I never got around to changing it."

He looked back at the photo. "That was a great night."

"Yeah, it . . . I'm sorry, can you give me a minute? Go ahead and pair the device. I'll be right back." I hurried into the bathroom that adjoined the bedroom where I'd slept the night before and gripped the shiny porcelain of the pedestal sink. *What* was the matter with me? It was as if the realization that yes, I wanted to be with Alex had completely upended my entire world. I had to get a grip. I forced a long breath in through my nose and out through my mouth. Then followed it with another, and another.

Back in the pool house kitchen, Alex was standing up, waiting for me. "Are you all right?"

I nodded. "Just nervous, I guess."

He held up the Bluetooth. "Maybe you could wear it on this side?" He motioned to my left. "It will be hidden that way."

My hair was swept over to the side, pinned in a loose bun just below my ear. If worn in my left ear, it would be completely concealed by my hair. I took the device from Alex and pushed it into place. "Is it in right?"

His fingers brushed against my hair, moving it out of the way so he could look. I took another deep breath, hoping he didn't notice how his touch made gooseflesh rise up and down my arms. "Looks good," he said softly.

His fingers lingered for a moment longer, tickling my neck. He cleared his throat and stepped back. "Ready to go?"

The kitchen was bustling, the catering staff already at work in preparation for the day's events. We got a few odd looks as we walked through, but no one stopped us. I followed as Alex led me through the house, pausing at the bottom of the stairs we'd seen Victor come down the afternoon before.

"Up these stairs and to the left," Alex said. "You'll pass through a set of French doors and then the master suite is on your right."

I nodded. "Got it."

"All you have to do is push the button here"—he motioned to his ear—"and it will call me. My number is already pulled up on your phone."

I nodded. "Okay."

"And your phone is in your bag?"

I nodded, gripping my clutch a little tighter. "Yep."

He gave my hand one final squeeze. "Good luck."

Chapter Thirty

Alex

I watched her climb the stairs, hoping against hope she'd be able to get to the dress without too much groveling. I hated the thought of her kissing up to Sasha, especially knowing what Sasha really was.

Dani paused at the top of the stairs and turned back, her hand gripping the railing. She looked beautiful. I smiled and offered her a nod of encouragement, then reached up and tapped my ear, a reminder that I was only a phone call away. She nodded, then disappeared down the hall.

Seconds later, my phone buzzed with an incoming call. I pulled it out, smiling to see Dani's picture filling the screen. I had my own tiny Bluetooth paired to my phone, so I tapped the earpiece once to answer the call.

"In trouble already?"

"What if you stay with me the whole time?" she asked me. "Just in case."

"A good plan until you're talking to Sasha at the same time that I'm talking to Alicio. That would be a lot to keep straight."

"I know. You're right," she said, with a grumble of complaint. "I'm just freaking out a little."

"You've got this, Dani," I said. "I've got to go back to the pool house to get the folder, then I'll find Alicio."

"You left the folder?" she whisper-yelled. "Out in the open?"

"Relax," I said. "It's in my suitcase." As soon as I said the words, I wondered if they were true. Was it in my suitcase? Or had I left it on the counter when I helped Dani put in her Bluetooth? The fact that I couldn't remember said a lot about how distracted I was. I was a perfectionist. A planner. The guy who always remembered the details. I swallowed my doubts. Either way, it was too late to do anything but go get it. I couldn't confront Alicio without it.

Elaine emerged out of the kitchen, a mug of coffee, and a plate of muffins in her hand. She shot me a questioning look. And rightly so. I wasn't going anywhere, just standing in the hallway talking to myself.

"You need anything?" she said.

"Actually, I was looking for Alicio. Do you know where he is?"

"He isn't here. He and Victor went to play an early round of golf this morning. They should be back by noon."

"Ah. Okay. Maybe I'll wait for them in his study."

"Could you possibly—?" Elaine held up the coffee and muffins. "These are for Sasha. That woman's been bossing me around all morning, and I have a thousand other things to do to make sure the house is ready. If *I* walk this upstairs, she'll find something else to ask me to do."

I hesitated. "So you want *me* to carry them up?"

"Say yes!" Dani whispered into my ear. "Bring them to me and I'll take them in."

"Actually, sure," I said to Elaine. "I'd be happy to help."

She shot me a weird look, but it didn't last. She was clearly happy to be free of the unwanted obligation. "Thanks. She's in the master suite upstairs."

"On it," I said.

Halfway up the stairs, I paused. "You still there?" I said to Dani.

"Yep," she whispered. "Coming to meet you. You gotta work on sounding more casual."

"What? All I did was ask where Alicio was."

"But your voice sounded like you were elbow-deep in the cookie jar."

"We *are* elbow-deep in the cookie jar."

I found her at the top of the stairs; she smiled and reached up to end our phone call. "This is perfect," she said, taking the coffee and muffins from me. "I've been hiding in the hallway, trying to muster up the nerve to knock on Sasha's door."

"And you say *I* need to be more casual? When you're hiding in an upstairs hallway?"

She grinned. "No one saw me; it's fine. And

now—" She held up Sasha's breakfast. "I have an excuse to be here."

"Be careful," I warned her again. "And stay in touch."

She nodded, then disappeared down the hallway one more time.

I quickly headed back to the pool house to retrieve the folder of evidence I'd prepared for Alicio, which was, gratefully, still in my suitcase. I dropped off the bag, as well as Dani's, in my car—we likely wouldn't have time to retrieve them on our way out—then went to Alicio's study, settling into one of the leather wingback chairs to wait for his return. I hadn't had a conversation with Alicio since I'd walked out of his New York office, not unless you counted our brief encounter on Christmas Eve.

I half wondered if he'd even give me the chance to show him what I'd discovered. It was possible he'd shut me down before I began, especially if Victor was with him when the conversation took place. It would be better if the two of us were alone, but how could I guarantee that would happen? I could always ask to speak to him privately, but would he allow it?

If he didn't, or if I couldn't manage the conversation before Dani was ready to leave, would I be willing to walk away? I could always send the information to the authorities without confronting Alicio directly. In a follow-up email full of additional implicating evidence, Angelica had offered to do just that. But my pride had made me say no.

I wanted to see Alicio's face when I showed him the truth, when he saw that I had been right all along. Somewhere in the back of my mind, I knew it probably wouldn't make me feel better. It wouldn't fill the gaping hole left by my lack of family. It wouldn't make the LeFrancs the kind of people I even *wanted* as my family. But I still had to try.

Chapter Thirty-One

Dani

The door to Sasha's room was slightly open, so I pushed it with my knee, stepping into the lavish bedroom and trying to look like I belonged there. "Good morning," I said, my voice light. "I ran into Elaine downstairs and she asked me to bring this up to you."

Sasha looked up from where she lounged by the fireplace wearing a silk robe. "Dani? Oh, thank God you're here. I've been completely surrounded by idiots all morning."

An older woman wearing glasses and a tight smile sat across from Sasha. "I'm actually still sitting right here, Sasha. I can hear what you're saying."

I placed the muffins and coffee on the small table next to her. "Well, I don't mind sticking around a little while if you need some extra help." I looked at the woman wearing glasses. "I'm Dani. I used to work with Sasha."

"Katrina," she said. "I remember you. I'm Alicio's assistant."

"Oh. Right. Sorry."

"No omelet?" Sasha said, rubbing her fingernails across the silk of her robe. "I asked Elaine for an omelet."

I froze. "The kitchen is pretty busy with all the wedding food prep; I'm sure this is the best Elaine could manage."

"That's right. I'd forgotten." She eyed my figure and picked at the corner of one of the muffins. "You're one of those women who think carbs are an acceptable choice."

Think of Paige. Think of Paige. Think of Paige. "The coffee's still hot," I said, nudging the mug toward her.

"When are you coming back to New York?" Sasha asked, finally picking up the coffee.

I swallowed. "Um, I'm not sure exactly."

"Well, when you do, come and see me first. You know how much I appreciate your attention to detail, and you were such a great assistant. Maybe we can talk about you getting your job back." The woman was actually serious.

"I'd like that," I lied. Apparently my groveling the week before had done its job.

Over the next hour, Sasha's bridesmaids arrived, and I became the go-to errand girl. To the kitchen for more muffins—seemed carbs weren't so offensive after all—and several bottles of champagne. To the store for more bobby pins, except I didn't go to the store. I just went to Alex's car and retrieved my own stash. To the back door to meet the florist who was delivering the bouquets. By noon, my feet were killing me and possibly all for nothing. Sasha hadn't left the room one single time. And she had to be minutes away from putting on her dress; the wedding started in less than two hours. I had to act. And fast.

Back in the room, I put the flowers on the bed and pulled out my phone to text Alex. There was a message from him already waiting for me.

Decoy is upstairs. Linen closet across the hall.

You're my favorite, I texted back. *Is Alicio back?*

Just now, he responded. *I'm waiting for Victor to leave him alone, then I'll confront him. Are you ready?*

My stomach tightened. It was now or never. *Ready,* I responded. *Let's do this.*

I felt both completely invigorated—one doesn't get to star in her own spy movie every day—and completely nauseated all at the same time. I looked around the room, trying to calculate my first move. The room bustled with activity and no one was particularly paying me very much attention, but if I up and grabbed the dress, hanging on the outside of the closet door across the room, and walked out, someone was going to notice.

Sasha's phone rang. She reached for it, a flash of something like anger crossing her features before she stood and hurried to the balcony where she answered the call.

I only wasted a second wondering who had

called her and why it had seemed to bother her so much. I didn't care why she was upset. I didn't care about anything but getting Paige's dress and getting as far away from the LeFrancs as possible. Digging deep to find my very best acting skills, I crossed the room and reached for the dress.

I had an excuse at the ready—Elaine had texted me and asked that I bring the dress to her for one more quick steaming before Sasha put it on—but no one even asked. I'd been helping them all morning. I'd apparently earned their trust. Or, maybe just their disinterest.

I paused outside the door, heart hammering in my ears and took a deep breath. Almost there. Crossing to the linen closet, I pulled it open. Towels, towels, towels, sheets, sheets, sheets. No dress. I scanned the shelves up and down, shifting things this way and that, but it's not like a wedding dress is an easy thing to hide. There was nothing in that closet.

"Looking for this?"

I spun around. Elaine stood behind me, the decoy dress, in all its tacky glory, hanging from her hand.

"Um . . . I . . ." I had nothing. No explanation. No reason for why I'd hidden a spare wedding dress in a linen closet. Or why I had Sasha's *actual* wedding dress in my hand.

Elaine stepped toward me, fire in her eyes.

"I think you better tell me what you're up to."

"It's not what you think," I said, taking a step back. Except, it probably was. It didn't take a genius to realize I was trying to swap out one dress for the other.

Before either of us could say another word, Sasha's door flew open and the bride herself tumbled into the hallway, her cell phone still in her hand. Her eyes darted from me to Elaine, then back again. I pulled Paige's dress tighter against my chest.

"Solomon, dear," she said into her phone. "Find Alicio. Tell him we have a problem upstairs."

I stilled. Solomon. Solomon her brother who was helping her embezzle funds? It wasn't a very common name. But that meant . . . Solomon knew Alicio?

Time slowed. With sickening clarity, everything clicked into place.

Alicio hadn't caught Sasha in her embezzling because Alicio was in on it. That's why he'd threatened Alex when he'd come close to discovering the truth. He wasn't trying to defend Sasha. He was trying to protect himself. I didn't have any hard and fast evidence, just a feeling in my gut. But I was right. I knew I was right. Which meant the conversation Alex was about to have with Alicio was going to go very differently than Alex expected.

"You little sneak," Sasha said, her voice low

and menacing. "You better give that to me right now."

I took another step backward. "No." It was stupid to back up. I was cornered. The only way out of the house was to get through Sasha *and* Elaine. What did I think I was going to do? Fight her for it? Six months ago, I might have argued I was capable of out-punching the impeccably dressed Sasha Wellington. I mean, she didn't even like to open her own coffee creamer for fear of breaking a nail. But I had a feeling I'd underestimated the Alabama-born and bred Sally Mabel Rivers. If she'd made it this far, she was used to fighting for what she wanted. Fist for fist? I didn't stand a chance.

"You seriously think I'm going to let you walk out of here with that dress? Are you completely delusional? You're a nobody. One phone call and Elaine could have this whole place on lockdown. You're not going *anywhere*."

"I know who you are," I said, willing my hands to stop trembling. "I know who you are, and I know what you've done."

She narrowed her gaze. "You don't know anything."

My Bluetooth buzzed in my ear and I reached up, answering the call in a move that I hoped looked like I was simply tucking back a loose curl. Isaac's voice filled my ear. "I'm at the back door ready and waiting."

I closed my eyes. I could make a run for it. Push past Elaine and try and make it to Isaac before security could slow us down. But that would leave Alex on his own. And the thought of that? Suddenly the dress didn't seem all that important.

Paige had already forgiven me once. She didn't need the dress to know how much I loved her.

My hands dropped and the dress slid to the floor. "I have to go," I said softly.

Katrina appeared in the bedroom doorway, my clutch and phone in hand. "Heads up," she said, before tossing them my direction. Whether she was actually trying to help me, or just be rid of me sooner, I'd never know. But as I raced down the hallway toward Alex, I hardly cared. I had to stop him. I had to keep him from humiliating himself in front of Alicio. At the bottom of the stairs, I scrambled for my phone. Isaac was still on the line.

I ducked around a corner, pressing myself into a darkened alcove. "Isaac?" I whispered.

"Dude, what just happened?" he said. "Do you have the dress?"

"No. The dress doesn't matter. I have to find Alex."

"What do you want me to do?"

"Just get out of here. Call Chase and let him know. I'll get Alex and meet you back at the hotel. I'll explain everything there."

Chapter Thirty-Two

Alex

I paced around Alicio's study and watched the clock. He'd returned from the golf course, I knew that much, and had agreed to speak with me, but he wanted to dress for the wedding first. His timing couldn't be more terrible. I'd told Dani to move on the dress, assuming that now that Alicio was back, I could confront him immediately. The delay might be the undoing of our entire plan.

The study door opened, and I turned, but it wasn't Alicio standing in the doorway, it was Gabriel.

"Gabe," I said. "Hey."

He was already dressed, at least. "Alex," he said. "So you came after all."

"I don't know why everyone expected me not to show. I told you I was coming." I didn't even try to hide the irritation in my voice. I was tired of pretending it didn't hurt to have his family cast me aside.

Gabriel's face softened. "Alex, I think I know why you're really here." He glanced at the folder sitting on the coffee table in front of me. I willed my eyes forward, keeping them trained on his face. If I followed his gaze, he'd know for sure he'd figured me out.

"I don't know what you're talking about."

"I think you do. I'm not going to stop you, but I do think you should reconsider. The situation—it isn't what you think."

"It isn't Sasha embezzling millions of dollars from LeFranc?" I said, crossing my arms across my chest. I was done playing it safe.

"It's a lot more complicated than that," Gabriel said. "As a friend, Alex, I'm telling you. Don't get messed up in this. Walk away."

"Walk away when I was right about Sasha all along? How can you stand for this, Gabe? How can you let her do this to your family?"

"Alex, he's right."

I turned back to the study door. Dani stood there, her hand resting against her chest and her breathing heavy. Had she been running?

"He's right," she repeated.

I stilled. "What?"

She took a few steps into the room. "It wasn't Sasha embezzling the money. Or at least, it wasn't *only* Sasha. Alicio knows, Alex. He knows Solomon Rivers."

I looked at Gabe.

"Like I said. It's not what you think," he said. "If you go public with what you think you know, Dad's going to have a lot of reasons to make your life miserable. Walk away now? Nobody has to know you had plans to say anything at all. You go on with your life, and we'll go on with ours."

Dani was in front of me now. "Alex. Let's go. You don't need this. You don't need Alicio's approval."

I closed my eyes, her words cutting like knives. Because that's exactly what I wanted. And the realization made me sick.

She reached up and cupped her hand around my cheek. "Listen to me," she whispered. "Look at me."

I forced my eyes open, my heart instantly swelling at the warmth I saw in her expression.

"You don't need them, Alex. I'm your family now, okay? Me. Isaac. You aren't alone if you have us, right?"

"I know, Dani. I know. But this is—"

"Alex, I'm still in love with you." She closed her eyes for a moment and took a long, slow breath. Then she looked at me again, her eyes so full of love and hope I nearly lost my breath. "I never really stopped being in love with you. I don't need LeFranc. I don't need New York. I don't need Paige's dress. I don't need anything but you."

Before I could even process what she'd said, Alicio pushed into the study, a wide smile on his perfectly tanned skin. "Well isn't this a nice family gathering," he said.

I reached for Dani's hand, her fingers gripping

mine with an intensity that kept me grounded. "Actually, we were just leaving."

"You aren't staying for the wedding?" Alicio said. "Isn't that why you came?"

I looked at Dani, love and hope and courage reflecting in her gaze. "Something came up," I said. "We've got to head out early."

I reached forward and grabbed the folder of information off the coffee table, still holding Dani's hand, then walked to the study door. I paused, turning back. "You were never good enough for my mother," I said to Alicio.

His eyes narrowed, but then his face fell into a frown. "I agree with you on that point."

"I think she's probably happy to be rid of you now," I said. "I wish you and Sasha the best. You two deserve each other."

I walked through the house and toward the back drive without slowing, though I could tell Dani was struggling to keep up with me. Still, she didn't complain. She just clung to my hand, running every few steps to keep up with my long stride. When we arrived at the car, she hesitated beside the passenger side door I held open for her.

"Alex," she said, still short of breath. She bit her lip. "Will you please just say something?"

I couldn't, actually. What would I say? Speaking would require me to make sense of what I was feeling, and I was too much a mess to do that.

Instead, I leaned in and kissed her. She responded immediately, wrapping her arms around my neck, pulling me closer than I would have thought possible.

"I've missed you," I finally muttered into her hair.

She hiccoughed a laugh. "Yeah. Me too."

"Sorry you didn't get the dress."

She shrugged. "It doesn't matter. I'm leaving with something much more important."

Chapter Thirty-Three

Dani

Six months later

Alex and I walked down King Street in downtown Charleston. We stopped in front of a small fashion boutique, where an employee was resetting the window display with what looked like samplings from a spring collection: a knee-length dress with tiny cap sleeves and a pencil skirt in pale rose, a cashmere sweater set in the same color, trimmed with gold, and a pair of skinny-fit trousers in a loud, floral print, navy with oversized roses in varying shades of pink. A handbag in the same print hung over the shoulder of the mannequin wearing the dress.

"What do you think?" Alex said.

I shrugged. "A little on the safe side, but the print on the pants is great. I'd cut the sweater set. It feels a little too 1997. The dress could work, but I'd add a gold belt, and recut the neckline into something a little more daring. Something asymmetric, maybe."

"You sound like an expert," Alex said.

I grinned. "More like someone with big opinions and nothing to back them up."

"You graduated from one of the top design

schools in the country, Dani. I'm pretty sure that qualifies as credentials."

"Yes. But I'll feel better when I've actually sold a few things."

We left the boutique's window and crossed the street, joining the line that snaked out the door of our favorite ice cream place. I breathed in the scent of homemade waffle cones wafting out the door and smiled. "How's that going?" Alex asked. "Any progress?"

I shrugged, wishing I had more to report. I'd been working retail at a design shop a few blocks away, designing in the evenings and on the weekends. But the progress was slow going. Even working full time, I wasn't making much, and I'd insisted Isaac start charging me rent as soon as I'd gotten a job.

I'd made several contacts with stores around town that were willing to sell my stuff on consignment but making enough pieces to sell took more cash flow, and time, than I had. I was slowly building my savings, but I was still months away from having enough to create the kind of collection a store would be interested in selling. It's not like I could go to a boutique and ask them to sell a single dress. I mean, I could, but that wouldn't do anything to build my brand. Volume was important. Impact was important. To make matters even more complicated, fashion was constantly changing. It wasn't like I could take three years to design one collection—not if I wanted to stay on-trend.

"Nothing new to report," I said. "Except I did finally take my design portfolio over to the bridal boutique on Church Street. She seemed pretty positive and said if I could make her a few samples to have on hand, she'd keep me in mind for brides looking for custom dresses. Oh! And Darius said his sister should have some logos for me to look at by the end of next week. So I guess that's progress."

It might have helped my cause if I'd been able to show the boutique owner the glowing praise Sasha's wedding dress had gotten within the fashion industry. Everyone had loved it; similar designs and copies were already showing up in stores. I'd held onto my sketches and had assembled a careful file detailing my design and construction of the dress. Someday, the timing would be right for me to expose what Sasha had done to me. When that time came, I'd be ready.

Alex grinned then leaned forward and kissed me quickly on the lips. "It makes me happy to see you so happy."

My own smile dimmed. "That got us in trouble before."

He furrowed his eyebrows. "What got us in trouble?"

"When we were in New York. You were happy because I was happy doing all the fashion things, the parties, the shows. But they didn't make *you* happy. I don't want to do that again."

Alex touched my back, urging me forward in the line. "But we aren't doing that again. We're getting ice cream in Charleston, talking about your plans to start your own brand. It's entirely different."

"I know. I just—I want you to be happy too, Alex. I want you to love where you live and love what you do and love the things we do together. I made it all about me for too long. That can't be how this works anymore."

Our conversation paused long enough for us to order our ice cream then move back onto the street. "I do love what I do," Alex said. "I've been talking to Isaac about opening myself up to additional clients. He doesn't need me as much anymore, so I have more time on my hands. I think I'd stay in the same industry. Entertainers, internet personalities. I've gained a lot of knowledge navigating Isaac's world; I think it could be useful to others who suddenly find themselves in the same situation. And of course I love where I live." He paused and took a bite of his ice cream. "It didn't snow one single time this year. What isn't to like?"

"Hurricanes," I said. "And palmetto bugs. And August. And—"

"A small price to pay," he said. "I'll take giant cockroaches and hot summers over icy winters any day." He nudged me with his elbow. "Maybe I didn't really love the fashion scene in New York, Dani. But I don't have any regrets about doing things that were important to you. I'd do it all again tomorrow if that's what you wanted. I likely *will* do it all again if your career takes off like I think it will. Is it so wrong that I want the woman I love to be happy?"

I'd heard Alex tell me he loved me hundreds of times before. He'd told me at least once a day for the past six months. Still, the novelty of hearing it again hadn't worn off. "I don't think I'll ever get tired of hearing you say that."

"What, that I love you?"

I stopped him on the sidewalk and leaned up to kiss him. His lips tasted like salted peanut butter and chocolate. "Yes, that you love me. Don't ever stop, okay?"

A phone buzzed and we both moved to see if it was mine or his. "It's mine," he said. He looked at his phone, then looked to me. "It's the attorney."

I stilled. *The* attorney was the attorney who had filed an anonymous whistleblower complaint against LeFranc with the IRS on our behalf.

Alex stared at his phone but made no move to answer it. "Alex, answer it," I urged, startling him out of his stupor.

He gave his head a little shake and swiped across the screen to answer the call.

I listened to Alex's half of the conversation, wishing we were in a place private enough for him to put the call on speaker.

"Right," Alex said. "I do understand. No, that is . . . we didn't expect it at all, but that's, that's amazing news."

My pulse quickened. What was amazing news?

Alex hung up the phone and turned to face me, his eyes wide with excitement. "You're never going to believe it."

"What? Believe what?"

He looked around the busy street. "You need to be sitting down. Come on." He grabbed my hand and led me down Broad Street and into Washington Square where we found a bench shaded by a sprawling live oak tree.

"Alex, what is going on? What did the attorney say?"

He took a deep breath and I noticed his hands were shaking. "LeFranc was found guilty of tax evasion. Over the past several years, they've hidden almost 50 million dollars from the government."

"Wow. So the twelve million we found in Sasha's accounts was only part of it."

"Right. That's a lot of back taxes and fees they owe the IRS."

Realization dawned and I swallowed, my hands suddenly trembling to match Alex's. We hadn't filed a whistleblower complaint against LeFranc for our own gain. We'd done it because it was the right thing to do; because the company had been defrauding its employees, its investors, its customers for too long. But we'd always known it was a possibility; that the IRS often awarded whistleblowers a percentage of the back taxes and fees owed as a result of the filed complaint.

I took a slow, deep breath. "How much?"

Alex started to laugh. "3.3 million dollars."

I closed my eyes. Then opened them. Then closed them and pressed my palms to my face. Beside me, Alex still laughed. "I think it's time you quit your job, Dani. You've got a design brand to launch, and now you've got the capital to do it."

Tears filled my eyes and I leaned forward, pressing kisses to Alex's lips and cheeks and ears and eyebrows. "Hey, Alex?" I said between kisses.

"Hmmm?" he answered, his lips finding mine. This kiss lasted longer than the others, long enough that a tour guide starting her tour at the foot of the George Washington statue looming in front of us cleared her throat until we separated, then shot us a scolding look.

My cheeks flushed, but I didn't let go of Alex.

I placed my hands on his cheeks and leaned my forehead against his. "Let's get married," I said softly.

He stilled. "What?"

"Marry me."

"Are you serious?"

"I don't want to live with Isaac anymore. I want a house. And a husband. And a baby with blue eyes and another baby with brown eyes and I don't want to wait anymore."

He smiled and kissed me again, causing another round of throat-clearing from the tour guide. "Oh, knock it off," Alex said, and I laughed. He always sounded more Southern when he was annoyed. "We just decided to get married. We'll kiss if we damn well please."

And we did. That day. And on our wedding day. On the day I sold my first wedding dress and the day I opened my own shop on King Street. On the day our twins were born. (Both with brown eyes, stupid genetics.) On Isaac's wedding day. On the day of my very first runway show in New York. On the day Paige and Reese moved back to Charleston full-time and on the day our twins started kindergarten. On the day Chase and Darius finally adopted a gorgeous (blue-eyed, of course) baby girl.

But more importantly, we kissed on all of the awful, hellish days that came in between the shiny, memorable moments.

Even when it was hard.

Even when we hated the world, and sometimes even when we hated each other.

Those were the kisses that mattered most of all.

Acknowledgments

If I've learned anything over the past ten years, it's that the process of breathing life into a book is never the same. This book will always be special to me for personal reasons and I hope it means something to you, too. Jolene, you read it first and told me it was good enough to keep working on it. Your insight, as always, was priceless. Melanie, I don't think I could do anything in publishing without your input. I value your opinion next to my own. Thank you for answering the countless texts, Facebook messages, and emails. Emily, the other half of my brain, my words will always be better because of you. Tiffany, Suesan, Wendy, Cindy, Brittany, thank you for beta reading and offering suggestions that tightened and polished the story. Camille, thank you for proofreading. It is second to none! Wilette, your ability to interpret my abundance of emails and turn my thoughts and (often misguided) opinions into such gorgeous covers is a testament to your brilliance. You've earned my loyalty to Red Leaf Cover Design for life. To my team at Four Petal Press, walking this road with you all is the BEST. I feel lucky to call you my friends and associates. To my kids, who are endlessly patient as I balance life and writing, thank you for getting me, for understanding me, for embracing the good and the bad of this job that I do. Josh, you're the reason I can write love stories—why I believe that love CAN change the world. Because your love changes mine every day.

About the Author

Jenny Proctor grew up in the mountains of North Carolina, a place she still believes is one of the loveliest on earth. She lives a few hours south of the mountains now, in the Lowcountry of South Carolina. Mild winters and of course, the beach, are lovely compromises for having had to leave the mountains.

Ages ago, she studied English at Brigham Young University. She works full time as an author and as an editor, specializing in romance, through Midnight Owl Editors.

Jenny and her husband, Josh, have six children, and almost as many pets. They love to hike and camp as a family and take long walks through the neighborhood. But Jenny also loves curling up with a good book, watching movies, and eating food that, when she's lucky, she didn't have to cook herself. You can learn more about Jenny and her books at www.jennyproctor.com.

Center Point Large Print
600 Brooks Road / PO Box 1
Thorndike, ME 04986-0001 USA

(207) 568-3717

US & Canada:
1 800 929-9108
www.centerpointlargeprint.com